WHISKEY ON THE ROCKS

WHISKEY WITCHES ANCIENTS BOOK 4

F.J. BLOODING

Whistling Book Press

Alaska

Printed in the United States of America

Published by Whistling Book Press

Whistling Book Press
Alaska
Visit our web site at:
www.whistlingbooks.com

❀ Created with Vellum

WHISKEY MAGICK & MENTAL HEALTH

S ign up to learn more about our books and receive this free e-zine about Whiskey Magick and Mental Health.
https://www.fjblooding.com/books-lp

To
My amazing husband.
I hate you a little.
You know why.

1

CONTINUES AFTER LIZARD WIZARD

Paige blinked blurry-eyed at the sprawling two story house that almost looked like it should be a small hotel. With as many people as resided inside, it almost was. Her *entire* family—minus her mother—lived under that roof.

Her mind scrambled through the bog in her mind to recall why she was standing outside her home. She couldn't immediately remember when it was or what had recently happened. It was as if...

...as if her memories had disappeared and were slowly returning.

Something was wrong. The cool air raised goosebumps as the sun rose.

Rising sun? Hadn't the sun been setting?

Oh. She vaguely remembered that. Yeah. It had been and then Roxxie had shown up.

Crap. She was in Heaven. This was...wow. *This* was Heaven? It felt an awful lot like home.

The air popped and Roxxie appeared beside her. She wore

her adult form more often. Her pink-tipped hair was pulled back in a single, severe braid down her back. Her jeans were clean, and her green shirt read "Save the Monkeys." Still immature for an angel, but Paige preferred the younger punk version she sometimes wore.

"Where are we?" Paige asked. Her memories still weren't fully intact. It was like there were still some big, gaping holes in it.

Roxxie glanced around, one hand out as she scanned the area. "We're safe."

Safe. Good. Something *was* wrong. This wasn't Paige's Roxxie. "Safe?"

Roxxie frowned at her for a quick moment, then shook her head. "Right. You're probably still...okay. Sorry. Quick run-down. You've been in Heaven for three weeks. Cooper is taken care of. Everyone is okay. And I managed to get you out of Heaven...safely."

Wait. "Three *weeks?*" How was that even possible? And what had the angels wanted with her for *three weeks?*

"Go inside the house." Roxxie gently set her fingertips on Paige's arm and pushed. "Go to your family."

"Not until you tell me what happened?"

The angel pushed a little more insistently, scanning the area. Again.

"Angels can't get through the wards. So, why are you looking around?"

Roxxie pressed both her long-fingered hands to her forehead and gave Paige her full attention. "I don't know much. Okay? What I do know...I mean, it isn't good. Raphael wanted a word with you. I had thought he just wanted to check in about the demons. I mean, they are on the rise."

Raphael was the douchebag angel who had created demon summoners in the Whiskey line to keep an eye on things. He had always kept his demon summoner on a short leash—that was until Paige. They had a hate-hate relationship. "Get to the point."

"Anyway, I took you up like he requested. And then? You...you disappeared." Roxxie's violet eyes were wide and desperate. "I've been searching for you for the last three weeks."

"Okay." This didn't sound good. "Do you know why I was summoned?"

"It wasn't for demons. That much I figured out."

Paige's memories of Utah returned. There she'd discovered the presence of ancients returning to their world. Shape shifters able to take on the forms of ancient beings like a griffin, a thunderbird, or a rajasi. Ultra-powerful. Mega strong.

There were already too many people afraid of shifters and witches mating and bonding. How would the angels react to knowing that Dexx—her shifter lover—and her were having power-twins?

"Why can't I remember anything?" This was fucking serious. And where the hell was Cawli? Her spirit animal was being quiet, though that wasn't irregular. She didn't know where he went all the time being as he was a spirit sharing her body, but...

Roxxie looked exhausted and her expression was almost ragged-hunter. "You'll be gradually getting your memories back. It's something with the trip."

"I am." And she was. Paige now vaguely remembered the situation she'd been pulled away from when Roxxie had abducted her. "Cooper." The psychotic shifter-witch who had been trying to destroy her family.

"Taken care of."

She'd said that. Right. Catch up.

There were three weeks of catch up.

Okay. She needed to stop harping on that. "Why are you looking around like we're about to be attacked?"

Roxxie rolled her eyes to the top of her head, batting her lashes, her lips tight as she gestured with wide hands on either side of her. "I just—" She met Paige's gaze. "It was weird. Okay? Just...weird...things. Something is going on and it's—" She shook her head.

If it was bad enough an angel couldn't put it into words? "What kind of things?"

Roxxie opened her mouth then closed it. She glanced over her shoulder. "I was standing in a hallway."

"In Heaven." Because it sure felt like Paige was going to have a tough time figuring this shit out if she didn't fill in some detail.

"Yeah." Roxxie took a deep breath, looking rattled. "And then it disappeared."

"Oh." Shit. "Really?"

"That's..." Roxxie licked her lips. "That's how I found you. I don't—" Her mouth opened again without sound. Her gaze looked lost. "I don't know if they were actually going to let you return."

Paige was about to leap out of her skin, but reigned herself in. That was just Roxxie's opinion. Didn't mean it was true. "Give me the facts. What made you think that?"

"You disappeared. I should be able to hear your soul no matter where you go."

Angel weirdness, but whatever. "And?"

The tip of Roxxie's tongue touched her bottom lip. "I found you in a cell unconscious. Your body was being nourished. You were being cared for but..."

Dread ran down Paige's spine. "Do you think they were after my babies?"

Roxxie's frightened gaze met Paige's as she whispered, "Yes."

The porch light flicked on at the front door.

Paige grabbed Roxxie's arm. "Why?"

Roxxie glanced as the front door opened. She leaned in closer. "The last time the ancients showed up, the portals between Earth and Heaven and Hell almost closed."

"What?"

"Paige!" Alma cried from the porch, her robe synched around her wide waist.

Paige didn't have time for her grandmother at that moment. "What do you mean? We can close the door? Be rid of angels and demons?"

Roxxie's shoulders shook slightly as she shrugged. "I've always been low in the ranks. I never got to see much or do much, but I do remember the griffin." She tipped her head to the side and gave Paige a pained look.

Alma scurried down the stairs gracelessly, walking toward them.

But she wasn't trying to butt into the conversation. Yet. "And?"

"And the wizard was using the griffin to close the door. That's what I heard."

"Okay." It was unlikely they'd find another wizard who would be able to use Leslie's griffin the same way. Paige had seen a vision of the previous griffin while in Utah. She'd seen the wizard pulling the griffin's powers, but the vision hadn't shown why.

Roxxie put her lips to Paige's ear and whispered. "But the thunderbird and the rajasi were the ones that nearly destroyed the heavenly host."

Paige stared in the angel's face as she pulled away. "You're shitting me." Because her twins were the thunderbird and the rajasi. Both had nearly been stripped from history. There was next to *no* lore whatsoever of the rajasi. He was just a lion with flaming paws and mane. The thunderbird at least had Native American legends that were remembered.

Roxxie shook her head.

Alma wrapped Paige in a tight hug. "Where have you been?"

Her grandmother's arms came with such an overwhelming sense of *home* that tears came to Paige's eyes. "Heaven."

Alma released Paige and turned on Roxxie in a rage. "This is your doin'."

Roxxie's lips flattened as she took in a deep breath.

"Grandma." Paige didn't need this. Not at that moment. "Just…back off."

"Back off." She snorted and moved to stand in front Paige, as if protecting her "What were you thinkin'?"

Seriously? Paige was the strongest damned witch in their coven. Well…coven. They didn't really *do* coven-like things. Whatever. That didn't matter. Roxxie had just dumped a frelling bomb in Paige's very pregnant lap.

One of the twins dug a toe into her diaphragm.

Yeah. Very pregnant. "Roxxie, could I have a moment."

"Paige!" Dexx flew out the front door wearing nothing but a pair of jeans.

Roxxie gestured to Paige.

"You need *another* moment?" Alma turned to her with raised, white bushy brows. "She's had three weeks of 'em."

"Grandma." Shit. She lived in a zoo.

Dexx's arms engulfed her, pulling her in close.

She melted into him, feeling a weight she hadn't even realized she'd been carrying lift off. She pressed her face into the crook of his neck and breathed deeply, inhaling his scent, grounding herself in him. He smelled like man and cars and, Goddess bless, she'd missed him. She may not remember the missing days in her mind, but her heart did.

He pulled away and scanned Paige's face. He lost his smile, then turned to Roxxie, his jaw tight, posture rigid. "I think we should take a break."

That...was probably the first time Paige had ever seen him as an *alpha*. She had to admit. It was rather impressive. "Dexx."

Roxxie took a step back, staring at him like he'd lost his mind. "This wasn't my doing."

Dexx shook his head, his lips pursed. "We've put too much trust in you. My trust bucket is empty."

A look of disbelief washed over the angel's expression. "After...everything?"

"Dexx." He still didn't even know how much Roxxie had done.

"And Bobby?" Roxxie asked as though Paige hadn't even spoken.

"He's the reason. That and our other kids. What happens when the angels decide they need Leah for weeks on end?"

Roxxie opened her mouth.

It wasn't fair he was taking this out on her, but Paige had the same fear.

Dexx slashed his hand and advanced on her. "Or when Raphael needs Tyler's voice? Or Kammy's mind reading abilities? Or maybe Mandie's fire starting ability. Or what about the new babies?"

Roxxie's pinched gaze fell on Paige.

His expression went even darker.

Paige...was a little turned on at the moment. Not in an "I'm going to take this man and strip off all his clothes" way. More of an "If I wasn't the size of frelling house, I'd seriously consider kissing that man" way.

But that didn't matter because he could potentially be endangering the kids. "Rox."

She held up a hand.

Dexx licked his bottom lip, his free hand shaking. "The gall. This had nothing to do with the demons in Portland, which you *should* be worried about, by the way. No. This had to do with my children."

"Dexx, they're concern—"

He released a growl that was more cat than man.

Alma set her hand on his arm and sighed. "Don't."

He breathed heavy, eyes set on the angel, hand pointing off the property. "Get out."

Roxxie held out both hands imploringly. "You need me."

He jerked his chin, his hand nearly shaking with rage, his jaw clenched, his jugular extended. "We have the wards."

"You will need an angel to *keep* those wards in place."

Dexx looked away, a deep glower on his face. "You are no longer welcome in our home or on our land. If I see you here without an invitation…" He let the statement trail off.

She met his gaze and held it, reminding the *man* she was an *angel*.

Good for her.

"I got her out." Roxxie's voice was hard and sharp.

"After I told you to."

"I was looking—" She cut herself off and let her hands fall to her sides. "Do you have any idea how much trouble I'm in?"

"The mother of my children was endangered because of you. Don't think I care."

Roxxie paused, her expression folded in frustrated alarm that was shifting visibly toward anger. "This is the wrong time to be pushing away allies."

Dexx pulled Paige closer with one arm.

Which was so disgustingly romantic. She pushed his arm away and stepped out in front.

"He wiped her memories," Roxxie's voice was small as she took a step back.

"Why?" Alma demanded.

"So, she couldn't give anyone the location. Same with

anyone else who goes, but Paige? It's a little more complicated."

As if she didn't already know that.

Roxxie raised one eyebrow as it shifted from pink to silver to white. "She has one daughter that can reach beyond the door between this world and ours. Raphael couldn't risk Paige telling Leah how to get to him."

"You can't be serious," Alma said derisively. "That girl brings souls across, not angels."

"The child reaches through the door in the same way Paige does."

"But I can only touch demon souls." Paige felt like she'd been hit with a sledge hammer. She had one daughter who could bring angels into their realm? Possibly? Maybe? And two unborn children who could close the door completely?

She was so fucked.

"As I've said," Roxxie said to Paige, regaining some composure, "you are safe. But keep your head down."

She didn't have to be told that twice.

Roxxie glanced down at Paige's belly, then met her gaze. The angel's eyes swam with silver flecks before she disappeared.

Alma released a breath and swept Paige up in another hug. "I'm glad you're back, Pea."

"Thanks." Paige was, too. She pulled away, touching Dexx's chest. "You're healed." Now that her memories were returning, Paige recalled the last time she'd seen him, he'd been hurt.

"Yeah." He blinked as if finally realizing what she said, then pressed her head to his chest.

That was where she wanted to stay. Her bulging belly wasn't making the gesture comfortable, but she didn't want to stop touching him. It was like half her soul had been returned to her.

"I'm fine." He pulled away.

She refused to let go of his hand.

He squeezed her fingers and lifted her chin, so she met his eyes. "We're all fine."

Paige nodded once and blinked. Reality slammed into her. If Roxxie hadn't been able find her, if…the corridor hadn't disappeared? That had to be a bigger issue. Part of Heaven had disappeared to show Roxxie where Paige was? Whatever. If it hadn't been for that, Paige might have been stuck in Heaven until she gave birth and then? She might never have seen her kids. That…was scary. She'd already lost one child. The thought of losing another—two—was terrifying. "What happened?"

"A lot." He pulled her toward the house. "Let's go inside and get you something to drink. Are you hungry? Thirsty? Did they feed you?"

Alma brushed Paige's deep brown hair with her gnarled hand as they walked. "It looks like they took good care of you."

Paige shrugged. She had to assume they did, given the size of her. "Roxxie said she found me hooked up to feeding tubes or something. I don't know."

Alma gave her a dry, dark look, but said nothing.

Paige was pissed. She wanted to face Raphael right then and there, pregnant or not. She wanted to hit him upside the head, box him around a bit. That fucking asshole took her and kept her… Getting pissed wasn't helping her. She was back. "What about Tuck?"

Dexx led her into the front door, by-passing the stairs, and going toward the back. The large living room filled with couches and chairs was devoid of people. "What *about* Tuck? He's fine."

Tuck was the chief of police and her boss. As the captain

of the Red Star Division, she answered to the human police force. He was a good man and a good mentor.

"How did you take care of Cooper?" The only thing she kept hearing from everyone was that it was handled. Great, but the details could ride her up the butt. "And he's not a threat?"

"He's in an elder jail." Dexx pushed her into a dining chair. "Trust me, he's no longer a threat."

"Anyone else?"

Dexx tipped his head and went to the fridge. "Celeste is dead, but Skye is in the wind."

Those were names she didn't know, but she assumed they belonged to Cooper's pack. More than that, she didn't care. "So, the one in the wind could still come back."

He lifted one shoulder. "She could. Wouldn't do her any favors."

Never stopped anyone before.

He retrieved a coffee cup. "Cooper was a shifter-witch."

Paige scooted back from the table, making room for her growing belly. She'd known that. She didn't remember how, but she'd known that. "We know that for sure?"

Dexx nodded.

Those who just thought she was a witch carrying shifter-witch babies were terrified because a shifter-witch was powerful. Crazy strong.

But her reality was a little more complicated than that. She carried ancients, powerful shifter-witches. She was so fucked.

Alma pulled out a carton of eggs and a package of bacon. She held them both up for Paige. "Good for you?"

Paige nodded. Eggs and bacon were the least of her concerns right now.

Tru strolled in, Kammy stumbling on his tottering toddler legs. "Has anyone seen Leslie?"

Dexx set the cup at the coffeemaker and pressed the button for hot water. "She didn't come home last night?"

Tru shook his head.

Bobby giggled as he ran into the kitchen, his tiny feet slapping the floor.

A wave of relief washed over Paige at that tiny voice. She pushed out of her chair and scooped him up in her arms, swinging him in a tight circle before hugging him close.

Bobby gurgled happily, slapping her face with his hands.

"Paige." Tru's lips were as pinched as his blonde brows.

What had she done this time? She missed the normal, dorky Tru. Ever since the Blackmans had kidnapped his wife and daughter to get at Paige, he'd become this…prude. She understood. She did. But they'd kidnapped *her* sister, *her* niece, *and* her daughter. So, he needed to find a cork for his butt. She put Bobby on her hip. "What's going on?"

"You're okay?" Tru pushed past her to the kitchen counter.

Paige nodded and moved out of his way.

He picked up Kammy and put him in the red highchair.

What the fuck? "What's going on?"

Dexx handed her a cup of steaming hot tea. "A lot, actually."

"Okay. Great. Fill me in." Paige let her tone inform everyone just how little patience she had. "Is my sister all right?"

"Well," Alma said, her gnarled hand flexing over the handle of the spatula. "We don't know."

That wasn't an answer. Paige looked to Dexx for more information.

He held up his hand. "Remember when she was bitten at school?"

Oh, for fuck's sake. Paige already knew about this. She'd discovered Leslie had been chosen by the griffin spirit when she'd been in Utah. She should...probably *tell* them what she'd learned there. Why hadn't she?

Oh. Right. Because they'd been busy and attacked and then busy and then...attacked. She was starting to see a trend.

Dexx shrugged. "There are a lot of people who fear her."

"Why?" She was *Leslie*. Of all the people on the face of the planet to fear, Leslie wasn't one of them.

"She's a shifter-witch."

She was *Leslie*.

Dexx widened his eyes, trying to get Paige to see. "Cooper was a shifter-witch and he was..." He kept nodding as he chose his words carefully. "...very powerful. He won against almost every alpha. He almost beat Chuck."

Shit. Their regional high alpha who was the high alpha because he was the *strongest* of all of them? "Seriously."

Dexx tipped his head.

"Is he all right?"

"He will be. But the fact remains that *she's* the *only* reason we won against him."

Okay. Fine. Paige could understand the scare. Maybe. "But she's Leslie."

"And she's been acting weird lately."

"So?"

"She's disappeared." Tru clenched his hands into fists. "She's abandoned her kids."

That didn't sound like Leslie. That was the only time you really had to be scared of her; when you got between her and her kids.

Dexx jutted his jaw to the side.

"Do we know if she's in danger?"

Dexx glanced at Alma.

Alma refused to look up.

Tru ground his jaw.

Why were they acting like this? *They* looked scared. "I'm gonna go find her."

Alma turned to the stove. "Eat an egg first."

Fine. An egg and then she was going to prove to them that Leslie was still…*Leslie.*

2

After feeding herself, then feeding her kids, Paige felt pretty good. She clung to Bobby and Leah a little more than she probably should. She didn't want to leave after having been gone for three weeks.

But her sister was out there, somewhere. She might be hurt, scared, or in need. If everyone feared her, *she* had to be terrified.

Dexx slid into the driver's seat. He'd already made it quite clear he wasn't letting her out of his sight. "Where to?" he asked, clicking on his seatbelt.

Paige didn't have an answer. Instead, she listened to Leah's car engine roar. Normally, they'd be riding in Jackie, a 1970 Dodge Challenger, and the center of Dexx's soul. However, apparently, Jackie was broke as fuck. She'd been a casualty of the Lizard Wizard Battle, as Dexx was now calling it.

Paige didn't know what this car was. It was black, only had a front seat, had a bed like a pick-up truck, but was low to the ground. Also, it was in the shape of a boat. He called it a Ranchero or Rancho or something like that. She had no idea where he'd gotten it.

And she knew better than to bring it up. They had more important things to deal with, like where in the hell she should she start looking for Leslie. "The soap shop."

Dexx didn't say anything as he put the car in gear and started the trek down the long, gravel driveway.

"How much danger is she in?" Paige asked quietly, her hand on her belly. "I get the feeling she's in more danger from everyone else than they are of her."

"After Cooper, everyone's a little on edge." Dexx's tone was dry and stiff. "He did a hell of a lot of damage."

Paige had to bite off her flippant reply. "The elders?"

"Are more than a little concerned."

Great. "How quiet have you been able to keep this?"

"A pretty tight lid, but it's harder and harder every day."

That couldn't be good. "Why?"

"If you're asking if we should be worried about the Shadow Sisterhood, the answer is yes. We should be."

The Shadow Sisterhood was an organization that kept the paranormal community secret. Honestly, Paige hadn't dealt with them too much. "Need to be worried? Why?"

"Yeah."

Was he being *coy?*

Dexx took in a deep breath. "She's a griffin, Pea."

"Yeah. I *know* that. I *met* the damned griffin in the spirit cave."

He sputtered. "You could have warned me."

"If I remember correctly, I'd *tried,* and you told me to stop telling you about my trip to Utah."

"You were telling me about the twins and I didn't want to hear about that. Some things should remain a surprise."

She'd gone to Utah to gain the help of another pack but

had discovered another shifter-witch instead. She'd also been introduced to the spirit cave, had been judged by a council of spirit animals and found wanting, and had met their unborn twins. They were a girl and a boy. The girl was a thunderbird and the boy was a rajasi. She hadn't even known what a rajasi was before that point. A very powerful lion who was always on fire.

And *now* she knew her unborn babes were capable of sealing the doors to Heaven and Hell. Shit. Should she tell him that part? Or should *that* remain a surprise as well?

"Is there something you'd like to tell me *now?*"

She probably shouldn't lead with the twins. "Well, Cawli chose me because he wanted to bring the ancients into the world."

"He—" Dexx pressed a thumb to his eye. "Why?"

"They wanted out?"

Dexx gave her a quick, flat look before returning his attention to the road.

Really, the story she'd received was full of holes and she didn't buy it. It seemed a little too…flat. "We're supposed to keep them safe."

"Keep them *safe?* When they're creating this much chaos?"

She couldn't disagree with him there.

"What else?"

"Well, you don't want to hear about the twins."

He shook his head, but then stopped, one hand raised. "Are they?"

"Ancients?" She nodded.

"Great. And witches?"

Blessed Mother, she hoped not. "I don't know."

"Do you know anything that could help us? With Leslie?"

"I met the griffin. He said he needed someone strong."

"So, he chose Leslie?" Dexx slid his hands along the steering wheel, but his voice said he didn't believe why the griffin had chosen her.

Which pissed Paige off a little. Everyone underestimated her big sister. Well, frankly, so did she and that shit was gonna have to stop. "She's the strongest damned one of us."

He tipped his head in acknowledgement. "She's not herself lately."

Leaving her kids behind? Yeah, that didn't sound like Leslie. She didn't believe that women had to worship their kids, but she didn't abandon them, either.

Dexx parked behind the shop.

Leslie had opened Whiskey Wine and Soaps in downtown Troutdale when they'd arrived in Oregon. She'd felt a great deal of guilt opening the store because it took so much time away from her kids, but she loved that place. Paige got out of the car without saying another word and walked into the back of the shop.

The rear was set up as a work room. The right half was where Leslie made her soaps. There were racks and racks of soaps waiting to be cured. Paige had never seen so many soaps before. "She's been busy."

"That's the thing," Dexx said, stepping in behind her. "She goes through periods where she's hyper alert, super focused. She gets lots of things done."

"That's great."

He rubbed his head with the palm of his hand. "But then she'll forget her own kids. She won't pick them up. She'll forget to feed them or put them to bed."

That didn't sound like her sister at all.

"She forgets to come home."

Nothing would make Leslie forget to come home. At least, that's what Paige thought.

Paige walked from the work room to the sales floor, listening for the sounds of… anything. She passed the wine section and unlocked the front door, stepping outside.

Quiet.

The light post directly in front of her was covered in multiple layers of papers.

Dexx walked to the light post and pointed to one of the flyers. "Missing pets."

What did *that* have to do with *anything*?

"You don't understand, Pea."

"Then make me." Before she punched someone, namely him.

He swallowed, looking around before leaning in. "We're pretty sure she's eating them."

Oh—gawd. Oh…gross. Wow. Pets? Wow. Shit.

She hadn't expected that one. She pulled herself together.

Dexx ducked his head and looked up through his lashes as the rising sun washed warm light along the sides of the brick buildings. "Where do we start?"

Paige opened her mouth to say something brilliant. At least she'd hoped it would be brilliant.

Leslie's voice stopped her. "Baby sister, you're back."

Paige spun.

Leslie had appeared in the middle of the sidewalk, fully clothed, her hair slightly mussed. "I see the angels brought you back in one piece. That's something, at least."

Well, she *looked* like Leslie. "Where did you come from?"

Leslie shrugged and gestured around. "Were you looking for me?"

"We need to go home."

"No. I have other things to do." She squinted toward to the street.

This didn't *sound* like Leslie. The Texan drawl was gone.

Her posture was different. She almost had a haughty pose to her stance. "griffin?"

Leslie blinked slowly, returning her attention back to Paige. "Great Cawli," she said with a slight sneer. "It took you long enough to make this happen."

Cawli stirred in the back of Paige's mind.

Leslie raised her eyebrows and turned away. "It's nice to see you were brought back, but I have other things to attend to."

Other things to attend to? "Where is my sister?"

"I'm right here, Pea," Leslie said, her drawl back. She put her hand on her hip and rolled her eyes.

"Les?" Shit. This was going to be confusing.

"Yeah." She sounded for all the world like she didn't understand what all the fuss was about.

"Do you know what's going on?"

Leslie took in a deep breath. "I know."

"Where have you been?"

"Out."

"Out where?"

Leslie's expression pinched as if trying to remember. She ran her tongue along her teeth.

"Do you even know?"

She shrugged, though her eyes were still unsure. "I've been busy."

"Okay. What about your kids?"

"Tru has them. They're fine."

"You're just going to..." Something was very wrong. Maybe there was a reason the ancients had been away so long. Maybe the humans of before had known better. "What do you remember?"

"I remember everything just fine, Pea." A frown flicked across Leslie's brow. "But you know what?"

No. She didn't know what.

"Cawli lied to you."

Lied to her. "Okay."

"You *can* shift."

"I figured." And she had. Since Cawli had chosen her, he'd told her repeatedly she couldn't shift. It seemed odd she'd be chosen by an animal spirit and be unable to shift.

When she'd gone to Utah, a few things had come to light, and her doubts on his honesty had grown.

He'd told her he'd been in a sticky place. He wasn't supposed to be helping her, inviting her and her family in.

"Yes." Leslie took a deep breath and turned toward the street, her chest out. "This is so freeing."

"griffin," Dexx said with a tired sigh. "What did you do?"

"Nothing." Leslie turned toward him and gave him a carefree smile. "This is amazing."

Dexx glanced at Paige, set his shoulders, and turned his attention to Leslie. "griffin, I'm telling you to fall back."

Leslie frowned. "But I didn't do anything wrong."

"You said it yourself. You need someone to keep you under control."

The griffin shrugged Leslie's shoulder.

What the hell was going on? "Wait. What?"

Dexx raised his hands as if in surrender.

Paige turned to the griffin. "Why *did* you choose my sister?"

"Because," the griffin said happily, sounding just like Leslie, "she is the strongest of you."

True.

"She brought a fire maker into this world."

Yeah. She had.

"And a story teller of amazing talents."

That was one way to describe Tyler's abilities. He could also destroy a room with the sound of his voice.

"And she had the faith to carry a soul reader into this world."

Commonly known as a telepath.

"She is the only one we have found in millennia who is capable of giving me refuge." Something shifted in those eyes, like the griffin was hiding something. "Shelter. A chance at life."

"If that's what you want, then you should be able to give her a little breathing room," Paige said. "Leslie needs to come out. Her kids miss her. She misses her kids, or she would if you allowed her to."

"She does, but we have so many other things to care for. The children will be children later."

"No. They grow, and then they're not children." It was like talking to a big, powerful child.

The griffin shook Leslie's head. "I chose her, but she had to choose me in return."

Dexx frowned. "That day with Cooper."

"The spirit stealer." The griffin growled low. "Yes. Leslie was desperate, and I gave her the power she needed to overcome him and save you."

Dexx closed his eyes for a long moment. "I'm the reason you're here."

"And I am eternally grateful."

"Well, then," Dexx snapped his finger and pointed. "Eternally grateful yourself to the background."

The griffin smiled. "Of course." With a blink, Leslie's familiar expression returned. "Paige? Holy fuck."

Paige's eyes widened in surprise at the rather sudden shift.

Leslie pounced, hugging her tight. "Where the hell have you been? I've been worried."

Dexx put his hand on Leslie's shoulder and propelled them both to the shop. "Let's get her home."

Getting her home wasn't going to solve this. They needed a real solution and fast.

Angels wanting her babies.

Her sister eating Fluffy.

The world trying to get their hands on the Whiskeys.

This had to be leading to something bad. She didn't doubt that in the least.

3

Paige's phone rang before they'd even made it to the car. With a sigh, she swiped the icon and put the phone to her ear. "Whiskey."

"Tuck."

"Hey, Chief."

He led the Troutdale Police Department, both the human and the paranormal divisions. When the Whiskeys had arrived in town, Chuck, the high alpha, had asked Paige to start up the paranormal division, and the best way to do that while sharing expenses, and authority, was to umbrella under a department already in existence. It helped they got along so well. Chief Tuck was good people, something Paige had once thought in short supply.

"Hey." His tone was brisk but pleasant. "Where are you?"

"Soap shop." However well they got along, though, whenever Tuck called, it meant troubles she had to take care of. "Why? What's up?"

"Well, I heard you were back, and we need to catch up on a few things."

Was back? As if she'd been on vacation. Well, hell. What story *had* everyone told Tuck? "Okay. When?"

"Now. Your office."

Which was in the opposite direction. "Okay." Crap. "Sure. See you in a few." She hung up, shoving her phone—which had a full charge somehow—into her back pocket.

"What's up?" Dexx asked.

"Tuck wants to talk." Paige looked at Leslie who was starting to lose her Leslie-ness again. "What are we going to do about her?"

Dexx rested his forearms over the top of the car. "I'm her alpha."

"You're what?"

He nodded. "So, I'll figure out what to do with her. You go talk to your boss. We'll be fine."

Saying he was an alpha and stepping up to *be* the alpha were two totally different things, but what choice did she have? She'd seen him with Roxxie earlier and that had been…well, Dexx on drugs, really. But…crap. "Hey, Les?"

Leslie looked up, her expression foggy, her eyes darting from place to place. "Yeah, Pea?"

Paige didn't know what to say. "What do you think?"

Leslie looked at her as if not quite sure what the question was about.

Yeah, maybe she didn't understand the question either. "What I mean to say is, do you feel okay? Does it feel like whatever this—" Paige gestured at all of Leslie. "—is bad?"

Leslie let out a long breath. "No. It doesn't feel bad. It just feels weird. It's like I'm finding new parts of myself I never knew existed."

That didn't quite make sense. "You are not the kind of mom to forget about her kids."

"You're right. I'm not that mom, but I happen to know my kids are okay. I have a grandmother who can take care of them when I'm not around. I have a husband who's actually around more often than he's not."

"That's not the same." Paige didn't know how she was going to get through to Leslie. She just knew she had to. "You're their mom. You should be there for them."

"And I am." Leslie took a step towards Paige.

She looked like her sister but at the same time she didn't. There was a distinct set to her shoulders, a stronger stance when she walked. She looked like a warrior almost.

It didn't matter what was inside of her sister. Paige was not going to back down. "If that's the case, then where were you last night?"

Leslie lifted one shoulder and shook her head.

"Because you weren't there to change your son's diaper. You weren't there to feed your kids this morning. You weren't there to put them to bed last night. So, where were you?"

"Where was I? Where were you? You've been gone for three weeks."

Paige almost felt bad about that, except she couldn't. She'd been taken against her will. And she still didn't completely understand why.

"The angels had me." Paige gestured with her hands palms up. "I have no idea where they took me. The only thing I do know is that it was bad and I was in some serious trouble."

Leslie raised her eyebrows.

"So, yeah, you may not know where I was for the last three weeks, but what I do know is that if I'd had a chance, I would have been here for my kids." Not that she had *any* room to speak. Paige was on par for the Worst Mom Award herself.

A smile blossomed on Leslie's face, one of derision. "Oh, really." She snorted "So, then, where have you been for the last, I don't know, year? Because it hasn't been here. It hasn't been with your kids. I've been taking care of your kids, Paige. Dexx has been taking care of your kids while you've been gallivanting all over the world."

Well, she wasn't wrong. "I haven't been *gallivanting* all over the world, Leslie. I've been doing what I can to keep the family safe. To keep our town safe. To keep our *people* safe."

"Our people?" Leslie looked less than impressed. "Your *people* are your family. Your grandmother and your sister and your kids and your boyfriend. What other people do you think you have?"

"Do you honestly think that the paranormals aren't our people? Do you really think we can exist in this world and not claim them?"

Leslie looked away, her lips curled up in a sneer. "I think that just a few weeks ago, we nearly died. I think just a few months ago, other paranormals tried to kill us. And, where were you? You weren't here trying to protect your kids. You weren't here trying to protect your family. You were off trying to save the world. And why is that?"

Leslie wasn't talking about what had happened three weeks ago because she already knew Paige had been a ward of Heaven. This was more. She had an answer, but she didn't think Leslie would appreciate it. Or the griffin, for that matter.

"You're saving the world because you need to be the hero."

And there it was. Paige had always wondered when she would see Leslie's resentment. Leslie always kept a cool head. She was the Whiskey pillar. She was the one everyone went to, could rely on. Paige had always wondered if there was a little bit of resentment hiding in the background just waiting to come out. Well, she guessed she had her answer now.

Leslie's sneer grew. "Did I hit a little too close to home with that one?"

Paige didn't know what else to say. Her reality was that, yes, there were other things out there more important than her family. There was an entire world of people that needed her. And if Leslie didn't understand that? Well, Paige didn't need to find a solution to that question right away.

She did, however, need to go talk to her boss. Because, while the angels might've been holding her for three weeks thinking nothing important was going on, there might have been. Maybe nothing newsworthy for an angel, but for a witch? For a new mother trying to ensure the safety of her kids? For a police captain trying to start her new police force? Yeah, there was a lot that could have gone wrong.

She met Dexx's gaze. "Get her home and see if you can keep from losing her again."

Dexx raised one eyebrow but didn't say anything to her sharp tone. He just got in the car and closed the door.

Paige opened the passenger's door for Leslie and plastered a reassuring smile on her face. "I'll see you at home."

Leslie didn't move for a long moment. Then, she got in. "I guess I will."

Paige closed the door and took a step back, listening to the rumble of the beast's engine disappear down the street.

What was Paige more pissed about? The fact the angels had taken her against her will for three weeks, or that her sister was out of control?

She fumed about both issues as she waddled down the street towards the precinct.

The Red Star Division had taken up residence in an old municipal building just off Main Street. She had no idea why a building that size had even been built in the first place, but it had made things quite convenient when she'd moved herself and her family to Oregon.

When they had first arrived, Paige had been assured she had a job in the Portland PD. However, when she reported for work, she discovered there was no job. Her new boss didn't want anything to do with her or the types of trouble she would bring. He knew all about the paranormals. He knew about the Whiskeys, the Blackmans, and the Eastwood's—the three largest covens in the area. He even knew the repercussions involved with having a member of one of the prominent witch families on his team. He probably understood the politics better than Paige ever would.

So, she'd gone home without a job, failing again in her ability to support her family.

That's when Chuck had come to her with a new plan. He wanted a paranormal police force, one run by someone who knew how a police force was supposed to operate. Initially, she turned him down. Until she realized it was the best solution for everyone. Not just her family, but for the paranormal community at large.

She'd spent weeks building up her team and the policies that would make the Red Star Division a legitimate operation. Their first task had been to bring down the Eastwood witches.

And they'd succeeded. Mary Eastwood was in prison thanks to them. They had taken the case to the Elder Council and won. Their mundane evidence had been practically useless. In cases like that, where magick was key and instrumental to the case, using mundane evidence was ridiculous. There wasn't a swab for picking up a magick trace. Just like there wasn't mundane test to use to determine the magickal signature from one witch to another.

That case had been a success. And it was great. Except now the Elder Council was keen on getting the witches back under elder control. For the last several months, they'd been sending Paige out to remote areas to speak with other covens, trying to get them to understand that being under the protection of the council was for everyone's benefit.

That wasn't the only thing she had to deal with, though. They'd also been sending her to out to talk to the paranormals who wanted to move away from the council. Many of them were terrified of witches. And not just because of the Eastwood's, though they were admittedly the worst. There were other witches out there, other covens who enjoyed lording over the power they had. There were those who enjoyed tormenting the paranormals around them, enslaving them, keeping them under their thrall.

Paige had made many promises to many people over the last several months. Some of those promises were of protection. Some, however, were not. She wasn't sure everyone would appreciate some of the bargains she'd made.

She stepped into the precinct and the familiar bullpen filled with desks and living vine walls.

The only person in the bullpen was Detective Michelle Gomez. She looked up as Paige walked in and moved to rise.

Paige raised her hand and kept walking to her office in the back. She could see through the window that Tuck had beat her there. She really didn't want to make him wait any longer.

Michelle stood up anyway and intercepted. Crossing her arms over her chest, she raised a dark eyebrow. "How long are you back for this time?"

"I really don't know." And Paige didn't. That was the crappy part of this mess. She sincerely hoped that things would eventually get better. She really needed them to. She had a life, a boyfriend, kids, family, a team. Babies growing in her damned belly. Leslie had brought up a good point. She couldn't just go gallivanting all over the world — or even the continental United States — when she had so many commitments at home. She just didn't have that luxury anymore.

Michelle quirked her lips. "So where were you for the last three weeks?"

"Angels. No choice." She fucking hated angels.

Michelle released her stance, letting her arms fall beside her. "Roxxie told us absolutely nothing."

"Dexx banned her."

"Good. Ever since the grove, I've had a bad taste for demons *and* angels."

Not good for Bobby, Paige's adopted prophet son.

Michelle turned toward Paige's office and gestured towards Tuck. "He's been in there for quite a while."

"How long is quite a while? He just called me."

Michelle shrugged. "About an hour?"

An hour? That's about the time she'd made it back.

"Maybe longer? I don't know."

Ugh. Paige may be in more trouble than she'd initially thought. "Well I probably better go figure out what he needs."

Michelle put her hand on Paige's arm. "We need you. Here."

Fuck. "You've got Dexx."

"Yeah." Michelle took a step back and perched on the edge of her desk, moving the large leaf of the philodendron out of her way. "And he's good, but he's not you. And he doesn't know squat about police procedure."

"This isn't news, Michelle." Paige had a problem with sarcasm. "We knew that when we put this team together."

"Yeah, we did." Michelle pushed off the desk and took her seat again. "But maybe you could at least train him how to do his job right. He's doing the best he can, but we need a leader who knows what he's doing."

Great. Just what she needed. She hoped the conversation with Tuck would go a little better.

4

P aige shut the door to her office behind her and took her seat. "Hey, Tuck, been waiting long?"

He gave her a friendly smile, playing with the brim of his hat. "Not too long."

Chief Tuck looked like the Most Interesting Man in the World, crossed with Sam Elliot. He was a bit of a cowboy with his snakeskin boots and his old Ford pick-up. Not that the pick-up was in the office, but Paige had seen it before and she'd given him a tough time about it more than once. He was an easy-going guy—for the most part. He had a long fuse, but when his temper flared, he was like a case of dynamite.

Well, not really. He could whisper forcefully, and you felt beat up afterwards.

Paige had no idea how he did that, but it was something Leslie was good at, too.

She stretched her legs out under the desk, grateful to take the weight off her swollen feet. "Should I get out some whiskey or something?"

That was something she'd seen on the movies and something she'd seen other captains do with difficult higher-ups, but it wasn't something she felt comfortable doing. She kinda got the impression she was already on shaky ground.

He pushed his lips out, accentuating his mostly salt, less pepper mustache and shook his head. "Nah."

Paige took in a deep breath and leaned back in her chair, folding her hands over her bulging belly.

He nodded curtly. "I need to know where you've been lately."

"Well—"

"And know I ain't talkin' about this last one. I already got that something weird happened. You're not off the hook, but you seem okay, and it doesn't sound like you were hurt. So, we'll deal with that later."

Great. "Well, the Elder Council has pulled me to help them with a few other cases."

Tuck nodded slowly but didn't say anything.

Fine. He needed to know. It made sense. He *was* technically her boss. "After the Eastwood case, they wanted to get witches back into the paranormal society."

"And you think that's a good idea?"

"Get them to follow a few basic rules? Yeah, I do." After what she'd seen, they needed it. "Look, most of the covens out there are good, wouldn't hurt a fly. You know, they have gardens and help with the community."

"Sounds good."

"Yeah. But then there are a few others who feel they're above the rules."

"Like the Eastwoods."

"Maybe not quite like the Eastwoods, but yeah. Like the Eastwoods."

"So, you're tellin' me you brought them in, and now you're good?"

"Well..." She wished it was that simple. "They've also been sending me out to talk to the paranormals who are threatening to leave the elder council protection because they're bringing in the witches."

Tuck tipped his head and scrunched down in his chair. "What does that mean? For us, I mean?"

"If they stay outside the council, it means if they break laws, you have to convict them in your court, not mine. But, that's just one thing."

He tapped his bearded chin with the tip of his thumb three times, then let his hand fall. "That ain't any good."

"No. It's not." Because there were certain things that needed to stay out of the human papers. The human world wasn't ready for werewolves living among them.

"Where all they been sending you?"

She released a breath of a chuckle. "It started with Portland."

"Because I agreed you could help them out over there as a favor to Captain Banes.

"Yes." It sounded like he was trying to make a point. She could guess what it was. She wasn't dumb.

"But then you were supposed to come back and work here."

She sighed and glanced at her clean desk. "And do what? Catch burglars?"

"That is what you signed up to do."

It was. She didn't know what to tell him, how to say it. "The elders need me to help them with a larger problem."

Tuck raised a bushy eyebrow.

"The president is making a huge societal shift."

"I thought you'd be happy to have a female president." His frown said he had no idea how the conversation had taken this turn.

"I would be if she wasn't dead set on sending us back to the Dark Ages."

Tuck waited in confusion.

If Paige could lean forward without jamming one of four tiny feet into her diaphragm she would. "I don't have enough evidence yet, but it really does look like she has a secret organization set to wipe us off the earth."

"You're kidding."

Paige shook her head. "That's only one of the things I've been working on, trying to track *those* assholes down. Paranormals have been disappearing all over."

"Great."

"That's not what I said. Vampires are gathering in Kansas."

"What did they want?"

It had sounded like a promising trip, but it petered out pretty quick. "To remain alive."

Tuck rubbed his mustache, his eyes flaring wide for a moment. "But you didn't come back and do your job after that, either."

She had checked in for a day or two. "Director Lovejoy needed my help in Seattle with a mermaid problem."

"You're..." He paused, his eyebrows high. "...kidding, right? Mermaids?"

"Really. Mermaids."

That had been an interesting adventure, but short because most of it had happened under water. She'd been there as an intermediary, really. The merfolk—and a lot of other waterborne creatures—had banded together to clean up Seattle's harbor. They'd just been doing so in ways that drew attention and made headlines. She'd helped with the negotiations, which sounded fun, but would have been a fast-forward scene if her life was ever made into a TV show.

"I spent a lot of time up in Alaska, but not for bad

reasons." She let her head fall against the back of her chair. "They're kinda cut off from everyone else up there and they make their own rules. Did you know—"

Tuck gave her a look of interest, though his blue eyes said he was starting to lose patience.

"—that they have wood witches up there? I didn't even know there was such a thing, but their magick is able to ward off danger better than the Whiskey wards. Do you know what that means?"

He shook his head, his eyes pinched.

"We've got demon magick, earth magick, all the elementals, bard magick, door magick—I mean to other dimensions, like, Hell—and angel magick in our wards." She pulled her head forward. "Pretty damned impressive, right? Totally surpassed by one witch with wood magick."

His lips disappeared in his mustache.

"Yeah." She let her head fall back again. "That's what I said. Also, 'can you help?' to which they said, 'nope.' But, they said it very nicely. So..." She sighed.

"Hmm. Did you succeed in bringing them under the elders?"

"Nope. I don't think that's ever going to happen, but they take care of their own anyway, so I don't think they'll really be a problem. That was more of a political thing, I think. The elders really want Alaska, but they aren't coming. They have their own ways of doing things."

Paige wanted their wood magick in her wards. Those things were amazing.

"When are you coming back here?"

That was a good question.

"You came back to Portland for the third time since you've been here. Banes said something about a demon problem, and I hear you're the gal for that."

As the demon summoner, yes. She was.

"But then you get back and disappear again, right when the whole damned town is literally blown to shit."

No one had told her about that. "More than what happened when the djinn attacked the ash grove?" Because there had been some pretty big explosions during that. Frankly, Paige didn't know how Michelle was still functioning. That had been her family, her grove under attack.

How many times had Paige's family been under attack? She was still okay. And none of her family had died.

Michelle had lost people she'd loved.

Okay. Paige could see why Michelle might be a little pissed at her for leaving.

"Yeah. A damned witch came through, a shifter-witch. Took out the packs like they were nothin'. Took down Dexx."

She somehow knew that happened, but it was foggy.

"Took Chuck down, too."

So, Dexx hadn't been exaggerating.

"And we needed you—the most powerful damned Whiskey witch of the Whiskeys, and the captain of my damned unit."

There wasn't a lot she could say to that. "The angels took me."

"Okay. What did they want?"

"Wish I could tell you." She clenched her hand into a fist of frustration. "They wiped my memories."

"That ain't helpin' you."

"But they think it's helping them."

Tuck sat up and leaned forward. "I'm gonna be straight with you, Whiskey."

That's usually what she liked most about him, but she had a feeling she wasn't going to like what he had to say on this one.

"We need a captain who can stay here and do the damned job."

She nodded sharply, because what was she supposed to say to that? He had a point.

"The chases. Endangering the public. The cases aren't being handled like you would have them handled. You have members on your team who haven't served, or been trained, and it shows. And they're all being led by a man who's a better rule breaker than enforcer."

Valid points. "What do you want me to do? Tell the elder council to stick it?" She was close to doing that anyway. She doubted they'd give her maternity leave. The thought was probably foreign to them.

"You and I both know you can't do that."

True statement.

He pointed at her with his hat. "You make a choice. You either work with them or you work here. And if you work with them, you either train the man tryin' to fill your shoes, or you find someone else to do it."

She narrowed her eyes at the desk, mulling it over.

"Dexx is a good man, but he ain't a leader. He gets the bad guy, sure, so let him do that with guidance, someone who knows how to do this job and lead."

"Have someone in mind for the job?"

He shook his head. "I was hopin' you would. You know the people like you in enforcement better'n I do."

She did, though she could count them on one hand.

"You did a respectable job getting all this started, but it's time. Paige."

Ouch. She let her head fall back against the chair again. "I hear ya, Chief."

"Get it fixed before you get called out again."

"Yes, Chief." But that could be at any time. Angels could swoop down and just abduct her again. She had no idea.

She was getting some damned angel wards set on her, something they couldn't see through or something. She wasn't going to be taken away just because Raphael got another feather up his ass.

"Anything else, Chief?"

Because he wasn't leaving.

He winced with one eye and nodded. "I sent you a file. I need you to open it."

She turned on her computer. "I haven't had a chance to start it up, so it might take a while."

He nodded. "We've had a lot of missing pets lately."

She didn't realize she was supposed to care about that.

"It's a sign there's a new shifter," he said in a tone that implied she should know that.

"Oh, right. Yeah." Like, how was she supposed to know that? Dexx hadn't shared those kinds of details with her.

"I have a feeling we have a new player in town." His expression said he was hiding something.

She turned her attention to the computer, which chirped at her. She took it through its start-up paces and then opened her email. Sure enough, there was an email from Tuck. She clicked the link.

A video filled the screen. A small room built on top of a flat roof. She glanced at Tuck in question.

He shook his head and gestured to the computer.

Okay. Whatever.

A raven swooped in, landed on the door, and opened it with its beak. It hopped inside, and feathers flew. Something came out of the door that might have been the end of a rope. A rope that lashed back and forth by itself.

No. A *tail*.

The tail disappeared, and a bald eagle flew out. But before it could go off frame, it shifted into something small like a hummingbird.

A chill washed over her. Witch-shifters were able to shift shape, into anything.

And that tail…could have been a griffin.

"Let me ask you something."

She could tell by the tone of his voice that she wasn't going to like where this was going.

"Do you know of any witch-shifters? Maybe newly bitten?"

Paige pretended to watch the rest of video. She didn't want to meet his gaze. Yes. She knew of a witch-shifter and, no, the situation wasn't under control.

"Because the last witch-shifter that came through town nearly destroyed us."

Paige's heart raced. What would happen if Tuck ordered her to arrest her sister? Or if the elders found about this? Would they make her bring Leslie in? For what?

Tuck's expression said he knew what she wasn't saying. "Leslie hasn't been acting herself lately."

Paige wasn't about to open her mouth and insert her foot. If that was a magickal gift, she'd be an adept. It was the one thing she was consistent with.

Tuck nodded. "Dexx told me she's the reason we won against Cooper McCree. Won't be long before others figure it out, too. Dexx owes that woman his life. Chuck too, for that matter, but if we're in danger, I need to know."

"She's a Whiskey." And she wished to hell that being a Whiskey meant something.

"I know it. Just makes it harder if you gotta do something."

Like what? Arrest her sister? For eating Pomeranians and —that was a pigeon coop. Who kept pigeons anyway?

"I ain't lettin' what happened last month happen again."

She couldn't either. She forced herself to meet his gaze and swallowed hard. "I understand, Chief."

He thumped his hat with his thumb and nodded. "Good." Turning, he put his hat on and left.

Paige blew out her cheeks. "What the hell am I going to do about Leslie? Hell. About everything?" Because...for shit's sake. She'd *just* gotten back.

5

When it came to work, Paige almost always knew what to do. And she knew she had to handle Red Star. There were two conversations that had to be had.

She pulled out her phone and stared at it for a long moment. She'd basically dropped Red Star in Dexx's lap and told him to do his best. Would he be upset if he found out she was looking for someone to replace him? She'd give him the offer to train into the position. Of course, she would.

But she doubted seriously he'd say yes.

He was well outside his comfort zone and it showed. Being a detective on the team was one thing. He could fly under the radar that way, but this? Running the department? That was totally different. She knew that, and now he did, too. His pride might push him to try to be the lead, but at some point, reality did have to rear its head.

Debating it wasn't helping. She flipped through her contacts and pulled up Tony Guerrerro's number. He'd been her partner for five years down in the Denver PD, and he was a vampire. In Denver, he'd already been in a position of power. He'd kept the vampires and shifters playing nice.

He picked up on the third ring. "Hey," he said, his tone filled with surprise. "I didn't expect to hear from you."

She really *was* bad at keeping in touch with people. "Yeah. How are you? Did you take the position in Texas?"

Her old boss had made an investigating force just for her, and she'd stayed for a few months. She'd just won custody of her daughter, and the courts had made her stay in Texas to complete the necessary assessments and tests and training. As soon as they cleared her, she'd packed up her family and relocated across the country.

But that had left her old boss with a job opening. She'd offered Tony up as the sacrificial lamb but hadn't heard one way or the other.

"No," he said. "I had obligations here in Nederland."

Nederland was a town very similar to Troutdale, in that it was full of shapeshifters and other paranormals.

But if he'd had obligations then, that meant he probably still did. "Oh." She tried to make her voice sound cheerful. She really didn't know too many people who could replace her in Red Star. If Tony turned out to be a bust, she'd have to go to FBI Director Lovejoy and ask her if she knew anyone. "What sort of stuff? Anything we need to know about up here?"

"Nah." Something closed shut on the other side of the phone. It sounded like a car door. "I handled it."

Past tense.

"It sounds like you're fishing, Paige. What's going on?"

"Well, I am." She sucked at tact, and she wasn't great at negotiations. "I have a possible job position up here."

"In Troutdale." His statement held a note of surprise.

"Yes."

"Really."

He sounded interested. Perfect. "It's actually my job. I'm the captain of the Red Star Division."

"Yeah. I heard. You're big news. Why do you need to find someone to do *your* job? First Texas. Now, this? Tell me you're not quitting."

"I'm not. The elders have me running in other directions and Red Star isn't getting the attention it deserves."

"I see."

He hadn't turned her down outright. "Red Star is attached to the local PD. Chief Tuck knows about the paranormals. We have a pretty good division of labor up here."

"Okay." Now *he* was fishing.

Shit, what else? "You would answer directly to Tuck. We also have the regional high alpha up here and you'd kinda be working with him, too."

"I've had dealings with high alphas before."

"Chuck?"

"I know of him. I hear he's fair."

"He is. We don't have a lot of vampires."

"No. You wouldn't."

Something about the way he said that made her do a double-take. "Is there something here we should know about? Something that would keep you away?"

He paused for a moment before saying bluntly, "The Eastwoods practice blood magick."

"I am aware."

"That's good." His tone implied *finally,* though he was kind enough not to say it out loud. "Their magick can send my kind into a feeding frenzy."

"Oh." Well, crap. "They're in Portland. I put up wards around Troutdale that warns us when the Eastwoods come. We don't put up with that kind of crap in our town."

"But Portland?"

"Probably wouldn't be safe. I took down Merry Eastwood last year, but the coven's still going."

"The *rest* of the coven?" He sounded incredulous. "It's still going?"

What did he expect? "We didn't have time to build a case against them, too." Well, they were... it was just a lot of stuff to sift through, and it was technically Captain Banes' jurisdiction. "But you could get up here and build a case against them."

He paused. "I want to see the place first."

"The team would want to interview you."

"Okay."

"And I still need to see if this might go to someone else."

"Oh? Anyone I know?"

Barely. "Dexx. He kinda stepped in when I couldn't be here, so it's only fair I give him a shot. But, I wanted to see if you were even available."

"I can be there tomorrow."

Whoa. "Seriously?"

"Yeah. I—" He clucked his tongue. "I need money. The situation here went sideways."

"In a way I should be concerned about?"

"No. I just made a few people angry that I probably shouldn't have."

"Like?"

"Important politicians who want to control the paranormals through threats and intimidation."

"The new president."

"Exactly."

"Oh." It amazed Paige what one person could do. "I see. Will that follow you here?"

"Shouldn't."

"Right, well, when you get up here, bring all that information with you. I'll give Tuck a head's up. Be ready to be grilled."

"Roger that. And, um, thanks for thinking of me."

"Anytime. See ya tomorrow." Paige hung up the phone and stood. There was a lot of stuff she needed to do in the office, but it had to wait.

She shoved her phone in her pocket and stopped at Michelle's desk on her way out. The green vine walls offered some privacy and sound dampening, much like a forest. It helped they practically *had* a small forest in the bullpen.

Michelle leaned back in her chair, shoving the end of her pen onto her canine. "What's up, Boss?"

"I'm heading out."

Michelle's expression pinched around the edges.

Paige held up her hand. "I have to go take care of a case Tuck just handed me, but I also need to deal with my replacement."

Michelle straightened, tossing her Bic pen on the desk. "What?"

"I'm going to offer it to Dexx. I feel I should at least give him a chance."

"Or? Tell me you have someone else in mind."

"I do." Paige nodded deeply and clasped her hands in front of her. "And he will be here tomorrow."

"Tomorrow." Michelle's eyes narrowed, and she pursed her full red lips. "Won't that make things awkward?"

"It's just an interview. I'm doing my due diligence."

"Okay." The corners of Michelle's lips pulled down and her focus grew distant. "Do I know this other person?"

"You don't. He was my partner in Denver."

"Oh." Her unfocused dark gaze landed on Paige. "What is he?"

"Vampire."

Alarm crashed over Michelle's features and she sat bolt upright. "But the Eastwoods."

"I know. He told me. He's coming to see if he can make it

work. He might have to stay in Troutdale and you might have to watch over him just like he'd have to watch over you."

"But less than I currently have to watch over Dexx."

Paige tipped her head with a sigh, looking toward the front. "When I started this, I had no idea what I was doing or what was going to be in store for any of us. I didn't know how much involvement the elders would want from me. I only knew I wanted to keep my family safe."

Michelle leaned back in her chair, putting her feet on the desk beside Paige. "You know, Dexx is doing better at that than you've been."

"I know."

"Angels?"

That was a sharp conversation change, but Paige understood what Michelle was really asking. "Demon summoner."

Michelle frowned but didn't ask anything further.

"Just know that I heard you, and I'm working on it." Paige stood. "Okay?"

Michelle nodded.

She left, not meeting anyone else on her way out. Her car was still in the parking lot, which wasn't uncommon. Sometimes, she'd start out on her own, but would catch a ride with someone else back home.

She was thankful for it as she reached into the rear wheel well and pulled out the spare key. It didn't take her long to drive through the small town, down the narrow, two-lane road on the west bank of the Sandy River, and down her dirt driveaway. Green surrounded her in the form of trees and tall grass. The farmlands on the right were tall with something she couldn't name. It didn't look like corn and that was all she could tell. She'd never make it as a farmer.

The canopy cut out much of the light, shielding her in cool shadow. She slipped through the wards which whispered a rippling greeting as she passed and parked her car in front of the house. She didn't always get a parking spot in the garage. As the part-time car, she often times found herself relegated to the circular driveaway.

The house was a two-storied monstrosity with a wrap-around porch on each floor. She could see the French doors that led to her and Dexx's room, but the light was off. Which she expected, but she always looked up anyway. She didn't really know why.

One of the babies moved in her womb, shoving a little foot into her diaphragm.

Ugh. She pushed the heel of her hand into her stomach, moving the little guy's foot away. Tuck hadn't even mentioned the pregnancy.

Which was a relief. When she'd been pregnant with Leah, she'd been put on light duty almost immediately, and everyone treated her like she had an incurable disease. To have her boss—for however much longer he remained her boss—treat her like a human being meant a lot.

Chaos attacked her as soon as she entered the house.

Mandy screamed at Tyler. Pounding feet thundered overhead. "You take it back!"

"No fire!" Paige shouted. She shouldn't have to remind her niece of this, but she was a teenager now and she didn't always remember. "Get out of the house if you're going to throw a fit."

"I'm not taking it back!" Tyler shouted. He appeared at the top of the stairs, and as he hurtled himself down them, his socked feet slid on a few of the steps. His outspread arms kept him pretty balanced as he gripped the banister and the wall on his flight down.

"I'm going to *kill* you!"

"Figuratively," Paige cautioned as Mandy followed her brother like a raging harpy. Though, to the girl's credit, there were no flames.

Mandy gave her aunt a 'well-duh' look and continued her pursuit, brother and sister disappearing down the hall to the kitchen and out the back door. Dexx had made a sort of proving grounds out there. At first, Leslie had been opposed to them even existing, let alone allowing the kids to use them. But now? They were a godsend.

Dexx stepped out of the living room to her left and pulled her gently to him, glancing around. "I have Leslie contained for now."

"What do you mean, 'contained'?" It didn't sound good.

"I don't know if you remember Ripley and Joe?"

The padfoot and the bear Dexx had just recently accepted into his growing pack. "Yeah."

"Well, when they were trying to cure his twin of rabies, they kept him contained in a bunker."

"A bunker." Yeah. That definitely didn't sound great.

"It's not far. She's safe. She can't get out."

"Can *we* get her out?"

"Yeah. Its easily opened from the outside."

"What was this thing used for?" Paige demanded. "A jail?"

"Probably a place to house uncontrollable paranormals until they could get them under control. I don't know. I didn't ask. I just said, 'Gift horse? Great. I'll take it.' And then used it."

Paige released a long sigh. "Fine. We need to have a conversation about what to do with her anyway."

"Exactly, but while she's not trying to kill us or eat the kids. That was my thought."

As much as she hated to admit it, "Good thinking."

Bobby wobbled into the hall on his toddler legs, giggling madly, little arms flailing.

Leah walked in after him, a smile on her face. Light

streaming in from the door shined on her long blonde hair. "Hey, Mom."

"Hey, Lee." Paige felt complete when her daughter was in the room. She gave Leah a quick hug and pressed a kiss onto the top of her head. "You doing okay?"

"Yup." And she looked like she was, too. Her body language was carefree and everything. "Oh, hey, Ash is coming over tonight to look at Bringer of Doom."

"Okay—what?" Paige liked Ashlynn, Leah's best friend, but…Bringer of Doom?

"That's what I'm calling the car because Ranchero just sounds stupid." Leah narrowed her blue eyes in thought. "Nah. I've gotta think of something better."

"Yeah." Dexx made a shooing motion with his hands. "Take Bobby out back."

"Okay." Leah gathered her brother in her arms and disappeared, talking to him about car names.

Paige crossed her arms over her chest and narrowed her eyes at Dexx.

"Yes. She needs a car," he said, his arms wide. "Can this be a conversation for later?"

She'd known he'd been thinking about it. But a car was a big thing. She didn't even *know* what a Ranchero was. "Fine. We need to talk about something else anyway."

"I was just joking. I *want* to tell you all about the car."

"Yeah. I know." And she did. That man could go on for hours talking about engines and firewalls and, oh gods, the gaskets. "But there's something important we need to discuss."

Dexx grimaced, his shoulders sagging. "What happened this time?"

Paige understood how he felt. "I'll get to that in a minute, but first I wanted to discuss something with you."

"You're repeating yourself."

"Alright, smart-ass." How to broach the subject so that it wouldn't wound his pride and force him to react defensively. "I called Tony."

"Your partner?"

"Yeah. Him."

"Okay, why?"

She took in a deep breath, watching him. "To take my place as captain."

Dexx went still for a long moment.

And then every bone in his body seemed to melt. "Great. When does he start?"

6

That really was one of the remarkable things about Dexx. He knew how to keep things simple. "If you want the job, Tuck and I will consider you."

Dexx chewed on his lip.

What she wouldn't give to know what was going on inside that head. Scratch that. She probably really didn't want to know. "Tony's just coming out to interview and see if he wants it."

"Why wouldn't he? Wait. Didn't he take your job in Dallas?"

"He had obligations in Nederland he couldn't get away from."

Dexx pulled a face. "Okay, and those aren't going to hold him up here?"

Paige shook her head. "But apparently he's going to have troubles with the Eastwoods."

"Who doesn't?"

Valid.

"Why?"

"Blood magick puts vampires into a feeding craze."

Dexx tipped his head to the side, his eyes squinty. "That seems like a problem to me."

"Could be, which is the reason I want to be very clear that a decision hasn't been made yet. If you *want* it, it *could* be yours, but we would really have to train you."

Dexx quirked his lips but didn't say anything.

They'd already had so many conversations lately about the way he handled things. Dexx thought being a cop meant going after the bad guy, to hell with the risks. An idea he had probably gotten from Hollywood and cheap TV because that for sure wasn't the way the real world worked.

In the real world, cops could end up seriously maimed or dead if things went wrong. Or, worse, they could harm those they were sworn to protect.

Sworn to protect. Shit. She hadn't sworn any of them in. That hadn't even been something she'd *thought* of. Fuck. She sucked at this.

Leading cops meant finding ways to keep them safe while giving them enough freedom to do their jobs, which really was to keep everyone else safe.

How could she teach him that when she sucked at it herself?

Though… he was starting to get that.

"You really do have a natural talent for this kind of thing." Just maybe not being a leader, which was odd since he was supposedly an alpha. Okay. She wasn't going to say supposedly. She *knew* he was an alpha. He just wasn't a particularly *great* alpha. He had his moments. Sure. But for the most part?

He kinda sucked at it.

"Yeah." His tone told her to shut up. "I hear ya."

"I don't think you do." She'd been good at handing out the harsh criticism but hadn't offered anything else. She realized it was because she loved him. Sounded stupid, but that was the truth of it.

He sighed and stared at her lips.

Oh, yeah. He wasn't feeling the love. "Look, you've got natural skill. You've got a way of bringing odd couples together. People who shouldn't be able to work together, like Tarik and Michelle—" Who were mortal enemies, being djinn and dryad. "—or Frey and Rainbow."

"I think you did Tarik and Michelle."

"No. I threw them together on a team." Paige had brought Michelle with her from Dallas. She'd asked Michelle if she could work with Tarik. The djinn destroyed ash groves for their power.

Dexx had made that relationship *happen*.

He raised both shoulders, more of a gesture to shut her up than a shrug. "I know I messed up."

"No, you don't." And that was true. Dexx Colt was a stubborn man with a thick head. "You know that you got yelled at and you *keep* getting yelled at no matter how many bad guys you put away."

He daggered her with his gaze. "It's like you know me."

About as well as he knew her, which was saying a lot. There was no one she felt more comfortable being around. That man completed her in so many ways. "Maybe. Anyway, truth of the matter is, we would be lost without you on the team and I want to make sure that whatever happens, we don't lose you."

"I won't leave."

"Physically? Great. Because I'm carrying your kids."

He rolled his eyes. "Now, I feel trapped."

"Good." She took his hand and put it on her belly.

One of the twins kicked his hand.

His eyes widened, and an almost boyish smile lit his face.

Oh, that man. She'd melt into that smile if she could. She reached up and touched his face because she *had* to. "I love you, so damned much, but I know you. If you feel you're being pushed out, you'll disappear in other ways. And I need you here, Dexx."

"I feel like I'm in trouble when you say my name." But the look on his face just said that while the words cut, he loved her back with his whole heart.

She pulled his face to hers and touched her lips to his murmuring, "Understand me, Dexx."

He breathed her breath.

"You are mine."

He raised his chin minutely, at least as much as he could without pulling away from her.

"But you're theirs as well. They need you just as much as I do."

His green eyes brightened as the corners drooped marginally.

She kissed him quickly and pulled away. With him handled, she needed to figure out what to do about her sister. People were work. "Where's Alma?"

"Kitchen. Tru, too."

"Great." Because those were the two she needed to talk to. "Come on. Let's figure out what we're doing with Leslie."

He followed her through the large living room, meandering around the two sofas. The dining room was separated by the chimney that rose through the middle of the house.

Alma stood at the table, a cup in her gnarled and shaking hands. Her eyes blazed an eerie white and her grey hair frizzed around her head, making her look like a wild woman.

Tru closed the garage door to their right and glared a little at Paige. "You back for a bit?"

"I don't know." Ever since Leslie and Mandy had been kidnapped in Dallas—along with Leah—he'd been a different person toward Paige. Colder, more reserved. "We need to talk about Leslie."

Alma raised her face as if she was rolling her eyes as

she pulled out a chair and took a seat. "That's something we've all been talking about, but none of us got an answer."

"Great." Paige went to the stove and checked the kettle. It was still hot and lifting it, she determined there should be enough for one more cup. She rummaged through the tea cupboard and pulled out the box of peach tea she hadn't been able to get enough of lately. "Talk to me. What the hell happened?"

Dexx took a seat and sprawled his legs wide. "I already told you."

"The basics and most of it didn't even make sense. She was bitten by a *kid* several *months* ago. Why is this happening now? How is it happening at all?" She knew a bit of this from talking to the ancients back in Utah, but she didn't know how much Dexx and the gang knew.

Tru took the seat opposite Dexx, his back to Paige. "The kid had alpha potential. Apparently, Leslie was chosen then."

"Then, why are we just seeing it now?" Paige filled her tea cup with water, dumping the tea bag in with her other hand.

"Because," Dexx said, his tone light, "she was chosen by a griffin."

"Do you know what that means?" Because that's the point she needed to make. Dexx was her alpha and he needed to grasp the significant issues involved with having not one ancient, but three, join his pack.

One of her baby ancients decided to jam his damned, fucking foot into her diaphragm like he was digging a tunnel to her heart. For fuck's sake, that little shit.

Meanwhile, the other baby ancient decided to use Paige's bladder as a pillow for her head.

"Hold that thought." She set the cup down, half-filled. "Gotta pee."

She didn't wait. She just left because pissing one's pants

wasn't something that was cute or funny. It was just wet, smelled gross, and was mildly embarrassing.

Or so she imagined.

Stepping back into the kitchen, she walked to the stove and resumed operations. She was *ready* to give birth. "Back to the question. Do you know what that means?"

"He's some ancient spirit or something that can only be housed by a witch-shifter." Dexx raised his hands and let them fall back to the table. "Or something. I don't know."

Well, that was part of it. Paige carefully took her cup to the table and set it down beside Dexx. "So, this thing has been done before?"

"What thing?" Alma asked.

"Witch-shifters."

Dexx nodded. "That's what Cooper was, and he was scary crazy."

Yeah. She realized she was interrogating her family, fishing for their answers, looking for their perceptions. She also realized that was a crap thing to do, but she had to. She needed to know what fears she had to mitigate.

"How many people fear that? Shifter-witches, I mean?"

Tru shook his head, his jaw lowered, his tongue at the roof of his mouth, his eyes dead. "A lot. Okay? The last one nearly destroyed us. You weren't...*here.*" He pressed a fingertip into the table.

Wow. To get Tru—goofy, joking Tru—this worked up, it had to be fucking scary. "And how'd she save you?"

Dexx frowned. "I didn't mention that."

"Tuck did."

Dexx's eyes widened. "What do you mean?"

She tipped her head to the side. "I'll get to that in a minute. Lots of fear. Everyone? No one's willing to have an open mind?" Because this was *Leslie* they were talking about. Not Mandy. Sure as fuck not Paige.

She was fairly certain she was a shifter-witch, too. Between the two, Leslie was the least scary. Paige had already done some pretty dumb stuff.

"Right now?" Tru shook his head.

"Including you guys?"

Alma's white eyes pinched. "What sort of thing has Leslie become?"

That was the thing with Alma. When she was scared, she tended to react badly. Decisively, but badly. When she'd heard that Paige was a demon summoner, she'd told Paige she couldn't practice magick inside the home. When she'd heard Paige had summoned a demon to kill her mother, Alma had banished her memories of Leah and her demon summoning gifts. She reacted out of fear…with force.

So, when Alma chose *those words* to describe *Leslie,* of all people, anger flared in Paige's chest like hellfire. "What sort of *thing?* She's Leslie, Grandma. I'd think you'd have learned your lesson by now, but no, apparently not. She's still your granddaughter."

Alma flinched. "It's just that Cooper was so…strong."

Paige's anger deflated a little at that reaction. She knew what she was saying was wrong. "And because *he* was so strong, now *Leslie* must be *evil?*"

"He could change into any shape," Tru said, his expression vacant, almost haunted.

She'd seen Leslie take on four shapes within minutes; raven, griffin or lion or something with a tale, an eagle, and a hummingbird.

"Anything that flies." Dexx grimaced. "Including…" He opened his hand with a chicken-head-bob nod. "…flies."

"Seriously?" She'd heard of shifters being insects, but she'd always pictured butterflies or something nice. A fly? They ate shit. Literally.

"Yeah."

"What are we going to do?" Tru's voice said he was afraid of hearing what everyone else thought.

Paige had a few ideas. She'd wanted to sit down and talk to Leslie when she'd gotten back from Utah, but they never had the chance. "What have you guys tried so far?"

"Training her," Dexx said, tapping a rhythm on the table with his thumbs. "But that only works for so long. She does good and then it's like she and her spirit short circuit again."

Short circuit? "What happens then?"

"She disappears," Tru said, his voice thin. "And more pets go missing."

As much as Paige felt sorry for the poor pooches, she was glad it hadn't gone to human disappearances. It wasn't that it was less wrong—well, it kinda was, even though Paige knew it really wasn't because a life was a life. She was a witch, after all—but it meant she had more freedom to handle the situation the way it needed to be handled.

Paige looked at Alma.

The old woman shrugged. "I said we needed to lock her up. But I also said we needed to shut off your gift, so I ain't the best one to make this call."

Paige nodded. "Okay. I learned a few things when I went to Utah."

"I'd wondered." Alma's tone wasn't condemning. They really *had* been busy.

Dexx quirked his lips to the side. "Anything useful?"

"Immediately? Probably not." She took a sip of her tea. She didn't like sugar and there were lots of people who told her she was crazy for it, but she just loved the taste of tea with a slight hint of peach. "The ancients are powerful beings that have been in hiding for millennia."

Alma frowned.

Dexx double-tapped the table. "Because they're a worry or because we are?"

"I was shown the griffin being syphoned off by a wizard."

"Oh."

"Yeah. But I get the feeling it's mutual. The griffin itself needs someone strong to...well, tame is the wrong word. Keep under control is wrong, too."

"It's like us." Dexx gestured between them. "You keep me level and I keep you unbalanced."

That was one way of putting it. Before Dexx, she'd kept her feet firmly on the ground, thank you very much. "Yes. Leslie and her griffin need to do that."

"And what about me?" Tru slammed his hand on the table. "Don't I get a freaking say in this?"

"No." Paige had to be blunt about it. "You give Leslie balance and support."

"Well, right now, I'm just her freaking babysitter."

"You're her *husband,* taking care of *his* children." But Paige understood where he was coming from. If Leslie'd abandoned her kids, how did her husband feel?

He bared his teeth, glaring at the table.

"That griffin is powerful and needs balance. Right now, Leslie is out of control because everyone is fighting her."

"We're scared." Alma held up both of her hands, shaking her head. "What should we be?"

"Supportive." And that was the truth of it. The Whiskeys did better when they were together and united. Unlike the other covens or witch families, they didn't have one single gift-type to bind them. The Eastwoods had blood magick. The Blackmans had door magick. The Whiskeys didn't have a strict coven or leader to reign them in. They performed better when they could be a little wild and act on their own.

Until they were at each other's throats.

When Alma had turned the family against Paige because of what Rachel had done, the Whiskeys had fallen apart. Sven had been released and he loosed chaos.

It wasn't until Paige had brought them back together that things started to settle down.

"Let's remember when we were divided the last time, Sven was able to grow in power. He wrecked a town, very similar to this one. He killed people to get to me, so he could carve a gate to Hell inside my soul. And he was able to do that because *you* didn't back *me.*"

Alma blinked, her wrinkled lips pursed.

"So, what horrible thing are we going to unleash by not having Leslie's back?"

Tru closed his eyes, his shoulders sagging. "I want my wife back."

Dexx frowned at him but said nothing.

Alma met Paige's gaze. "What do we do?"

Paige couldn't agree with locking her sister up, no matter how weird things got. "We're going to go let her out."

"We have other things we need to consider here, Pea." Dexx stretched out his neck. "People got to see how powerful a shifter-witch can be. And that was with a witch who trapped a shifter, who hadn't been chosen."

What the hell was he saying?

"People are going to be watching," he said carefully. "And not just her." He glanced significantly at Paige's growing belly.

As if on cue, the little parasite almost seemed to reach for his father. Or her father.

She put her hand on her belly, not wanting to think about what Dexx was implying. She already had people after her kids. Merry wanted Leah because technically *she* was the heir to the Eastwood Coven and Rachel wanted her because…who knew why. Angels, demons, and who knew what else wanted her adopted son. And now she was bringing two children into a world where people would fear them for being shifter-witches and ancients.

Paige swallowed, looking down at her belly. "They're ancients as well."

Alma's expression went slack, and she shook her head. "I wondered."

"They want back into the world of the living. And they think we're the best ones to help with that."

"And are we?" Dexx met her gaze, his green eyes blazing.

She saw the thread of doubt. "Yes." She knew it in the pit of her being.

Alma's white eyes narrowed in fearful concern. "What does it mean that all your babies come out strong? That you and Leslie came to your gifts early? What's goin' on that needs that kind of balance?"

Paige didn't know, and it worried her. The Whiskeys were Wiccan witches for the most part. They believed in a balance and that balance, they believed, was how gifts were chosen. They were handed the arsenal they'd need.

And it had worked in the past, but...Leslie and Paige had gotten their abilities in school. Paige had no idea when Nick had gotten his. Leslie's kids had all been born with theirs, and Leah had only just come into hers. Something clicked. "Grandma, Leslie's kids are the only ones that came really early. Lee just got hers last year, which is right around puberty, so right on time."

Alma blinked. "So, you think it might have something to do with Leslie?"

"I think she's not as weak a witch as everyone likes to think." Paige stood up, taking in a deep breath. The little ones *really* didn't like it when she sat. "I'm going to get Leslie out. Would someone like to show me where she is?"

"I will." Dexx stood up and led the way to the garage.

Because Leah's car had the privilege of being parked there. That irked her a little. *She* paid rent and had to park outside. Leah didn't and got to park in the garage?

The ride was quiet. Dexx drove them back toward town but took the bridge that crossed over the west side of the Sandy River. The road became windy as it rolled up the winding hills. He pulled off a rutted driveway cover with tall grass and weeds dominating the middle section. That was a clear indication that the property belonged to shifters. They used cars a lot less than everyone else did.

Eventually the pines and cottonwoods broke and revealed a small cabin in a wide meadow filled with tall, big-headed dandelions.

"How'd you guys find this place again?" She couldn't remember if he'd told her or not.

"Ripley and Joe. They used it when they saved his brother from the rabies."

"Who?"

"The padfoot. Though, technically, Leslie did the saving. But Rip did an excellent job, too."

There was a lot Paige needed to catch up on apparently. She got out of the car and carefully shut the door, massaging her lower back. She was over carrying around babies, though, it *was* easier to carry them in the belly rather than in the arms. It just went from one discomfort to the next. "Where's Les?"

"Around back." Dexx led the way with long, swift strides. "She's probably going to be pissed, so be ready with the witchy stuff."

Like hell. "You're her 'alpha'." She dipped her tone low. It kinda pissed her off he was claiming to be her sister's alpha. The nerve of the man. Near as she could tell, he still didn't want to be alpha, so what right did he have taking responsibility for Leslie's life?

Dexx stopped suddenly, his hands out.

Paige barely managed to stop herself from careening into him. "What?"

He held his finger to his lips and motioned ahead.

A door hung open. It opened to a dark room built into a hill.

"Where the hell is my sister, Dexx?" Paige asked in a whisper.

Dexx tipped his head to the side, listening.

Cawli, Paige said with a growl. *I need to know what we sense.*

Cawli rose to the surface, sniffing the air. He smelled something that tasted musky on the back of her tongue. *Kangaroo.*

You're kidding me.

I assure you, I am not.

"Cawli says kangaroo," she said.

Dexx nodded. "Hattie does, too." He stepped forward carefully and stooped to retrieve something from the ground. He held it out to Paige and narrowed his glowing green eyes. "McCree is back."

"Who?"

"The shifter-witch." He ground what looked like a grasshopper carcass in his fist and spun, his shoulders tight. "And he has your damn crazed sister."

Shit. What the hell would a shifter-witch want with…

…another shifter-witch?

7

One would think that as a powerful witch and the current captain of a pretty kick-ass police team, finding one man would be an easy task. One would be wrong.

Later that afternoon, Paige was still waiting for one of Rainbow or Ethel's searches to come up with something. A credit card hit. Anything. She'd caught up on her paperwork, something she didn't even know was possible. Turned out Dexx had somehow managed to not destroy the town while she'd been a captive of the heavenly host.

That was still something she needed to deal with. What the hell had they wanted? What had they been looking for? What had happened? Were the babies okay? What information had they gleaned from her?

Was Bobby safe?

Her heart hammered to a standstill. What if they'd found out about Bobby? She doubted they'd be looking for him anywhere near her. He was God's prophet in the house and care of witches. Which was the most sacrilegious thing on the planet in some eyes.

She and her team had gone above and beyond. They'd had

to falsify records and modify memories because, technically, Paige hadn't given birth to Bobby. Her best friend had.

But, the angels weren't just average people in search of babies. They could see magickal tampering. If an angel dug just a little, they would discover Paige hadn't been pregnant, like everyone believed. She'd been fired from Denver, not pregnant. Then she went to Texas, and miraculously "gave birth" to a bouncing baby boy.

The next prophet of God, whatever that meant. She wasn't going to profess knowing anything about the Bible or the faith. She tended to see the ugly side of organized religion. Whenever her witchiness was brought up, she could immediately tell which ones belonged to the Church and which ones had true faith. One was ugly and judgmental.

The other side had amazing and real people.

What would Bobby mean to that world, and did Paige want to release her son to it?

There were too many people out there who had too many opinions on religion, God and the Word, and whatever else. How many people would cast Bobby aside, or elevate him higher than he needed to be, or use him for their own benefit? There was just as much money to be made in the word of God as there was in sex. One was just a lot less hygienic.

Making money off people's "salvation" disgusted her.

But just like not all prostitutes were whores, not all God-fearing folk were money grabbers.

She pressed her fingertips into her closed eyelids, the ragged edge of the nail she'd broken on her left hand digging in a little too much.

Normally, she tried to veer away from religion. She wasn't a great spokesperson for either side. She wasn't the most forgiving or the most understanding. She tried. Sure. But the fact was, her family had been attacked in Texas by a "God-fearing" person intent on getting all the paranormals out of his city.

Paige sat back, slouching in a way that made the kids press into her should-be-empty-because-she'd-*just*-peed bladder.

She feared people of organized religions, yet she was raising their next prophet. This wasn't going to end well. It couldn't.

She had bigger apples to fry anyway. She was on a witch hunt.

A secret organization she knew almost nothing about was going after paranormals who made headlines and wiping them out.

At first, Paige had thought it was a group of hunters, like Dexx had been.

But after Kansas? She wasn't so sure.

She'd gone to Hopkinsville to talk to a group of goblins. They didn't have a huge presence. They'd done a fantastic job of staying off the radar.

But a group of kids had pulled a prank, removing their glamour at a haunted house.

And then got caught on camera.

Apparently, the reason there was no paranormal activity in Kansas was because it was a ginormous hub of paranormals, but not the kinds they had in Troutdale. There were a lot more of the fairy-type creatures there who kept news down. They called themselves The Hill because...why not?

But while she was working with one of the Hill representatives—an elf, with the pointy ears and everything—their people had started disappearing. Security footage only showed men in either hoodies or full military gear converging on the paranormals and taking them. None of the missing had been found.

Paige'd offered to stay and help but she'd been invited—forcefully—to leave.

This organization frightened her. She was almost certain it was somehow connected to their new president. Maybe not directly.

And was this organization already in Oregon? Would they start kidnapping people from Portland? Troutdale? What if they found the school and attacked the kids?

Honestly, those kids could defend themselves. They were all pretty powerful, and not just the Whiskeys.

But it had been beaten into them since they were all small that they were not to use their powers outside of the protections of the compound. What if they were attacked in the grocery store parking lot?

Paige was pushing herself into a fear-fueled frenzy. What was she going to do next? Force all Christians out of Troutdale? All humans? Where did it stop? Where would she draw the line?

No. She couldn't allow herself to fall for any of that. She had to do what was right, whatever that meant.

Even if that meant endangering her children.

She put her hand on her belly, her heart heavy. She had no idea what the "right thing" for her kids was. She didn't know what move she should make.

She only recognized the small, tiny warning signs. They were all over the place and if she just put those pieces together...

She could either hide under her bed with her kids…

Or she could find a way to head it off at the pass.

Whatever that pass would be.

Her hands stilled, her mind moving faster than she could track. She *could* put the pieces together. She was still a detective, and not a horrible one, either.

But it was getting her nowhere. She needed to focus on

her sister. Why was it easier to solve world problems than her own family issues?

She shifted gears, moving the casefile on the McCrees over the stack of other notes on her desk. She'd dug in a little way, but the file was pretty substantial.

The McCrees were a big family with considerable influence in Australia. The file didn't have a great deal of information on the types of magicks they performed, but the family had been in Australia for several generations. From what she could tell, they were an influential witch family.

The elders made a habit of keeping records of the major witch families, documenting their traits, powers, and abilities. It had annoyed Paige when she'd first found out about it, but now she understood it. And it was fairly helpful. This one time.

Tom McCree was the patriarch of the three witches who had shown up and destroyed so much of Troutdale. Cooper, Celeste, and Skye were all siblings with the same shapeshifter mother. The shifter spirits had claimed the twin sisters, who had no witchcraft abilities. Cooper was a witch and, as far as they knew, hadn't been chosen by the spirits.

That gave Paige some slim hope for her babies. She knew they'd both been chosen, but it was possible they wouldn't be witches as well. If that was the case, maybe, just maybe they wouldn't be hunted like the rest of her children.

Tom McCree was a powerful witch in his own right, though. The elders didn't know exactly what his gift was, but he could summon three of the four elements. He was also a caster of real spell work, something Paige was not good at.

The man had money and lots of it. More, even, than the Eastwood's. Tom was nearly as old as Merry Eastwood, so far as they could tell. Did that mean he was into blood magick too? Or did he have another way?

She wasn't sure she wanted to know. But if this guy was a threat?

And why wouldn't he be? One of his twin daughters had been killed, the other close to death, according to the reports. And Coop? Well, he was rotting in an elder prison and probably would be for the rest of his life.

The more she read of the file, which Dexx had proudly labeled Lizard Wizard, even though the man-witch could take the form of any shifter he killed, the more pissed Paige became. How dare the angels kidnap her when her family had so obviously needed her help? Yes. They'd survived and that was good.

Because if they hadn't? Well.

Before she could get into it, her office door opened, and Ethel flew in so fast the air of her passing actually moved the tips of Paige's hair.

"Do you have something?" Paige asked at the same time Ethel blurted, "We found him!"

Ethel stopped and held out her hands to keep Paige from speaking. "We have a hit on his credit card."

"Where?"

"Mac's Edge Farm."

"What is that?"

"It's a really swanky resort." Ethel closed her eyes and shook her head. "Like super swanky. It's been on my list of places to visit since I got here, but there's no way I can afford to step a toe in there."

"Great. Where." Paige stood, keeping her belly out as a baby woke, stretching. Those damned kids had the best damned timing. She could already tell they were going to be a handful.

Ethel handed her a sticky note. "I already told Dexx."

"Great."

It was time to find her sister. And get some answers.

8

It didn't take them long to get to the resort Tom McCree was staying at. It wasn't far from Troutdale, located in the middle of flourishing farm lands. The place looked fit to house royalty.

They were met at the front door by a very thin man who wouldn't be able to kill a fly with his bare hands, but his attitude might have been able to suppress a bear. Well, if Paige knew a bear. She didn't.

Wait. Didn't they have a bear in their pack now?

Oh, whatever.

The man led them to an opulent lounge filled with a mix of comfortably stuffed chairs and harder chairs that surrounded small tables.

Paige opted to stand.

Dexx pulled out a chair and gestured for her to sit, an eyebrow raised.

She shook her head. She didn't need anyone getting the wrong impression. One being that she was weaker for being pregnant. Yeah, sure, the babies did take away some of her energy. There was no getting around that.

But she was *not* weaker for it.

Dexx smiled and nodded curtly, pushing the chair back in.

It was as if he could read her mind.

Or maybe he was thinking of something else and had no idea why she wanted to remain standing. She didn't know.

She only wanted to know where her sister was.

She'd taken a smelling sample—a handy bit of magick she and Cawli had discovered in Kansas—of the magick at the scene. All she needed was one whiff.

There it was. Musky and aged, like walking into the old part of a building or archive.

The same scent she'd found at the bunker where Leslie was supposed to have been in earlier.

A cold calm rolled over Paige.

Tom McCree was a tall man, making Dexx look short in comparison. He had dark hair that curled around his ears and shoulders, and his black eyes lit with laughter. He looked personable, but professional. His slacks were pin-striped and freshly pressed, and his blue button-up shirt looked like it had just come off the hanger. He stopped in front of them, still working on rolling up his right sleeve.

Good lookin' man.

"Hello." He had an Australian accent that rounded his vowels and r's. "I heard you wanted to see me."

Paige narrowed her eyes.

Dexx took a step forward and offered his hand. "Dexx Colt. You've probably heard of me."

Tom stiffened, and the congenial expression on his face faded away almost instantly. He stopped, his hand in the action of accepting Dexx's handshake.

Dexx smiled grimly. "I see you have."

So, he might be holding a grudge.

Tom shoved his hands in his pockets. His cold expression added sagging years to his face. "What can I do for you, Mr.

Colt?" His accent smoothed out as if he'd practiced repressing it.

"You can tell us where Leslie Whiskey is."

Tom's gaze slid to Paige and stayed there.

Paige stared back solidly.

He lingered for a moment then looked back to Dexx. "I'm here to receive my daughters' bodies, thanks to you."

"Celeste was killed by your own men." Dexx spread his hands wide. "I have no idea where Skye is. Last I saw her, she was still breathing."

"But was she well?"

"Nope. Split her right up the middle." He drew a line with his finger up his belly to his chest. "But she was good enough to disappear, though."

Tom blinked slowly. "And my son is in jail."

Dexx nodded. "Did you get to visit him?"

"You should know. There are no visitors in elder prison."

"Yes." Dexx clucked his tongue. "That is rather unfortunate, isn't it?"

"What are we doing here?" Tom asked Paige bluntly.

"Like he said," Paige said, her tone dark, "we're here to see where my sister is."

"And how would I know where she is?"

"Because you were there."

He raised his chin. "Was I?"

Paige tapped her nose. "I'm a shifter and a witch, which means I not only have an excellent sense of smell, but that I can smell magickal signatures."

The confidence slowly drained away from his face.

Paige took a step closer. "Where is my sister?"

"You're her alpha, aren't you?" Tom asked Dexx, his accent growing in strength again. "Can't you tell?"

Dexx ground his teeth. "Things are complicated with Leslie."

"Yes, well." Tom rolled his head on his neck for a half turn. "I don't have her."

Paige was just supposed to believe that? "Do you know what happened?"

"Yes."

A couple walked into the large room, but after glancing their way, left almost immediately.

"Care to share?" Dexx asked, leaning forward.

Tom took in a deep breath. "I followed a lead and located the bunker. After a brief conversation, I released her."

"What were you thinking?" Dexx pinched his nose and took a step back.

Tom's expression hardened. "I was thinking there was someone trapped inside that hill."

"I don't believe you." Dexx let his hand drop as he leaned in. "What brought you up there in the first place? Why would you go *there?*"

Tom turned his full attention to Dexx for a long moment before taking a step forward. "I believe you know, Mr. Colt. You destroyed my family and I heard that one of your pack was unprotected and alone."

Protective rage roared to life in Paige's chest. "She wasn't alone."

"She wasn't protected."

Dexx raised his head, his lips pinched. "She doesn't need it. Found that out for yourself I bet."

Tom took in a deep breath and nodded. "Yes." He straightened, clasping his hands behind his back, and looking around the room. "She escaped."

"Unscathed?" Paige needed to know what condition Leslie was in. "You used magick against her."

"Powerful magick." Tom nodded, looking at Paige out of the corner of his eye. "I didn't even phase her. She stepped out and my attack slid right off her."

"You attacked her?" Paige was going to kill him.

"After she started sucking my soul dry?" Tom tipped his head. "I've heard about that but never felt it. We don't allow that in Australia."

"We don't allow it here either." Dexx glanced at Paige, concern making the crow's feet at his eyes deepen. "She really did that?"

Goddess, what was Leslie even thinking? Because the Leslie she knew would never stoop to something like that.

It had to be the griffin spirit inside her.

Tom's Adam's apple bobbed. "You need to get your house in order, Mr. Colt."

Dexx gave him a dark look.

"And I will have the money you took from my son."

"You mean the money I turned over to the elder council?" Dexx smiled and hopped on his toes. "Good luck seeing that money again. It's as good as gone."

Tom glared. "That money was not yours to take."

"It was part of an investigation." Dexx clasped his hands together. "And did I forget to mention that he'd stolen it from Oliver Eastwood? If anyone's going to collect that money, it'll be him."

Tom narrowed his eyes which lingered on Dexx as he turned back to Paige. "She was fine when she left."

"*How* did she leave?" Because that was important. Did she fly? Run? Human form? Shifted? On a broom—because, hell, *that* might be possible now.

"As a hawk." Tom spread his hands wide. "I am not your enemy."

Dexx tipped his head to the side. "Your kids seemed to think differently."

"They were under the impression they were doing as I wanted." Tom rocked his head from side to side in a deep contemplative movement.

"And was it?"

"If they'd won?" Tom arched an eyebrow.

Dexx nodded. "Well, we're not as weak as your kids thought."

"You're not as strong as you think, either." Tom smiled sickly. "They discovered your weakness."

"Trust me," Dexx said, "we're working to plug those holes."

"Excellent. Then, as I see it, my children provided you a service."

A service? She'd provide him a service if he kept talking.

"You want my advice?" Tom asked, turning away.

"Not really," Dexx said. "But I feel you're gonna give it anyway."

Tom turned at the door. "Kill her. She's too powerful. A witch-shifter is a deadly thing to begin with, but that one? She's a powerful witch and the spirit that chose her is almost stronger than she can handle."

Paige needed to re-think Leslie's "power" levels. She might have been over-looked a little too long.

"My son is proof enough of that, don't you think? And he wasn't even chosen."

"No," Dexx growled. "He trapped his spirit animals to him, tormented them. He killed shifters to steal their shapes."

Tom's eyebrows rose, and he sucked in his cheeks. "Well, we can't all raise perfect children, now can we?"

Paige stared as the door closed behind him. Why *had* such a powerful spirit animal chosen Leslie?

She needed to find Leslie first and make sure she was safe.

9

Before they'd even stepped outside the resort, Paige's phone rang with her standard ring tone, the *Wonder Woman* theme song. Looking at the display, she swiped the green call button. "It's the house," she told Dexx.

He stopped in the carport in front, giving her time to concentrate on the conversation.

He knew her so well. She *could* talk and walk, but it made her grouchy. She wasn't the best multitasker in the world. "Hey," she said into the phone.

"Aunt Paige," Mandy said, her tone a little urgent. "Mom's home. When can you get here?"

"We're on our way." Paige tapped Dexx's arm and walked briskly to the car, forgetting for a moment they weren't driving Jackie. What was that new damned car called? The thing was ugly, whatever it was, and easy to pick out in the parking lot. "What's going on?"

The sound of a door closing sounded over the line, and Mandy continued in a hushed voice. "Aunt Paige, why is Mom acting so weird?"

"Sweetie, I wish I knew all the answers, but I just got back."

"You've been back for hours."

True, but she had a *lot* of things to take care of. "The only thing I know for sure is that she was chosen by a very strong spirit animal."

"A griffin." Mandy sneezed. "Yeah. I know. I've been doing some research of my own."

Smart girl. Okay. Time to start treating the kid like a partial adult. "Great. What did you find and what are your resources?"

"Old stories, really. The ones about some of the older creatures like dragons and unicorns and griffins."

"The make-believe creatures."

"Yeah. Except they aren't so make-believe." Mandy actually sounded a little like an adult in that moment. "So, according to Chuck—"

"Who is an *excellent* resource, by the way."

"Thanks. Anyway, he said that the griffin is an ancient spirit that only chooses a very select few."

"Okay. What are the qualifications?" Because this was useful information to have.

"They have to be powerful."

Time to go fishing again and see what Leslie's own daughter thought. "But your mother isn't powerful."

"Well," Mandy said with an intake of breath, "maybe not like you. But she's the most powerful medium we've met."

"Which isn't saying much."

"No, but she also does very clean and great spell work, something even you can't do."

"I can't do a spell to save my life."

"Which is the reason your locator spell didn't tell you where my mom was."

Ouch. "Yes."

Mandy said something, but Paige couldn't hear her over the engine turning over and roaring to life. "Mandy," Paige yelled. "You're going to have to talk louder. We're in Leah's car and it's loud."

"The Black Mobile of Death?" Mandy shouted. "Give me a sec."

They pulled out of the long winding driveway and got onto the highway, the road noise so loud she'd have a tough time having a conversation with Dexx, and he was right next to her. She reached into her pocket and pulled out her noise cancelling Bluetooth. She didn't like using it. The thing drained her phone battery like crazy, but she needed to be able to hear Mandy. Putting the girl's voice directly into her ear seemed like the best idea.

"Okay," Mandy said loud and clear. "Can you hear me?"

"Yeah," Paige said. "Can you hear me?"

"Yeah."

"Where are you?"

"Garage. Mom doesn't come out here anymore. There's something in the air she doesn't like. She doesn't even like being around Leah or Dexx after they've been working on the cars."

Then there was probably a smell in there that didn't sit well with her griffin. "I don't always like it either."

"Meh," Mandy said. "You get used to it. Leah smells like gas a lot."

Great. "You were saying. The ancient spirits need someone who's powerful."

"Oh. Yeah. Right. Also, some of the ancient spirits need a witch."

This was something she *hadn't* learned in Utah. "A witch."

"Yup. Like the dragon and the griffin. They're pretty sure the unicorn, too, but there are other things involved with the unicorn and its all very post Sex Ed and I—well, it was interesting, but I felt uncomfortable."

"Because you haven't had Sex Ed?" Because Paige was fairly certain she and Leah both had gone through it by the age of fourteen.

"No, because Chuck was making it weird. *He* was uncomfortable, and Faith was laughing at him, and I just wanted answers."

So, Mandy was a Whiskey after all. "That's hereditary."

"Whatever. Anyway. So, a strong witch and they have to be able to partition their mind for the griffin."

"Why? Because it's so strong?"

"Kind of. Mostly because they're very scatter brained."

"What do you mean?"

"I don't know." Something clanked as if maybe the girl was playing around with the tools. "But it makes sense. Mom's been acting all kinds of weird. Sometimes, she has ultra-focus, like 'get off my back already' focus, and then other times you can't get her attention with a pry bar."

"I don't think pry bar is what you're looking for."

"Okay a lawn mower."

It was obvious the girl needed to do more chores. "Okay. What's her mood like right now?"

"Super focused." Mandy paused. "She's alphabetizing the cupboards."

That...wasn't bad. "Well, we're almost home."

"Great. I'll—"

A loud crack pierced painfully through the earpiece. It sounded like gun fire. "What was that?"

"I don't know," Mandy said quietly. "The wards, I think."

Then why wasn't Paige getting anything? Oh, shit. Because she hadn't been there the last time the wards had to be re-built.

"Shit—shoot. Aunt Paige, where are you?"

"Are you under attack?"

Another loud crack popped in Paige's ear.

"Yeah? I think so?"

"Can you look out the garage door and tell me what you see?"

Dexx pressed his foot to the gas, gripping the wheel.

"Uh, yeah."

"What is it?" Dexx asked.

Didn't he just hear her ask?

Mandy took a moment to answer. "Uh. It's…oh, god, Aunt Paige, they're…human."

A cold chill swept through Paige. "Are they dressed in black?"

"Yeah. Like military black-ops stuff. The stuff you see on TV."

"And are they getting through?"

"Nope. I don't know why. The wards don't protect against the military."

No. Normal humans would get through with ease. The Whiskeys weren't allowed to ward them out. The Shadow Sisterhood didn't allow anything that would tip a human off to magick or anything out of the ordinary.

"I don't know, Aunt Paige, but they're—oh, god. That's a big gun."

Gun fire rattled over the phone.

Paige gripped the handle of the car door, power surging through her. "They're shooting at our kids," she growled.

The world went red. One moment, they were on the highway. The next, they were in the driveway. The engine sputtered to a stop.

Dexx gaped at Paige, but she didn't have time for that.

The door nearly came off the hinges when Paige stepped out of the car. Power flared in her hands, her inky-black magick extended in oozy hands.

Cawli's soul roared with hers, eager to smell blood on the wind.

The gunfire, which sounded muffled, like it was far away, stopped.

A dozen or more men were spread out in front of her in black uniforms, their black helmets strapped to their heads. They turned, pointing their rifles at her and Dexx.

Paige didn't think. The trees, the air, the car, the skin on their faces.

Wind roared around her.

Clouds darkened the skies.

Tree branches bent, swooping down. They plucked men from the ground, flinging them into the air.

The earth rumbled.

A strangling bellow of Earth's fire ripped upwards, filling the air in front of her with incredible heat.

Through the flames, she watched as the man right in front of her lowered his rifle, one hand out imploringly. His lips moved as if he was trying to talk to her.

A man's voice filled the air, his cry cut short as he flew between them and crashed into a tree.

The man directly in front of her unclipped his helmet and dropped it to the ground. He spread his hands out, low, his rifle falling to his side as it hung from the strap. His lips mouthed words she couldn't hear.

She could *taste* the magick on him. Witch.

A witch attacking witches.

Cawli crept forward. *We could eat his soul.*

The thought was tempting, but she couldn't. She'd taken one shifter's soul on accident in self-defense. She didn't want to do that again. *No.*

Well, then, Cawli said with a sneer in his voice. *If you're not going to kill him, then calm your wind and hear what he has to say.*

The cat had a point.

Paige cooled the anger in her chest, letting the wind die.

The earth stilled.

The storm lightened minutely.

The fires dipped back into the earth, though only so far as she couldn't see real flames anymore.

The man looked around, his pale brows high, bright blue eyes wide. "Impressive."

Paige strode toward him. She wanted to rip him apart. Her emotions were out of control. "You shot at my children."

"No bullets went in their direction."

"And how do you know? Maybe they were in the woods."

He held his hands up.

All this time, she'd been trying to find one of them to interrogate. But before she could get to that, she had to take care of the fact he'd been shooting bullets at her house, at her kids.

"I have information for you." He tipped his head. "How about you put away the fireworks, and we talk."

"You put away your guns."

He nodded and pulled the strap to his rifle over his head. "Sounds fair." He held his rifle out in front of him, his other hand out in a motion of surrender as he lowered himself to the ground. He stopped, staring significantly at her hands.

Could he see her witch hands? Even the others in her family couldn't see those. "And your men?"

"You mean those you haven't already killed?'

She hadn't killed any of them. The trees—she stared at them in wonder. The trees had acted on their own. She'd never been able to get trees to do anything. It was as if they'd answered her call and had come alive. She swallowed and quelled her magick. "You fired bullets at my children."

"Your children were not harmed, I can assure you."

Like hell. "Why?"

He narrowed his bright eyes and set his rifle on the

ground, rising, his hands out to his sides. "You'll have to be more observant than that."

He had a faint English accent. What the hell was someone from across the pond doing here? "Why were you firing bullets at our house?"

He licked his lips and raised his head. "We're part of an organization meant to keep your kind… on a short leash."

"My kind?" she asked incredulously. "You're a witch. You're firing on witches."

Fuck it. She wasn't going to get the fucking answers from him. She pulled her phone out of her pocket and dialed the house.

Mandy answered. "Aunt Paige?"

She sounded fine. Scared, but fine. "Yeah. Is everyone all right?"

"Yeah."

"Anyone hurt? Injured?"

"No. Just…I don't know what they were shooting at, but it wasn't at us, I guess. We're fine. The house is fine."

"Okay."

Paige moved to the pull the phone away from her ear.

"But Mom—"

Paige put the phone back to her ear and waited. "Yeah?"

"She's…" Mandy's voice lowered. "It's like she's watching something. She's not moving. She's just staring."

Well, she wasn't breaking things, so… "Okay. Keep an eye on her. I'll be there in a minute." She hung up. "So, asshole, why the *hell* were you shooting at my house?"

He gave her a dark look. "We were shooting at your wards. These aren't normal bullets, Paige."

Not…normal bullets. Great. "Why is a witch firing 'not normal bullets' at other witches' wards?"

He ground his teeth for a moment. "To get to the shifters. The paranormals. The tainted."

The...what? "You're trying to tell me you belong to..." She didn't even know what to call it. "The true blood faith?" She'd heard of that with the shapeshifters, but the witches?

She recalled the grimoires that had listed her family tree. Maybe she'd heard more about it than she realized.

"You're the product of two very powerful witch families. Your daughter is the delta of three. A very powerful witch in her own right."

Paige didn't like where this was going. Dread filled her gut. "And you were just firing on her."

"We were firing into the air to draw you out."

"Well, you managed that."

"Indeed. We did." He sighed heavily, dropping his hands to his sides.

"Next time, use a phone."

He quirked his lips. "We had hoped you would become an ally."

An ally. Not likely. Not with an introduction like that.

"But your wards."

Those wards had been an idea brought about by Chuck. He had packs and they were made stronger by the people in them. Each individual. So, the Whiskeys put each witch's power into those wards.

"You couldn't break through them."

"They were a test, the first of many. You've passed so many, but this? This is unacceptable."

The wards. "I don't understand."

"I can feel your spirit animal taint, Paige."

Paige. She sucked in a sharp breath. She didn't know his name, yet he knew hers, about her family, her daughter.

But he wasn't feeling *her* animal spirit taint because she wasn't in those wards. He was feeling Leslie.

Threatening Paige was one thing. Threatening her family?

Bad idea. "You mean how strong it's made me?" Because if he didn't know, she wasn't going to tell him.

The man stared at her for a long moment and then snorted. "Yes. It has made you strong, but it's also made you an enemy."

"Great." Paige gestured around her. "Get in line."

One of his men helped another who limped, held his side.

The leader pulled back with a frown. "Do you even know what you've done?"

Paige rubbed her nose, pissed. She wanted to rip him a new one. "No. Why don't you tell me."

He licked his bottom lip and took a step forward. "You've invited the ancients into our world."

Well, at least she wasn't ten steps behind on this one. "I'm aware."

Dexx came and stood behind her, a calm, warm presence.

The man blinked. "You know."

"Of course, I do." At least a little.

"Then you know how dangerous they are. The dragons, the griffins."

"The unicorns." Because that would never stop being funny.

He shivered.

Seriously. She took in a deep breath to calm her nerves, but Cawli was coiled inside her like a tightly wound spring.

"They were banished centuries ago and we've kept them at bay. Carefully, and with great reason."

"And why's that?" Because she needed to know their side of the story. Could they be swayed? Probably not, but at least then she'd have a better idea of how they'd attack her.

The man looked around the area. "Did you intend this?"

She looked around, too. The trees were still moving, their branches snapping and grasping toward the intruders. That...was odd.

"You are stronger than you'd ever dream."

And she wasn't housing the griffin.

Cawli paced in the back of her mind, growling.

She was, however, holding two ancients in her womb.

How had she been able to reach the elements so power-fully? She was a very powerful witch, but this? She'd *never* been able to do this before.

But if Leslie was part of her pack? If Leslie's griffin made the pack stronger, would that be enough to make the Whiskeys stronger too?

"You're dangerous."

"You really have no idea." Not even the half of it.

He took another step closer to her.

Anger curling in her gut, she closed the distance another step.

He stopped his hands raised. "I have a way to stop this."

"And keep my family safe?" She doubted that.

"And keep the *world* safe. Yes."

Not good enough. Whatever was going on, they could handle it. They were the Whiskeys. They could handle just about anything.

He reached into his vest.

She called the power of her inky magick to her hands.

He held out one hand, offering her a business card.

She let the magick cool, keeping it just within reach.

He flicked it toward her.

It reached her with a gentle breeze.

"My business card for when things get…" He licked his lips, glancing around. "…out of control."

She plucked the card from the air. "And you're that certain they will."

He shrugged then looked pointedly down at her bulging belly. Raising his gaze, he said, "Others are going to be inter-ested in that."

She put her hand protectively on her belly. No one threatened her kids.

No. Who was she kidding? They *all* threatened her kids. They just didn't survive long after the fact.

He gestured toward his men.

They slinked out of the tree line, their guns hanging from their bodies like limp noodles and disappeared down the driveway.

Paige maintained her magick in her hands until the men were out of sight.

"I'm keeping your guns," Dexx called.

Paige released her magick only when they were no longer in sight or smell.

The trees stilled.

The earth closed.

The fires receded.

The storm tapered to a slight drizzle.

She looked at the card.

Mario Kester, Director of the Department of Delicate Operations.

A hand-written note read, "Call me when you're ready for a real solution."

For fuck's sake.

10

P aige wasn't going to just let a threat to her kids and her unborn children go unanswered. What was she supposed to do about it though? She could chase Mario Kester down and demand more information.

She at least had a name and a phone number, which was more than she'd had for months. For right now, she knew she and her family were safe as long as they were behind the wards.

But what did he mean by "others would be interested" in her babies?

Well, her babies were half as powerful as she was, she could understand that. The babies weren't powerful yet, just had potential. They didn't throw tantrums that could destroy small city blocks. They didn't have the ability to hold or carry a gun or defend themselves. But they could be trained.

Crap.

And how the hell was Paige so damned powerful? She looked back at the car. She'd teleported them in a frelling car.

Because of having Leslie and the twins in their pack?

That could be a benefit, couldn't it?

Well, of course it could.

"What the hell was that?" Dexx asked quietly from behind her.

"What?" Paige asked, but only because there was a lot of "what."

"The magick." He gestured to the woods and the field.

Everything was back in order again. She couldn't even tell anything had just happened.

"Oh." She rubbed her brow. It had been so easy. She hadn't even realized what she'd done. "How did we even get here?"

"That's a really good question and the next one I was going to ask you."

She had no idea. *Cawli? Do you have any ideas?*

He was quiet for a moment. *I might.*

Did you want to share?

Cawli huffed a sigh. *Tell the demon hunter to have him and his cat meet us in the sacred space.*

What does that mean?

You'll see. Find some place comfortable.

Paige looked over at Dexx. "Do you know where the 'sacred space' is? Cawli wants us to go there."

He nodded. "It's a chore to get there, but yeah. I know."

"He said to get comfortable. What does that mean?"

"It's like a vision quest of sorts. Come on. Get in the car. We'll get on the right side of the wards and go."

"I'm checking on my kids."

"They are." Dexx walked around the front of the car and got in.

Paige followed, slamming the door closed. "How do you know?"

"I'm the alpha." He shrugged. "I just always know."

That was going to piss her off. "I need to know for myself that my kids are okay."

"And the fuzzy ones don't have a lot of patience. You can check on people when we're done. For now, we go." He turned the key, but the car didn't even sputter.

Paige looked at him. "Are we pushing it?"

He shook his head, his eyes closed. "Whatever you did when you magicked us here, you killed the battery or something. Are you okay?"

She pulled back, startled by his sudden attention. "I'm fine."

"You magicked us and a car several miles."

She lifted her shoulders and shook her head. She felt fine. Normally, a big show of magick would tire her, but not this time. She didn't know why. She still didn't fully believe it had been her. It might have been something else. It could have been Roxxie trying to help, even after Paige had banished her.

Though, she doubted that. She wasn't ready to hurl her toes, which was always a side-effect of travel-by-angel.

Dexx gave up on starting the car. He made Paige sit in the driver seat and steer while he pushed.

They managed to park, and huffing, Dexx dropped into the passenger seat next to Paige. "Okay, babe, just trust Cawli. Stay calm and do what he says."

"What are you talking about?"

"Just do what he says."

Paige jammed her back against the seat, irritated. She wanted to make sure Mandy and Leah and Bobby, and the rest of the kids were safe. *Cawli, I'm ready. What the hell am I doing?*

You must calm your senses. Release your anger.

I'm not angry.

Uncurl you fingers.

Paige looked at her fingers. They were balled into tiny little hammers.

Dexx could have been asleep beside her. He was already there? Damnit.

Fine, now what?

Relax, and come to me. Follow my words and see me.

This is insane.

Dexx had said to trust Cawli. Closing her eyes, she took a deep breath, then exhaled slowly. She felt something… move. With another breath Cawli appeared. At first, he was just a white fog, slightly glowing, then he took form.

Cawli was a massive white tiger with golden eyes.

That's what you look like?

It is. Now come to me and let go.

Paige laid her hand on the big cat's neck. They stood suddenly in the spirit cave she'd visited in Utah.

Dexx, Hattie, Leslie, and the griffin were already deep in conversation as the cave solidified. Cawli stood with her.

Hattie turned her even larger head to them, which she dipped in greeting, then her ears pricked forward. She looked… happy.

Cawli sank onto a rock, laying his massive head on his paws. *We need to discuss what has happened.*

The griffin snapped his beak, his lion's tale flicking.

Leslie walked around the fire pit and hugged Paige. "Where have you been?"

It felt odd seeing her sister there, but it was good, too. This was *her* Leslie. Almost. "Apparently, I've been a hostage of the angels."

"Hostage?" Leslie bristled.

There was her Leslie. "Maybe inmate? I don't know."

Leslie's eyes took on a slight glow. "Why?"

Glowing in a spirit cave. Just how much access did Paige have to magick? "That, I still don't know, but Roxxie says we're good now."

Leslie narrowed her glowing eyes. "And why don't you know?"

Hadn't they *had* this conversation before? What had Mandy said about griffins being flighty? "Because my memories were wiped."

"They were what?"

"That's kinda what I said."

Leslie growled. "Was this Roxxie's doing?"

"No. I don't think she really knew what was going on, and I get the feeling she's the reason I'm even back in the first place." But it didn't mean Paige was any less pissed.

"Well, at least there's that. And Bobby? Is he okay?"

Paige nodded. "We think so. No angel attacks yet, anyway."

Leslie licked her bottom lip, a frown furrowing her brow, her eyes no longer glowing. "She hasn't done wrong by us yet."

Wow. Those were almost teenager emotional curves there. "I know." But Paige wondered how long they'd be able to maintain that level of trust with the angels. It had been tentative to this point because they'd needed the angel's assistance in protecting Bobby. What would happen if they couldn't trust the angels, even Roxxie?

Paige pulled away and held Leslie's hand. "So, you were chosen."

Leslie released a puff of breath. "He's hard to manage."

Which is the reason I took so long to manifest. The griffin's voice hadn't changed in the spirit cave. He was still silky smooth and easy to listen to.

"We're going to need a few answers." Paige sat gingerly on the rock beside the pool. "Oh, and don't take your shoes off and dip your toes in."

Leslie blinked. "Huh?"

"Just sayin', you will lose your boots. Wait." Now that she

was back, she could look for them. She leaned back, trying to look around, but nothing seemed out place. "If they pop back up, I'd really like them back."

The griffin's stared stonily at her.

Perfect. A gigantic beast with a dry sense of humor. Just what they needed.

"Look, guys. We've got bad guys headed our way and we need to know how to mitigate this whole—" Paige waved her hand between Leslie and the griffin. "—bonding thing as quickly and smoothly as we can."

The griffin shifted his orange gaze to Leslie. *It has been going quite smooth. I am well pleased.*

"Boo for you." Paige let her head fall back, stretching her muscles. She rubbed her lower back. Making babies was arduous work.

Dexx sat behind her, wrapping a leg around her hips and massaged her lower back, batting her hands out of the way.

Pain exploded at his thumbs. "Man-hands." For fuck's sake. "I'm not a car. Treat me gently."

"This is the *only* time you need gentle treatment," he muttered.

Which was true, but not getting them anywhere. "You," she said, pointing to the griffin, "have got to stop wreaking havoc on the community. Stop eating dogs and birds."

I can eat the mundanes.

Hold up. "Is that how you got banned the last time?"

He blinked. *There were humans offered as sacrifice. I did not realize it was bad. I was hungry.*

Fuck. "Well, you can't eat people."

And dogs and birds are not people.

Shit. "Not…in the same way. No. Try sticking to beef like the rest of us."

The griffin snapped his beak closed and turned his huge eagle head away.

"What's it going to take to get you guys up to team-status?" Because that was the biggest question. "I get you're crazy and strong and a two-year-old in griffin's clothing, but how long is it going to take you to climatize?"

Paige, Cawli said reproachfully.

"What? It's the truth."

Hattie chomped her teeth.

Leslie shifted on the rock she'd perched on.

"Guys, we're in trouble. Okay?" Paige had to get them to understand the stakes. "We've got people coming after us. They're going to take us out, especially if we can't get our shit together."

Leslie jutted her chin forward. "They're scared of me."

Paige understood that more than anyone. "Cry me a river. You've gotta stop giving them reason. Did you even notice we were under attack just now?"

"What?" Leslie pushed off the rock.

"Exactly. Your daughter is terrified right now. Men in black were shooting at her and what were you doing? Alpha-betizing the cupboard."

Leslie clenched her hands into fists. "It was the only thing I could do. It takes everything I have to remain in control."

"Then find a way to cohabitate." Paige stood. "And quickly. Now, if you don't mind, I'm going to see how my kids are."

She didn't wait for anyone else to say a thing. She just got up and walked out the cave entrance.

When she opened her eyes, she was sitting in the car, Dexx napping peacefully beside her.

How in the hell had there been bullets flying and the Whiskey house wasn't a crazed ball of activity at that moment?

11

No one in the house had realized anything was going on outside their home. Mandy was the only one. When Leslie reappeared in the kitchen, she returned immediately to the cupboards and didn't stop working until the kitchen and the garage were both organized to within an inch of everyone's lives.

The only thing Paige could think of was that either she or Leslie had somehow warded the house, so no one heard a thing.

Their power was…insane and it terrified Paige.

It still haunted her the next day. She sat at her desk wondering, not for the first time, what she was doing. Was she going to live her entire life like that, wondering what she was doing? When would she know? When she was grown up? She'd have thought that by that time in her life, she'd be able to consider herself a grown-up.

She wanted to be home with her kids, but she had priorities. Tony was coming into town for his interview and she had to be there for that.

She organized the files as best she could, preparing for

Tony. She wasn't just interviewing him. She understood she was being interviewed as well. Dexx had a good team. He didn't agree with everyone he had on it, but he had a good team.

She just hoped Tony saw it that way, too.

She'd worked with him back in Denver, during the years she hadn't had any memories of being a witch or a demon summoner or a mother. It had been a guiltily stress-free time of her life. When she'd come back from Louisiana with her memories intact, she'd discovered he was just as paranormal and strange as she was. Except he was on the gross side.

Vampire. Ick.

But she'd always liked Tony. In Denver, he'd been the guy others looked up to. Granted, she hadn't known why. She'd asked. He hadn't told. Not all of his secrets anyway. She did know that coffee made him poop. That was one piece of information she'd never get out of her head. Ever.

Michelle knocked on her office door and leaned in. "Hey, boss, your replacement arrived."

Paige leaned back and smiled. "First impression?"

"He's not a newb." She tipped her head to the side, letting her dark, Hispanic-amazingly-dark-and-full-and-luscious hair cascade over her shoulder. "So far, I could be talked into being impressed."

Paige chuckled and pushed herself to her feet, feeling a slight pressure in her abdomen where her babies were.

She called Tuck on his cell.

He picked up on the second ring. "Yeah. Tuck."

"Whiskey." She closed the drawer to her right to get out. She hadn't even realized she'd boxed herself in. "Tony's here."

"On my way."

She hung up and stepped into the bull pen. Stashing her phone in her back pocket, she looked through the half-walls of vines. When she'd started this place, the first thing she'd done was create those walls. She was a witch after all, and people needed to get the feeling that they weren't in Kansas anymore when they walked into her police station. Also, she dealt with paranormals who handled or were highly connected to elements if they weren't elementals themselves. This was one way to keep them mollified. If only slightly.

Tony stood up straighter, looking over the wall at her. He beamed a grin and took the distance with large strides. "I'd shake your hand, but I've missed you," he said, wrapping her in a tight hug.

That man knew how to hug. She loved Dexx's hugs, don't get her wrong, but Tony's hugs? It almost felt like he was hugging her soul.

She pulled back and took him in. He was taller than her by a good five inches and string-bean thin. Not in a drug-addict way, but in a way that said he ate well and worked out. It might have something to do with his diet of blood, too. She just didn't know. He had the Hispanic facial structure— happy, rounded cheekbones, dark eyes, dark hair feathered back. The man was handsome in his grey dress pants and purple dress shirt. He even managed to pull of the funky, weirdly colored tie. "You haven't aged a day."

"It's only been a year." He raised an eyebrow, the other one lowering.

"I *feel* like I've aged."

"You've gotten fat." He beamed a grin at her and held his hands out to her belly without touching. "I'm so excited for you. How far along?"

"Seven and a half, I think."

"You don't know?"

"There was a fuzzy three weeks where I was abducted by angels. I'm still struggling to get my timeline back."

His eyebrows shot up. "Wow. Do you know what you're having yet?"

His damned hands just hovering over her belly was getting on her nerves. She appreciated the fact that he didn't want to touch without permission, but the damned man could ask. She grabbed one of his hands and stuck it to her belly. "Twins."

"Oh." Tony's lips rounded, and his eyes widened almost comically as one of the twins kicked his hand. "Well, won't you be busy? Is that the reason you're having me take over for you?"

She wished. "No. That's a later conversation." She turned around and met the smiling, intrigued faces of her—Dexx's team as they huddled around. "I guess we'll get this going. Meet the team."

Tony took a step forward and offered his hand to Michelle. "Tony Guerrerro. Vampire. Been in the Force over twenty years. Detective for eight."

Michelle's smile grew. She took a step toward him and grasped his hand in hers. "Michelle Gomez. Dryad. Been in the Force for almost fifteen years. Detective for four."

Well, at least Michelle seemed happy. For now. Paige had no doubt she'd find something else to complain about. Not because Michelle was a complainer, but because she always discovered ways to improve things.

"Rainbow Blu." Rainbow hopped a step forward, her afro bobbing with the movement. Her brown eyes brightened—if that was even possible—as she smiled up at him. "Rusalka. I don't eat babies and I don't go around drowning people. It's a long story I'd rather not get into, but I feel death. Usually around water, but other places too. Water's everywhere."

Tony's expression grew wider. "Experience?" he asked as he gripped her hand.

"Here. Mostly. Almost a year? Not quite a year? I don't

remember. It all gets so blurry so fast. But a lot's happened. Big explosions and witches and djinn. And we were possessed. Well, Tarik was possessed. I don't know. It's a long story and I shouldn't probably get into it right now, but you'll love it so ask about it."

"Okay." Tony sent Paige a worried look.

"She's a very good investigator." Paige loved Rainbow. Sure, she could talk the hind leg off a mule, but the woman was always in a good mood and she *was* good at her job. Dexx had even finally said so. "She's the key reason we were able to take down the Eastwood Witches."

"Oh."

"Frey." The blonde woman leaned forward, not leaving her place on Rainbow's desk, and offered her hand. Her platinum braid fell over her right shoulder and her blue eyes narrowed. "How's that vampire thing going with the Eastwoods right down the street?"

He nodded once, then twice, but took her hand. "Surprisingly okay. While in town, there's no pull. I will have to test it out while I'm here. See how close I can get to Portland before I have to turn back. How bad it might be for me if the wards ever fell. That sort of thing."

"Yeah," Rainbow said, her eyes wide, her expression comically grim, "because that happens."

Tony blinked. "It does?"

Rainbow nodded.

"There was a huge battle not long ago," Paige said. "All the wards went down, but we got them back up."

"I take it you won."

"You bet we did," Dexx said, entering the huddle. "Hey, Tony. Good to see you here and in one piece."

Paige loved Dexx and just having him close made all her nerves just…settle. She took in a deep breath and shoved her fingers into her pockets.

"Give me a minute," Tony said, holding up a finger. He turned back to Frey. "What are you and what experience do you have?"

"I thought you were being interviewed."

"Employers often think that." Tony smiled politely. "You're being interviewed, too. Species and experience."

Frey crossed her arms over her chest. "Valkyrie and... longer than you've been alive."

Tony's expression opened in surprise.

Paige didn't know what to think about Frey yet. She'd barely met the woman and hadn't had the chance to get to work with her. In her mind, she was still Gretta, but, apparently, she really didn't like the name. Well, Paige could kind of understand that.

Frey was all big balls and anger. She lacked honey, but Dexx loved working with her. They probably spoke the same language somehow, which was good.

Tarik stepped up. "Tarik Riyad, djinni and...several more years than you've been alive as well."

Tony gave him a pained smile and shook his head. "Wasn't there a djinn problem here earlier? How are you on the team?"

Paige ducked her head and smiled. "He's been cleared. Trust me. He's a good addition."

It felt odd to be introducing her team and not introduce Quinn Winters. She was a siren and had been hired because she'd been brought to Troutdale to teach Tyler, Paige's nephew, on how to use his voice. Quinn was a grifter, no doubt about that. But she'd disappeared with a whole lot of blood left behind at her apartment. The investigation was still ongoing, but with no leads, no witnesses, and no facial recognition, it looked like their siren was off the grid.

Ethel hop-skipped over from the stairs that led down to her lab. "Who's this?"

Paige knew that Ethel knew exactly who this was because they'd talked about him not long ago. "Tony, this is our lab tech, Ethel Mills. She's a mundane."

"Pleasure to meet you." Tony took her hand with a smile.

"Don't get any ideas," Dexx said low.

Tony rolled his eyes and shook his head.

The door opened, letting in the sounds of a garbage truck fighting with the dumpster on the side of the building.

Chief Tuck walked in and propped himself against Frey's desk, holding his chief's hat in both hands while looking at Tony. "You must be the new guy."

"I am, sir." Tony bowed his head in respect, a slight smile on his face.

Well, he was immediately un-impressed like he had been with Rainbow. "This is Chief Tuck, and who we ultimately report to. Tuck, this is Tony Guerrerro. He was my partner in Denver."

Tuck nodded, and quipped his lips, his mustache burying them. "I read your file. I have a few questions."

"Of course, sir."

"Let's go to the conference room." Paige didn't want to cram that many male bodies into her office. It wasn't that it was small. Far from it, as far as offices went. But she was developing a slight claustrophobia with her pregnancy.

The boys followed, leaving the rest of the team behind. Dexx didn't ask permission. He just pulled up the back of the group.

Which was fitting because this was his team. More so than it was hers.

They all sat down around the table. Tuck and Paige took either of the ends, leaving Dexx and Tony to take either side of the middle.

"So, Tony," Tuck said, taking off his jacket and draping it over the back of his chair. "Why don't you start by telling us where you were for the past year. Way I heard it, you were offered a pretty good job in Texas."

"I was, sir." Tony pushed his lips out in thought and folded his hands. "I had family matters I had to attend to in Denver."

"And now? If I offer you a job here, are you going to turn me down for the same reasons?"

Tony winced and shook his head. "Truth be told, I've been looking for a new position for the past several months."

"Can't have been looking very hard."

"Oh, I have been."

"There are jobs all around."

"You think so." Tony sighed. "My family is very influential. Politicians and big business owners with powerful lobbyists."

Really? Because Tony didn't seem like he came from money.

"Unfortunately, when you piss one of them off, they tend to end your career, especially if you're a civil servant."

Dexx leaned back and folded his hands over his abdomen. "Now I'm curious. Is it as good as being kicked out of Hell?"

That was Balnore's story, the demon who had taken Paige under his arm and trained her to be a demon summoner when she was still a kid.

"No." Tony flushed, embarrassed. "But maybe nearly as bad."

"I don't see how." Dexx smirked.

Paige rolled her eyes.

"My father wanted me to set someone up."

Tuck leaned forward, his interest piqued. "How?"

"For murder."

"That could be an easy thing to do for a vampire *and* a cop." Tuck raised the fingers of his right hand, tipping his head as if in apology.

"Yeah." Tony licked his lips and shook his head. "I told him no, and he turned everyone against me."

"I thought you were in good standing with everyone," Paige said. "The shapeshifters and the vampires."

"Yeah. Until that. My father was going to bring me into the business."

The business, huh? "I take it that the family business isn't all legitimate."

"That's what I'm guessing as well."

Tuck blinked for a bit, staring off into space. "Are you clean?"

"I am, sir."

"And the blood. Will I have to worry about my people winding up bled to death?"

"Not from me, sir."

Tuck gave Tony a frank look.

Tony held up his hands. "I don't drink much and when I do, it's bagged. It's all I need."

"We don't have a hospital. Closest one is in Portland."

Tony released a long breath. "I may need someone to help get the blood then."

"The blood craze."

"Yeah." Tony nodded and looked at Paige. "I'd really like to see if I can make it. Test it out."

"Trial period?" Paige had never offered one of those, nor had she ever been offered one. But in reality, every single time she'd taken a job, it had been a trial period. Just not the one that anyone ever talked about.

"Well, you'll have to talk to Dexx," Tuck said.

Paige nodded. That was a very true statement.

"If Dexx is okay with givin' you a shot, I'll back his play."

"As will I." Mostly because she loved her man, but also because she needed this to work.

Dexx studied Tony for a moment before grinning. "I promise not to break your face in the first week."

"Dexx," Paige and Tuck said simultaneously, in almost identical tones.

Tuck pointed a finger at Dexx. "You break my town while trying to break in your new boss, I'll do more'n break your face."

Paige covered her mouth to hide her smirk.

Dexx shot Tuck a look of innocence.

Shaking his head, Tuck got up and headed for the door. "Well, I hope you work out, Tony. But understand, I don't much care for the whole vampire thing. I watch TV. Not a lot, mind you, but enough. Don't make me regret bringing you on."

Like he probably regretted letting Paige and the Whiskeys make a home for themselves in his town. Oh, that poor man.

12

Dexx took Tony for a few rounds to show him the town, and probably to do a few tests on the range of his blood madness. Paige had decided to stay back. She was starting to feel a bit crappy. Her insides were being pushed around and things were uncomfortable.

Also, every time she turned around, she had to pee. Again.

She caught up on budgets. Dexx had done a pretty good job with things over the past few weeks, but he absolutely refused to do budgets. She wasn't great at those either.

So, she made sure everything was adequate. Just as she was getting ready to leave, though, someone knocked on her office door. She looked up to see Ollie.

Oliver Eastwood was the new coven leader after his mother had been put in elder prison. He and Paige should probably be enemies or something, but he was her daughter's uncle. Technically, Leah was the next matriarch of the Eastwood coven, but Paige was going to do everything in her power to make sure *that* never happened.

The Eastwoods were blood witches. Just like anything

else, that didn't make them bad. Guns weren't bad. Bullets weren't bad. The people who used them in the wrong way? They were bad. The people who chose to kill innocent people, or to have a shoot-out on the street, not caring about who got in the way? Those people were bad.

The Eastwood coven…was bad. They murdered people. Mostly because Merry had trained them to be that way.

When Paige had put Merry away, she'd asked Ollie if he had what it took to take over the Eastwood coven. He'd said he did. He'd begged her for the chance to prove himself.

But, in the time he'd taken over, there were just as many disappearances as there were when Merry was in charge of the coven. Paige had tasked Dexx with getting dirt on the Eastwoods to take them down. Maybe they could cleanse Portland of the blood magick.

And invite a bunch of vampires? That wouldn't be a clever idea. But something had to be done. Paige couldn't just let someone kill people when he knew exactly who they were and what they were doing. Okay. She didn't know *exactly*. She knew a lot, though.

"Hey, Paige." Ollie offered his hand.

There was a lot of handshaking going on. "Hey, Ollie." She rose to shake his hand, then retook her seat.

He gestured toward her stomach. "Did you catch something, and is it contagious?"

Oh, pregnancy jokes. They never got old. "That's classy."

He smirked. "Are you having a litter? Because I hear with shifters, that's a real concern."

"I hate you so much right now."

"So, yes, then." He chuckled good-naturedly and sat down. He really didn't seem like a bad sort. He grew serious. "I'm glad you're moving on."

His brother, Mark, had been the love of Paige's life. She hadn't thought that love would ever find her again, but then...Dexx had shown up. They'd know each other before, but they'd never really spoken. He was a demon hunter and a friend of her mother's, and he thought Paige was the coming of the end of the world—thanks to her mother's influence.

Once Dexx had gotten over that in Louisiana, however, things started to slowly shift. Until they made it back to Denver, and then to Texas, and Paige's entire life had changed. Just like that.

She was still sad about Mark, but it was a distant sadness. "I am, too."

"Seriously, though, how many are you having and how far along are you?"

"Seven months—almost eight—and twins."

Ollie made an "o" with his lips, then scratched his stubbled chin. "How's Leah taking it?"

"She's excited, though we're having to rearrange the house a bit. Kammy and Bobby still have the nursery."

"Oh, that's right. I've never made it inside your house."

"That's because you've never been invited."

He nodded, his lips pursed.

"This isn't why you're here, is it?"

"No." He ducked his head and looked at her through his eyelashes. "I have information on McCree."

Seriously? If he'd called beforehand, he could have saved himself a trip. "What do you know?"

"Only that he's very powerful."

"Monetarily or witch-wise?"

"Both. He married a shapeshifter, but none of their kids became shifter-witches." He glanced down at her belly, then brought his gaze back up to her face.

She didn't have to wonder what he was thinking. He was wondering just how much power the Whiskeys were going to gather. How powerful were her kids going to be?

Well, it seemed like they were super powerful, but the

Eastwoods were still stronger. She knew that. The entire damned witch world knew that. When Paige had gone to Kansas to confer with the fae, they'd mentioned it. It was all good and great the Whiskeys were joining forces with the shifters, but they were powering up a little late in the game as far everyone was concerned.

Everyone knew there was something on the horizon, but no one knew what that might be. Demons. Angels. Witches. Demon spawn children? No one had a damned clue.

"Look, Ollie. I really wish you'd called. I know this already. In fact, I've already talked to him. Just yesterday, actually."

He looked surprised.

"But I'd take it as a kindness if you just keep your eyes off my kids."

He crossed his legs and placed his left hand on his knee. "They may need protecting."

"From who?"

"Everyone." He gestured with one hand, then let if fall back to his lap. "If they don't want to kill them, they'll want to take them. Raise them as their own."

"Are you thinking that?"

He ducked his head and shook it. "I'd be stupid not to."

"You'd be stupid to get between me and my kids."

"Why? Your mother did it." He met her gaze solidly. "And she's still alive to tell about it."

That was a low blow and she knew he understood that. Her mother had taken Leah, and that was the reason Paige had lived in Denver for several years with no memories and no gifts. She'd summoned a demon to kill her mother. There hadn't been a hearing. Her grandmother and Balnore had simply done what everyone had so desperately wanted.

To take Paige off the playing field.

"I was alone then."

"And you're not now?" Ollie tipped his head and gestured with both long-fingered hands.

"No. I'm not." She really wasn't. "You pit your coven against mine, and you'll find out just how many friends we have."

Ollie met her gaze for a long, hard moment, then dropped it.

Paige really didn't want to play that card. She didn't know how many shifters would honestly stand behind her. Dexx? Sure. He was liked well enough in town, or at least it seemed like it, and he was one of them. Mostly.

There were plenty who still shunned him, or those in his pack like Ripley and her mate Joe. Joe had been kicked out of his clan for mating with Ripley. A bear and a padfoot. And Dexx had taken them in. That hadn't bought him a ton of friends and had definitely made an enemy of more than a few.

But Chuck, the regional high alpha, was on their side. And if they needed backing because of a threat, Paige was pretty confident they'd rise to the challenge. The Whiskeys were a small family and coven. The Eastwoods were not.

Ollie rolled his eyes. "I'm not interested in your kids, Paige. Honestly, but it's something you need to be very careful of. People all over the world know you. They know who you're attached to, who you're mated to—if you two ever mate—and they know where you live roughly. If you go out in public—and I mean outside of Troutdale—showing that you're pregnant—a powerful witch and a powerful shifter father—they will hunt you down and take those babies away from you."

She doubted they'd get the chance.

But for as powerful as she was, she'd been outmatched innumerable times. She couldn't say that and mean it.

"Whatever went down with McCree, don't think he's done with you."

Okay. "Why?"

"He was in Portland asking a lot of questions. I think he has ideas about taking your babies."

Great. "Okay. Thank you." But… "Why did you feel you had to come all this way to tell me this in person?" And… why hadn't her wards popped letting her know he was on his way?

"I wanted to…discuss another matter with you."

She wasn't really good with "other matters" because they were often personal. "What?"

"Your investigation."

There was no way he thought she'd tell him anything, did he?

"There are…" he looked away, licking his lips. "…a few key people who need to be removed."

"And you can't do that?"

"I risk losing the coven if I do."

"Wouldn't you lose the coven it they found out you helped the police take down even more members of your coven?"

"They need to learn there are rules, Paige. And they need to learn they have to follow them. For too long, Mother has had them believing they were above the law and that's just not the case."

"I agree with you, but how do you want me to help?"

He fished a thumb drive out of his pocket and held it up. "I have information that will help in building a case against them."

"The murders?"

"Some of them." Ollie leaned over and put it on her desk. "I don't know everyone involved in the disappearances, but I know these are the leaders. If I can get rid of them, I can gain control of the coven. I know it."

"Ollie." Paige picked up the drive and rubbed it with her

thumb, feeling the ribs press into her thumb. "You need to get control of your coven now."

"I'm doing what I can."

"If you don't, we will come after you."

Ollie shook his head. "If you do, they would destroy you. We are powerful."

"So," Paige said quietly, pointing to the door, "are we."

Ollie sighed but stood up and left her office.

She picked up the phone and called Ethel's extension. "Hey."

"Hey, yourself," Ethel said. She sounded distracted.

"I have a thumb drive for you."

"Aw. You shouldn't have."

"It's from Ollie."

"You should have said so." Her tone changed to excitement. "I'll be right up."

Ethel wasn't one of those gals who chased the cutest man in the room. She honestly wanted to catch the Eastwoods doing what they all knew they were doing and get them off the streets.

She hung up the phone and it rang again. Frowning, she answered. "Whiskey."

"Hey," a familiar female voice said. "It's Billie Black."

Billie Black was a wood witch she'd met in Alaska.

"Hey, Billie. It's good to hear your voice." And it was. The trip to Alaska had been interesting and humbling. But the bright side had been Billie Black. "What's going on?"

"Well, I heard a rumor that you have some pretty big stuff going down in your world."

That was the largest understatement...ever. "Like what?"

"Like...ancients and your sister and a mutual friend. Mario What's His Name from the Department of Delicate Operations?"

"Oh. Those big things." And she'd heard about that? How the hell?

"Yeah. Look." Billie paused. "I know things are about to get rough."

"How?"

"The trees told me. What does it matter? Anyway, go home right now, grab your sister, and get your butts to Alaska."

"Why?"

"Why?" Billie clucked her tongue. "They're on their way to you and they're not going to be gentle. And they're going to take Leslie and your babies before you have a chance to prove you're safe."

Well, fuck.

"I have your tickets. You leave in three hours. Be on the plane."

"Okay." Well, Paige guessed she knew what she was doing for the next few days then. Saving her sister and her babies from being the next residents of ... DoDO.

Seriously. She hadn't looked at the title quite like that yet, but...

She was really this terrified of a DoDO?

Yes.

13

Normally in a situation like this, Paige would call Leslie. Unfortunately, Leslie was the situation.

Alma wouldn't be able to handle this. So, Paige called the only other person she could think of.

Ripley.

It hadn't been easy because she barely knew the woman, but Paige knew that she was going to need more help with Leslie. It didn't help that she was almost eight months pregnant, so flying in the first place was going to be tricky. She was almost at the point where airlines wouldn't let her even board the plane. So, she'd tasked Ethel with getting her one more plane ticket. Before she left the station, Paige had everything she needed. Ethel was a miracle worker.

More than that, though, Ripley was a padfoot, which meant she saw death. Or something. That could come in handy.

When she parked the car at the Whiskey house, prepared to pack a bag, Juliet was stepping out the door.

"What are you doing here?" Paige asked, stopping on the bottom stair.

Juliet was a tall woman, and big boned. If it wasn't for her constant soft smile, she would be intimidating. Her spirit animal was a polar bear, so it made sense. "Doing what I can to keep Leslie calm on the flight over. Billie called and asked me to use my tea."

Juliet had an old, Alaskan tea that repressed the spirit animal when needed. They'd almost had to use it when a rabid wolf had bitten her husband. Rabies in shifters was bad news. It typically bypassed the human's physical body and infected the spirit animal instead, inciting it to madness and fits of wild rage.

Well that certainly sounded good. And it was something Paige hadn't thought about. It probably wouldn't be a good idea to have a woman who could change into the shape of a rhino or a bird decide midflight that she didn't want to be on the plane anymore. "Thank you. I guess I should've thought of that."

"Don't worry about it." Juliet took three steps down then paused, turning to Paige. "Are you really going to be able to help her?"

She had no frelling clue. "I hope so. Don't really have a choice."

"Do you even know what she needs?"

"Nope." With everything she had heard, she had no idea what to expect, and no idea what to do. She was sick and tired of being put in situations she had no idea how to handle.

Juliet blinked and ducked her head. "Leslie is one of the strongest women I know."

"Yup." That was the understatement of the year. "She'll get through this. We just have to make sure that she still has a family when she gets back. And a shop."

"Oh crap. I totally forgot about the shop."

"I almost did too." And Paige would never hear the end of

it if they got back and Leslie was again Leslie, and the shop had suddenly disappeared. "Do we have anybody who could watch the shop for her?"

Juliet lifted one shoulder and a half shrug. "I probably could. I just need the keys."

Yeah. Keys. Where the hell would Leslie put the keys? "We need to talk to Tru about that."

Juliet walked back up the stairs with her. "I guess I'll go with you then."

Paige put her hand to her lower back and heaved herself off the last step. She was really ready to have these babies.

"How are you doing?"

Paige rubbed her belly, a wave of happiness and contentment rolling over her. The human body was an amazing thing. It had a way of keeping the mother content through the most horrific moments of her life. "I'm doing okay."

"Dexx is going to be super pissed."

"Yeah." She knew. "But I don't have any other answers for him."

Juliet open the front door and waited for Paige to go through. "I'll go find Tru. You go find Dexx."

"Sounds like a plan."

Dexx wasn't the only person she needed to see, though. She needed to see her baby boy and her little girl. She stood at the bottom of the stairs listening. She didn't hear anything in particular, so she leaned back and belted out as loud as she could, "Leah, where are you?"

A muffled voice was heard from above. "In my room, Mom."

Paige pulled herself up the stairs, wishing she was about a hundred pounds lighter. "Meet me in my room."

Thunderous footsteps sounded two floors above.

"Where is your brother?"

The thunder footsteps stopped, retreated, paused, then

continued back in the same direction. Paige can only assume that Leah had went to retrieve her brother.

"Do you know where Dexx is?" Paige asked, almost to the top of the stairs. She didn't have really yell from here.

Leah met her in what Paige called the second-floor hallway. It wasn't really a hallway. It was a very wide room where all the bedrooms emptied out into. There were several chairs on one end, a series of pantries lining the stairwell wall, and then another hallway leading to Paige and Dexx's room.

Paige loved that house.

"I think he's out in the garage." Leah bounced Bobby on her hip.

Bobby was getting big enough to where he really didn't want to be carried around all the time. However, it was safer for all of his adults if he remained within arm's reach. That boy was a monkey. He enjoyed climbing on everything.

"Okay." Paige would have to go out there and say her goodbyes. And beg for forgiveness. Again.

"Do you want me to go get him?"

"No." What Paige really wanted was just to spend some quality time at home. She hadn't had a lot of that lately. In the past several months, she'd had precious few moments to spend with the people she loved most on the entire planet. "Help me pack?"

Leah sighed. "Where you going this time?"

"Alaska." Paige waddled down the hall. The room she shared with Dexx was big, open, and full of sunshine. It had one large window beside the bed. The adjacent wall had a large French door that spilled out onto the balcony that wrapped around the entire house. The windows let in more light than she'd ever had in one bedroom. It also allowed them to see the stars.

When there weren't clouds.

And when they were home to enjoy them.

Leah stopped at the door that led to the hall closet. It was the only other room on that floor that wasn't a bedroom. It lacked a window, but it was large enough that it could be a small office if needed. "Are we going to convert this into the new nursery?"

Paige stopped and looked at her daughter.

Leah was tall for her age, but she still had a lot of room to grow. Her long blonde hair had a slight wave to it, and her blue eyes were big and woeful. Her cheeks were soft, and Paige wondered if they would sharpen as she grew older. Both her father and herself had never been beautiful babies, but they had both grown into handsome adults. Paige wouldn't say she was a raving beauty, but she was aging fairly well. She hoped that her daughter would as well.

Leah was a great kid and Paige needed to figure out how to spend more time with her. "That's a really good idea. She opened the door and peered inside, turning on the light. "There's a lot of work that will have to be done."

"Honestly, none of the stuff in there hasn't even been looked at since we moved in. Why are we even keeping it?"

Paige and Leah often-times thought alike. And this was one of those things where they shared similar opinions. Neither one of them agreed with keeping things that had no purpose. "Well, none of it is ours. So, it would fall on everyone else to go through and figure out what they don't want."

Leah stepped through the door, pushing her way around her mother. With Bobby still on one hip, she peered into the closest box. "Do you have any idea how many boxes of Christmas stuff we have?"

"Do you have any idea what a fiasco it was last year?" Paige grimaced just recalling it. "We couldn't find any of this stuff."

"So, you bought all new?" Leah looked over at her mom

with raised eyebrows. "This is insane. It looks as though you lost Christmas at least ten years in a row."

Paige looked around the room. After last Christmas, they'd discovered all the decorations had been left in Texas. Nick and his fiancé, Mark, had fixed that by bringing them all up with them the last time they'd been down there. Leah had a point. "Is most of the stuff Christmas?"

Leah nodded giving her mother a look that told her just how ludicrous she thought the situation was.

Paige frowned at the boxes. They'd put in temporary shelves along three of the walls. And every single shelf was filled to bursting. If she was really paying attention, she would have recognized the red and green duct tape denoting Christmas. She shrugged a guilty shrug. "We won't have to buy new stuff this year?"

Leah shook her head ruefully and turned to leave. "You guys are hopeless."

Paige wasn't going to disagree. However, Leslie and Paige were very busy people. Between being moms, working, and being wise-asses, they just didn't have time to keep track of trivial things like decorations. "Can you grab my suitcase for me?"

Leah closed the bedroom door behind her and set Bobby on the floor.

Bobby immediately made a beeline for the dresser. His favorite thing in the world was to open all of the drawers and pull out as many clothes as he possibly could. It would keep him entertained for a few minutes. It had gotten to the point where Dexx and Paige didn't even use the bottom drawers because they knew it was pointless. So instead, they had condensed all their clothes to the top two drawers.

The bottom drawers were now filled with baby boy clothes.

"Are you ever going to stay home?" Leah set Paige's suitcase on the bed and opened it.

"I certainly hope so." And she really did. This was the hardest part about being a working mother. Working. Being away from her kids. Being away from the man she wanted to marry one day. However, she just didn't know what else to do. "Your aunt really needs this."

"Yeah, she does." Leah went to Paige's sock drawer. "Do you know how long you'll be gone?"

Paige sat down on the edge of the bed. She needed to get off her feet. "Well, I won't be able to fly in two weeks. So, I'm hoping it only lasts that long."

Leah grabbed two handfuls of socks, underwear, and a couple of sports bras. Dumping them into the suitcase, she looked over at her mother. "Aunt Leslie is really messed up."

That was an understatement. "You know what Dexx is." The biggest, most powerful animal they knew of.

Leah nodded, giving her mother a "duh" look.

"You know how long it took him to figure out how to work with her?"

Leah shook her head.

"Two weeks."

And if they were really, really lucky, Leslie would figure this out in less than two weeks because Paige was having her babies at home.

She didn't care what she would have to do in order to make that happen.

14

Paige found Dexx exactly where she thought she would. In the garage.

He didn't even look up when she came in.

That was a bad sign. If anything, it made her feel even worse. She hugged Bobby closer to her, then opened the door of Leah's car.

Bobby loved to play in cars. Paige didn't know if he if he got it from Dexx, or if it was just something he had picked up along the way. Bobby was an adopted son, but that didn't make him any less theirs.

Closing the door, she straightened putting a hand to her lower back, trying to give it some extra support.

Dexx had the hood up and was working in her engine compartment. The thing was roomy, that was for sure.

Frowning, she searched for Jackie, who had been crushed in the fight with Cooper McCree. Where would he have stashed her? Certainly, not in a junk yard.

"Hey," Paige called softly, knowing he knew she was there. "Where's Jackie?"

"In the shed for now."

"I was wondering if you were going to scrap her." Really, she was just pushing buttons, looking for a response.

He sighed and straightened, wiping off a—well, some shiny, silver tool with his red rag. "No. Doing work on all the other cars first. I've got some parts on order to bring Jackie back."

Paige didn't know a lot about cars, but… "After she was wrecked that bad?"

"Frame's still good." He put the—maybe it was a wrench? —on the bench behind him. "I've been looking to replace her heads anyway. Plus a few other things. It just speeds up the process now." He looked pissed.

But at who? "Are you going to keep her the same color?"

He flattened his lips and narrowed his eyes. "Haven't decided."

"Keeping the same engine?"

He shrugged. "I was thinking of going with a Demon Hemi."

She didn't know why, but he enjoyed the hemi, whatever that meant. It was a term she'd come to recognize as "engine." As long as she kept things simple, she could follow along. "What does she have now?"

"A stroked 440 V8."

"You'll get more horse power?"

"Honestly? I'll get more horse power with the new heads I want, and then changing out the cam should help some, too."

She attributed the word "cam" to meaning "things that moved." That wasn't super helpful, but if he was happy, so was she. "And that thing you were going to do to make her more fuel efficient?"

"You mean her exhaust?" The look in his eyes told her she wasn't passing the test too well, but his tone of voice said he appreciated the conversation. "Yeah. Might as well. She's practically getting gutted anyway."

Paige raised her eyebrows. She didn't enjoy car talk, but she liked *talking* with Dexx. He went places he didn't like to go—like Babies R Us—so it was only appropriate she at least try. "How long's it going to take to get everything you need to fix her up?"

"Not too long. Got most of it on order. Should see stuff showing up any time now."

Car stuff was expensive. "Did you rob a bank?"

He finally smiled. "I might have robbed a man who'd robbed a bank."

Dread washed over her. That man. "That's still a criminal offense in a human court of law."

"If they catch me."

There *was* that.

"Where are you headed?" His smile disappeared, replaced with upset.

"The *Men in Black* are after us." She hoped he would get the movie reference. It was something he enjoyed, and she never got. He could watch a movie once and quote it for months and months.

She could watch a movie eight times and still be unable to remember anything that was said. He could watch the same movie once and quote it months later.

He nodded and pulled another tool out of the engine compartment.

"You're not going to say anything?"

He set the tool down on the bench behind him and picked up another tool that she didn't quite see. "And what am I supposed to say?"

"I don't know." Because she felt like an ass. "Anything."

Something thunked in the seat of the car.

Paige looked.

Bobby was crawling back onto the seat. He must have fallen down, but he wasn't screaming so...

Dexx set the new tool down and stepped around the car. "Okay. Stay."

"And then what we do with Leslie?"

"What are you going to do with her in Alaska?"

Paige really didn't know. "Their wood magick could really help us."

"How?" He tipped his head to the side. "Because you were working some wood magick of your own with Mr. Department of Delicate Assholes earlier."

"I, honestly, have no clue what happened out there."

He closed his eyes before looking away.

"Look, she's out of control. So am I. I teleported us and the car."

He raised an eyebrow, baring his clenched teeth for a moment.

"I've never been able to do that, and I haven't heard of a witch who could, either."

"Telekinesis isn't a new thing."

"No, but on a small scale. I practically teleported an elephant."

He narrowed his eyes, still not looking at her. "A small elephant."

Was he serious?

He sighed. "I'm her alpha. I'll teach her."

"You've had the chance to teach her. And you haven't been able to because her power is too great."

He shrugged. "So, what do you think you'll be able to do in Alaska that I can't do here?"

She swallowed. "Billie and her wood witches are going to help. They...look, they take in challenging cases like this all the time. There's just something in their wood wards that...I don't know. It sluffs off the extra power somehow? It's hard to explain."

"And you can't do that here?"

"I don't know how."

"Then have her and her wood witches join you here."

"And what happens when the men in black show up again?"

"And they won't there?"

"You've…obviously never been to Alaska." She shook her head. "They could try, but it won't be healthy for them."

He strangled the red rag in his hand and turned to face her. "Why am I still here, Pea?"

Was he seriously thinking of leaving, or was he just having a hard day? Paige had always secretly felt Dexx would one day leave her. She kept that thought buried deep inside, but it was a fear she held onto.

"Why are you still here?" Dexx thumped his tool in his hand. "Are you even still part of this family?"

He wasn't wrong to ask, but she certainly hoped he wasn't being serious. "I'm hoping you stay."

He didn't say anything.

Because he'd never think of leaving? Because he didn't miss his old hunting days when he'd get in Jackie and just go? It had been just over a year since she'd pulled him away from all of that. Back then, he'd been confident and self-assured.

Now…he was cocky. Sure. But he floundered. With Red Star. With his pack.

Not with the kids, though.

She had no idea what was going through his head, and that worried her.

He was probably frustrated and tired of doing all the heavy lifting, which he had been. She needed him, more than anything. She just needed him to understand that. "I love you."

He snorted. "Are you sure about that?"

Paige shoved her hand in her left pocket her fingertips finding the one thing she had been holding onto for the last several months. She'd just been waiting for the right moment. That moment never seemed to show up.

But now? Looking at him right now. He needed to understand just how much she did love him. She pushed herself off Leah's car and straightened as much as her bulging belly would allow her to.

Technically, Dexx had already proposed, but true to his nature, they had no rings, no date, and no idea when they'd actually get married or how.

She pulled the ring out of her pocket and held it in her fingers. It was black tungsten steel and heavy. She'd figured she needed to find something that could withstand all the crap Dexx put stuff through. He was the ultimate killer of pants and satin underwear. She hoped he wouldn't destroy the ring to.

A frown flickered across his forehead as he stared at her.

"I need you to let me talk." One of the reasons they never got the real information out there was because they always got interrupted.

If it wasn't outside interruptions, then it was them interrupting each other. They just wanted to tell each other everything. And sometimes that meant going down tangents only to forget why they'd even started the conversation in the first place. It didn't help that they could finish each other's sentences.

"Okay." He didn't sound too sure.

Well, that certainly wasn't helping anything. "After Mark, I never thought I could feel this way about anybody. I...

thought the world of him. He was my sun, my reason for being."

Dexx raised an eyebrow, opening his mouth to say something, and then closed it again.

Tears stung her eyes and she blinked them back, swallowing hard to keep the words coming.

Dexx's eyes rimmed red in response. There were no tears there, but she could see they were close.

"I have no idea why you stuck with me. All the crazy shit I put you through. Moving you from place to place. You were bitten because of me. You've always had to play second fiddle. You had to pick up where I dropped the ball. And I've been dropping the ball a lot. The kids? Red star? You?"

He ducked his head and sniffed.

"But through it all, I don't think I've made it quite clear just how much I care for you. When you enter in a room, I just feel better. Your voice is like a blanket. Your arms make me feel as though the world doesn't suck."

He pressed his lips tight together, the green in his eyes brightening.

"You make me feel whole and complete in a way I never thought was possible. You are more than just the sun. I really don't want to see what life is like without you, and I hate you a little bit for making me feel that way."

He released a chuckle, shaking his head.

She had to stop because she couldn't say anything anymore. She didn't know if it was hormones making her more emotional, or if it was the power of the truth in her words coming out.

He took a step closer to her and took her hand.

She hadn't even realized she was trembling. He'd already asked *her,* and she'd already said yes. It wasn't like he was going to give her a different answer now.

Unless he did.

Every single part of her knew how much she wanted him. She wanted him to be a part of her life forever.

But a voice in the back of her head asked why he would want to be a part of hers. What if he said no? Granted, she was carrying his children. But she knew from experience that meant absolutely nothing to some people.

She swallowed hard to clear her throat. Tears were falling from her cheeks. But she didn't care. She just needed him to understand that in this moment he was the only thing that she could think of.

"I love you, Dexx Colt."

He just stared at her, not saying a damned word.

While that was infuriating, his face and his eyes told her what he felt without words. No snarky comebacks. No witty returns. Just honesty and a bleeding, open heart. His eyes glistened a brilliant green against the red rims of his eyes.

Clearing her throat, she held out the ring. She took in a deep breath. "Will you marry me?" The words barely made it out, her emotions were so strong they nearly buried her breath. "Not for the kids or the Division. But for me."

He caressed her face with his fingertips. "I think we got this a bit backward." His voice was ragged.

She released a ghost of a chuckle and shook her head. "Well, you forgot the ring last time."

He licked his lips and reached into his pocket, pulling out a black box. "I was…I was planning on asking you tonight. At dinner. I had the evening planned for us."

That explained why he was so upset.

He got down on one knee and opened the box. "I know you don't like diamonds."

She didn't. She thought they were empty and ugly, and she hated that everyone felt they needed to have one. The ring inside the box was simple with a single blue stone. It was perfect.

"Paige Whiskey," he said in a clear voice, so much stronger than hers had been. "Will you be my wife?"

She chuckled once, then twice, then a flurry of giggles that would have made her teenaged daughter proud erupted from her. Pushing the ring she'd gotten for him onto his finger, she said, "Yes. You silly man."

He gave her a pained smile and this time, tears did fall from his eyes. He slipped the ring on her finger and stood. "For your information, I hate you a little too."

His arms held her close. They hated each other for the same reasons. Two strong, independent people were now desperately dependent on the other.

But it felt amazing.

He pulled back and looked down at her. "How much time do we have?"

"Not long. My plane leaves very soon. Ripley is on her way. Juliet has Leslie drugged."

"You've said good-bye to Leah."

"See ya later? Yeah." Paige loathed the word good-bye. "We have a very bad situation on our hands."

"What else is new?" Dexx leaned against Leah's car, and brought Paige close to him.

She snuggled close, raising his T-shirt a little so that she could feel his skin against her fingers. She didn't understand why men were so hairy. And at one point, she had found that to be quite disgusting. But now, she didn't care. It just meant she was that much closer to the man she loved.

"You're about to be a really crappy wife."

She chuckled. "You're such a jerk."

He hugged her close, pressing her head to his chest. "I'll trust you. Because I always do. Then, you come home to me."

"Always."

And she meant that.

She pulled away, looking up at him with a grin. "You do

realize of course that you're going to have to change your name to mine."

He wrapped her shoulders and went for the door to retrieve Bobby. "In your dreams, babe. You're going to be a Colt."

Paige retrieved her son from the seat. "Oh no, babe. You're going to be a Whiskey."

Dexx pressed a kiss onto Bobby's head. And then looked at her, his eyes soft. "You can hyphenate."

"Not on your life."

He put his arm around her shoulders again. "You're such a jerk."

Things were going to be okay.

15

Paige hadn't been able to sleep on the plane. Those seats weren't designed for anyone above "average" size, including pregnant women.

Paige just wanted to cry. She knew she wouldn't. She'd keep it together, but she was just so overwhelmed; at work, at home, with the elders and DoDO, with the new babies, with Leslie. She needed…

What? Time?

She doubted that.

She needed to get a handle on the situation, but what would that take? How much did she really think Billie Black was going to be able to do? The wood witches were incredibly powerful. That was true, but were they powerful enough to stand up to DoDO? And why would they do that? They had no reason to do that for the Whiskeys. They weren't going to get anything in trade from it. Though, Paige would offer, she doubted Billie would accept anything.

And why were the Whiskeys getting so powerful?

That thought absolutely terrified her. What was coming

that was so big and bad? Would they even make it? Would they beat whatever was coming?

What would need *this much power* to defeat it?

A pack of demons? An army of angels?

Both?

All of Hell? All of Heaven?

Demigods.

A virus breaking out on the paranormals? The zombie apocalypse?

If they survived all of this, would she even want to be a part of that life? What they had was what she wanted. A normal life. Would she ever have that? It didn't look likely.

They landed and got off the plane, which was a sight to see, mostly because Leslie was still unconscious. They'd had to tell the flight crew Leslie hated flying. They'd gotten strange looks, but Paige was sure they'd had odder situations.

Juliet's mojo—brew, whatever—had worked like a gem.

But it looked like it was finally starting to wear off. She raised her head, her eyes blazing orange before her head fell forward again.

Ripley looked over at Paige from the other side of Leslie. "We could be in trouble."

That was an understatement. So many of those lately.

Paige kept her eyes out for DoDO agents. She didn't know where they were or might be. She didn't know how they operated. They could be attacked right there in the airport for all she knew, though that was a Federal offense, and Paige doubted even the elders could help make that situation disappear.

"Where are we ending up?"

Paige hadn't really given Ripley much information about the trip, mostly because she didn't have much information. "I have no idea."

"Well, I hope it's close."

Paige did too but doubted it. When she'd been there the last time, she'd had to drive for hours before getting to the wood witch territory.

Leslie's eyes opened in slits, orange light shining through her lashes.

Ripley was average height with wavy, wild brown hair and dark eyes. Currently, they shone silver as her padfoot came forward a little.

That couldn't be good. The padfoot could see death. "Are you seeing anything?"

"Not yet." Ripley's voice was distant, but strong.

"That's good." Right?

"It is." In one blink, the silver eyes disappeared and were replaced by a dark color Paige couldn't quite decipher—not really brown but not black either.

Ripley had entered Dexx's pack after her mate had been thrown out of his bear clan for mating with someone other than a bear. She was sassy, wore ratty jeans, and t-shirts designed to irritate people. She had her customary red flannel wrapped around her waist plus a jean jacket, which had only appeared after Paige told Ripley they were headed to Alaska.

"Why am I here again?" Ripley asked as they maneuvered to baggage claim.

Paige had checked her suitcase because, even as an officer of the law, she couldn't carry a gun on board a plane, and she hadn't wanted to lug it, her sister, her two babies, and her laptop bag around the entire friggin' airport.

"I needed an extra set of hands." And really, she might have thought about bringing one more set because Paige was tired. She was already carrying two extra people around. "And I've wanted to get to know you for a while."

Ripley pulled back, almost hiding behind Leslie's semi-prone body. "Should I be worried?"

"Blessed Mother, I hope not." Ripley might be worried that Paige wouldn't like her, but Paige was equally worried. Ripley was part of Dexx's pack, a pack Paige hardly knew. Ripley was sharing the other half of Dexx's life, and frankly, was probably spending more time with him than she was.

"You're not worried I want to take your mate, are you?"

That thought hadn't even crossed her mind. She found their carousel and propped Leslie against the column, waiting. "Hell, no. I just haven't had a chance to meet you. I've either been gone or busy or doing other things."

Ripley didn't say anything.

Which didn't mean she wasn't thinking something.

The baggage started flowing. What was the likelihood her suitcase would be one of the first to come through?

Paige sighed. "This is the closest thing to a vacation I've had in a while and you seem cool and everyone in my family likes you and the pack adores you."

"Adores me?" Ripley's tone was genuinely surprised.

It was true. "Leah wants to *be* you."

Ripley chuckled. "That's a bad idea."

"It's probably better than having her turn out like me."

"You really think that?"

Paige remained quiet until they'd gathered her suitcase and made it through the double doors to the outside.

It was still light outside even though she knew it was late out. She wouldn't say it was bright, but it was lighter than dusk. She'd read about this but had never seen it for herself. The last time she'd been there, it had been the middle of fall and about to snow. They'd had almost normal daylight hours.

"I do. I know me," Paige said, looking around. "Billie said she'd be driving a red Bronco."

"Do you know her?"

"Yeah. We met the last time I was here."

Ripley motioned to a column and they propped Leslie

against it. "You are a very mysterious woman, Ms. Whiskey. Back to that mom thing."

It wasn't something she wanted to get into a lot of detail on. "I don't want to come off like a whiner, or like I'm looking for sympathy. I'm not. Bottom line, I'm not Mother of the Year."

Ripley raised her face to the sky, the corners of her lips pulled down. She pulled in a deep breath and let it out. "At least you're willing to admit it."

Paige appreciated the fact that Ripley just accepted her truth at face value. Too many people wanted to pry or enable, trying to be sympathetic in a vain attempt to appear to be the nice person. Paige was at the point in her life where she could see right through people like that. And she really appreciated the fact that Ripley wasn't about putting on airs.

"I sometimes wish my mom had admitted to that," Ripley said.

"Me, too."

Ripley quirked her lips then glanced at Leslie. "What are we doing?"

Paige shook her head. "Aside from following my gut, I have no idea."

"Do you do that a lot?"

Paige opened her mouth to say no. She thought of herself as a very strong person who had a plan and followed it. But then she changed her mind because that just wasn't reality. "Yeah. Actually. I do that a lot more than I probably realize."

Ripley narrowed her eyes. "I don't."

"Good to know. So, we can rely on you to come up with our plan?" Because Paige needed someone to do that.

"I thought you were the alpha female."

"Oh, sure." Paige set her bag and her suitcase against the column then leaned against it herself. "As soon as I figure out what that means."

Ripley chuckled. "You and Dexx aren't normal alphas."

"We aren't normal people, either." And they really weren't.

"There's got to be a reason why you're here, dragging a suitcase, carrying a bag and your sister while you're that—" Ripley gestured to Paige's bulging belly. "—pregnant. What's got you scared?"

Paige was beginning to understand why so many people in their pack liked Ripley. She was refreshing to be with. No pretenses. Honesty was allowed *and* asked for. "Well, have you heard of ancients?"

Ripley thought about that, but then shook her head.

"Okay. Well, they're the old mystical creatures that disappeared a long time ago."

"Like the unicorn."

"Yeah, them and griffins."

Ripley snapped her fingers and gave Paige a wide-eyed smile. "The sphinx."

"Sure." Though Paige hadn't heard of that one coming back. "Anyway, they're super powerful and they're coming back."

Ripley leaned forward and gave Paige a deadpan look. "You're giving birth to a unicorn."

Paige chuckled, letting the stress roll off her a little. "No. A thunderbird and a rajasi."

"A raj-a-wha?"

Paige shrugged and shook her head. "Fiery lion thing."

Ripley's eyes narrowed, and her mouth fell open as she thought. "India."

"Yeah." The woman knew some stuff, or maybe she had enough worthless information to keep things interesting. Dexx could do that, and it was annoying. "Anyway, there's a lot of people who want to either capture the ancients and use them or destroy them."

"Which one of those are we running away from right now?"

Nothing got by that woman. "Destroy." Paige cleared her throat and resituated against the column. "Department of Delicate Operations."

Ripley snorted, chuckled, and then burst out laughing. "We're running from DoDO."

Paige chuckled, too. "Yeah."

"Okay." Ripley sobered. "Should we be on look-out?"

"I've been watching but haven't seen anything. And you had your padfoot look and you didn't see any death. So..." Paige shrugged.

"You think we're okay."

"I *hope* we're okay."

Ripley nodded sharply. "Why are you always away from home?"

Paige shrugged. "It really depends on the week." And it did. "Sometimes, it could be a demon outbreak. Other times, it's an attack on a paranormal community from DoDO, if you can believe that, and other times, it's the Elder Council trying to get other paranormals back under their control."

Ripley raised her eyebrows, her expression dry.

"What do you know about the Elder Council?"

"Me? Not much. I've spent most of my time as a padfoot in other countries."

"How much have you heard?" Paige really had no idea.

"A lot. They're quite loud about their beliefs."

This was good information to have. "Good or bad?"

"It's like anything. It's both. Their plan is to keep people safe. They just have particular ideas and laws to do that and not everyone believes that they'll work."

"So, just like our own government."

"Yeah."

Well, on one hand, it was nice to know that some things

were similar. And that someone close knew things. She really did need to make a point of getting to know the pack. "How far does their reach extend?"

"Most of the Americas. Canada, Mexico, and Brazil. Australia and New Zealand a little, but the UK and Russia have other governing factions. There are others, too, but those are the biggest ones."

Neat.

Billie's red Bronco pulled up in front of them. Billie leaned over and yelled through the passenger window, "Need a lift?"

Billie looked like she had some sort of Native American heritage in her, but Paige didn't know enough about heritage or bloodlines to know specifics or if she was just "exotic." She had deep brown, almost black hair that was full, thick, and straight. Her skin had color to it—a natural tan Paige was almost jealous of—and her eyes were big and brown.

She was also a complete sweetheart as long as you weren't trying to push your way onto her turf.

Which had been exactly what Paige had attempted to do the last time she'd been there.

Paige and Ripley managed to get Leslie into the back seat of the Bronco. Ripley let Paige have the front seat.

Billie looked over at Paige's large belly. "Wow."

Paige nodded. "Yup."

"Okay." Billie put the vehicle—Paige had learned not to call it a car because it wasn't a sedan, but she didn't know what to call a Bronco—into gear and pulled away from the curb.

"Where are we going?" Paige asked.

"Home." Billie threw Paige a smile. "Trust me. It'll be okay. Just don't go having babies on the flight over."

"Flight?"

Billie nodded. "Unless you want to drive for another three hours."

Paige really didn't. "I'm ready for a bed."

"I'm ready for wine," Ripley said from the back seat.

"We have both waiting for you. It'll be a quick flight." Billie drove around the terminal of the airport to the hangars on the far side. She parked the Bronco just inside one of them and got out.

Paige had never been inside a hangar before. They were massive buildings. It made sense they would be. After all, they housed planes. Entire planes. Sometimes plural, like this one.

"We're flying in one of those?" Ripley asked, stopping dead in her tracks.

Paige gestured through the passenger door to her sister. "You want to help me with Leslie?'

"No." Ripley stood on the other side of the vehicle, staring inside the hangar.

"What is this?" Paige stared at the woman like she was out of her mind. "You can *see* death. Do you see any now?"

"No."

"Then, why are you freaking out right now?"

"I'm not freaking out."

"You're not helping."

Ripley gave her a dirty look.

Billie turned to them both. "You two figure out how to get you and your stuff on that plane and I'm going to do finish the pre-flight checks."

Ripley clamped her lips shut, her nostrils flaring. "I don't like this."

"You were fine before."

"That was a real plane before."

"This is a real plane, too." And Paige was pretty okay with

getting on it and shaving time off their travel. She really wasn't looking forward to traveling another several hours.

Ripley shook her head then reached for Leslie, pulling her out of the door.

Leslie mumbled something.

Ripley muttered something back.

Paige grabbed the two backpacks, the laptop bag, and her suitcase, feeling more like a pack mule than a human, and waddled to the plane.

It took a bit of maneuvering, but they all managed to get on the inside. It was pretty tight. It wasn't a luxury liner, this plane. It was a bush plane. An actual, honest-to-God bush plane.

And they had it packed to the max.

Ripley sat in the co-pilot's seat, leaving Paige and Leslie in the middle of the plane with the gear.

Flying.

Paige enjoyed looking out at the scenery. For all that it was well after nine at night, there was still plenty of light to see the landscape below them through her small window. The mountains were amazing. They were everything she expected from the Rockies, which was what she compared *all* mountains to. The Rocky Mountains of Colorado were harsh and sometimes unforgiving. They challenged a person, and they either lived up to the expectation of the mountain, or they got out of the way.

Overall, the flight was pretty smooth. A little bumpy in spots, but otherwise fine.

Billie brought them down in elevation while they were in the middle of the mountains. Paige couldn't find a landing strip or where they might land at all.

The last time she'd been there, she hadn't made it out of Anchorage because she'd been invited not to leave it. Rather forcefully. Billie was a nice woman, but you didn't want to cross her either.

Billie said something, but Paige couldn't hear it over the drone of the engines.

She only saw that the mountains were getting bigger.

But, she had to trust that Billie knew what she was doing, even if it was freaking her out just a little.

Her babies, still in her womb, were quiet and calm.

Leslie stirred and looked around her blurrily. Her lips moved, but Paige couldn't hear her. Between the elevation changes which had clogged her ears, and the noise of the pane, there was no way of hearing anything.

She smiled at her sister and gripped her cold fingers, giving them a squeeze.

Leslie nodded slowly, then turned her attention out the window.

The landing wasn't anything exciting except that it really did look like they were landing on the side of a mountain to be exact.

Billie taxied to a large shed just big enough for the plane, and she stopped the engines. She turned toward them and motioned for them to get out. "Ladies, we have arrived. Thank you for flying Black Air."

Paige closed her eyes. She was ready for a nap.

1 6

Alaska was gorgeous. Everywhere Paige looked was another breathtaking view. The mountains were *mountains*. The air felt *good*.

The magickal currents even felt fresher up there.

Billie led them to two pick-up trucks parked outside the shed. "Which of you is the least tired."

Ripley took one look at Paige and raised her hand.

Billie tossed her a set of keys. "It likes to stall at stop signs. If it does, give it a minute before restarting it."

Ripley shrugged, re-situating the backpack on her right shoulder. "I understand that. I've got a truck that has more personality than go. I'll follow you."

"Will you take Leslie?"

She nodded.

Paige was about to drop. She hadn't been this exhausted since…Louisiana. But she'd done a lot more in Louisiana. All she'd done this time was paperwork, get on a plane, and sit. There'd been a lot of sitting.

Billie took Paige's suitcase and led her to the blue truck.

It was older and looked like something Dexx would appreciate. It had the kind of character he enjoyed in a vehicle. But more than that? Paige just didn't have it in her to care. She pulled herself and her two kids into the passenger seat and rested her head against the headrest, closing her eyes.

Billie got in and started the truck. "I was wondering how you'd sleep here. A lot of people struggle with that."

She was talking about the constant sunlight. "I was, too." Paige didn't even bother to open her eyes. She rubbed her belly as the twins decided it was time to wake up and kick around again. Awesome. "But I'm tired enough, I think I could sleep through a tsunami."

"Well, we don't get those this high up in the mountains, so you should be safe."

Paige dozed off after that, until the sudden quiet of the engine cutting off drew her out of sleep. She opened her eyes to find a series of cabins were sprawled out in front of them.

"I went ahead and booked these for you guys."

"For how long?"

"A month."

"Hopefully, we can get somewhere sooner than that or I'll have to drive all the way home in order to have my babies there, where they belong."

"And that's if you carry to term." Billie tipped her head. "Which most don't, carrying twins."

That was true, but the idea required too much energy to think about.

Billie nodded and pointed toward the cabins. "Pick one. I have one for each of you."

"What about Leslie?" Ripley asked. "Shouldn't we set up a watch for her?"

"Probably not." Billie narrowed her eyes and pursed her lips.

"She's standing right here," Leslie said, flopping her hand against her thigh.

The Leslie looking at Paige through Paige's blurry gaze looked a lot like *her* Leslie. "You don't understand."

"I feel fine."

Paige took in a deep breath of clean mountain air and released it. "Okay. Bill, look. She'll be fine one moment then she'll just disappear. And then? There's paperwork because people are looking for their lost pets. Dogs, cats, birds. And I've seen the footage. She eats them."

"I don't eat people's pets."

Except she really did.

"Trust me." Billie raised her free hand. "I brought you here because we can help in more ways than just keeping off DoDO's radar."

"Wait." Leslie snorted. "DoDO?"

Billie ignored her. "Just relax and understand that we have ways of keeping the energies repressed."

"Repressed?" Leslie asked, her Texan drawl coming out a little.

"Don't you feel more relaxed?" Billie gave Leslie a frank look. "More yourself? More in control?" She looked at Paige and Ripley. "All of you?"

Ripley narrowed her eyes then tipped her head to the side. "Decima is actually joking with me right now. It was a horrible joke, but she let one out."

Just the way she phrased that made Paige picture the spirit animal releasing a fart.

Leslie blinked rapidly then straightened. "I—I can think clearly for the first time in weeks."

"See?" Billie gestured to the cabins again. "Now, please. Get some rest."

Paige barely had enough energy to make it up the three semi-rickety steps and into the cabin. She found the bed, slipped off her shoes, found a blanket, and was down for the count.

She woke up feeling like a new woman. She took a quick shower in the small bathroom and finger-combed her hair, deciding to let it air dry. She didn't like blow drying it, but she didn't enjoy having a huge mess, either.

She changed her clothes, looking forward to being able to wear real jeans again. She was out of her jurisdiction, so she didn't need to carry her badge with her—it was actually best if she *didn't*—and considered leaving her gun there as well. She couldn't wear the hip holster. Not because she couldn't reach it but because it made her pants fall down.

Real pants. She was really looking forward to it.

She tucked her suitcase aside, with her gun, then stepped out of the cabin.

The sounds were amazing. Wind in the trees. Birds. A squirrel.

The smells were refreshing. Forest. A distant storm.

No planes. No traffic.

Just…nature.

She carefully stepped down the stairs. They weren't rickety like she'd thought the night before. They were just uneven because they'd been made from real logs. She didn't see the pickup trucks, so she went around to the second cabin. She sent a tendril of thought inside the cabin and found Ripley.

"The door's open, Paige," Ripley called out.

Stepping inside, Paige found a cabin very much like her own. Same layout. Same color scheme. Different furniture. It looked like whoever owned the cabins had gone to garage sales or had used what they'd collected over the years. It wasn't bad. The furniture was still in decent condition, but it was just an odd mismatch of stuff.

Ripley was sprawled on a loveseat straight from the 60's, big floral patterns and all. She looked up at Paige and smiled.

"Billie brought over breakfast earlier. Coffee's there and you can reheat the eggs."

Paige was ravenous. "Is Leslie awake?"

"Yeah. And she's already out with Billie."

"Why didn't you wake me?"

"You're living for three people. We thought it best to give you the time you needed. Also, it gave me a chance to read a book."

Paige hadn't realized Ripley was a reader. She lifted the paper plate covering the blue ceramic plate and took in the feast of eggs, hash browns and bacon. It looked amazing. She plopped the plate in the microwave and turned back to Ripley. "What are you reading?"

"This book, *Fall of Sky City*. It's about this guy on another planet. He's pretty stupid, but he's just now figuring that out and I kind of dig that. It's pretty cool."

Paige listened to the microwave nuking her breakfast. "What do you like about it?"

"The place."

Paige chuckled.

"Man, you should see this place. It's really neat. They use jellyfish to travel in. Can you believe that? Jellyfish. And I can *smell* it." Ripley shook her head with a smile as she stared at the cover. "I didn't expect that when I picked up this book. I just wish Synn wasn't so clueless."

"Can you imagine what would happen if you were put in a book?"

"I dread the idea." Ripley snorted.

The microwave dinged. "Me, too." She took the plate to the table and snarfed down the food. "Do you know where Billie and Leslie are?"

"Yeah. They're just down the way a bit. It's a short walk. You bring boots?"

Paige gestured to the ones on her feet. "Just regular ones."

"You're probably going to want to wear them because it rained after we went to bed and it's going to rain again."

A sense of relaxation ran through Paige. She loved the rain. She had worried when they'd moved to Oregon that she'd start to hate it, but it just hadn't happened. If anything, she loved it more. She missed it when the sun was out for more than a few days in a row.

Well, with nothing urgent in need of doing, it was time to get to know her a little more. "Why did you join Dexx's pack?"

"Billie brought these for you just in case." Ripley glanced over at Paige as she pointed at a pair of muck boots. "Dexx offered to let Joe in."

"And that was enough?"

"You probably don't understand this, but there are a lot of people that don't like padfoots. They don't trust us."

That was something Paige understood. "You do realize who you're speaking to, right?"

"That's another reason why I accepted." Ripley stood, muck boots in hand. She smiled and handed them over. "I had a funny feeling you would understand more about acceptance than most."

"Do you think we're actually going to need these?"

Ripley shrugged. "I'm wearing mine. Figured it couldn't hurt."

Paige stared at them for a moment, but not because she was trying to figure out if she needed them. She was trying to determine if she *should* wear them. There was the whole very-large-belly thing to consider, and it wasn't looking promising. "What was your life like?"

Ripley smirked. "I'll write it down in a book someday and let you read it."

"So, you're admitting there's a story."

"You've got more than one."

That she did. Setting the boots down, Paige turned.

"Living life adventurously?"

"When you're the size of a house and can't bend over to put on regular boots, we'll talk."

Ripley led the way through the door with a chuckle. "What were you doing in Kansas?"

Paige carefully walked down the uneven stairs in the front of the cabin. "Shouldn't we lock the door?"

Ripley gestured with one hand dismissively. "Were out in the middle of the woods if you hadn't noticed. No one's around to steal anything."

And if they did show up, Paige was pretty sure they'd be shot. "Kansas. That's one question I don't get asked a lot."

"Probably because it was the quickest adventure you've been on. Usually you're gone for at least two or three weeks."

That was true. "There were a bunch of disappearances, but by the time I got there, they'd decided I wasn't welcome."

Ripley walked down what might have been a driveway, but it was hard to tell. Mostly, it was just dirt with fewer flowers growing up along two tracks. "I don't know you very well, but I can tell that you're not a person that would take that as an answer."

"Normally, I wouldn't." And that was the Goddess's only truth. "However, I realized elves weren't something I should play with."

Ripley chuckled. "Elves? Seriously?"

Paige shared in the chuckle. "Seriously. They are very powerful, and they seriously are not people you want to cross. Ever."

"I always thought they were only a myth."

"I thought werewolves were only a myth."

Ripley held up a finger. "Werewolves *are*."

Paige grinned. It was easy for her to like Ripley. She was just a down-to-earth kind of girl. "It sure was a shock."

"What was the first shifter you ever saw?"

"That's a trick question." They stepped off one lightly beaten track and onto more of what Paige would consider a dirt road. "Because, technically, I can see the shapeshifters spirit animal when they're still human."

Ripley looked back over her shoulder. "Seriously."

That wasn't a question. "Yes. I really can't remember the first one I saw. I think…" Paige really had to think hard on that one. So much had happened in one year—had it only been a year? — since she'd first seen her first shapeshifter. "I think… It was Sheriff Carl."

Ripley gave Paige an interested frown. "Sheriff?"

"Yeah. It was over in Nederland. An entire town of shapeshifters and other paranormals, kinda like Troutdale."

"Except Troutdale has a human sheriff."

"Except he's not sheriff. He's the chief."

"He used to be the sheriff." Ripley shrugged, looking more like a schoolgirl than the self-confident young woman. "Back when he was raising me, that was the title he had. Got the title of chief about the time you came along."

Right. She'd forgotten about that. There were so many things she was forgetting. Was it because she was over-whelmed? Or was it because the babies were eating her brain?

That last one was a real thing. She vaguely remembered losing a lot of her memories when she'd been pregnant with Leah. Oh, this could be bad.

"Well, she was the sheriff and she was a pink fox."

Paige recalled the pink fox. Sheriff Carl's ability to make other people feel comforted was something she would prob-ably never forget. It was also something Paige wished she was capable of. But the only thing Paige was really good at was pissing people off.

"A pink fox?" Ripley turned off onto a walking path that was nothing more than a very narrow line of dirt surrounded by short grass. "What kind of shapeshifters do they *have* in Nederland?"

Paige chuckled and followed. "I can see the color of their souls, I guess. I think it has something to do with their abilities, and the elements they're closely associated to? Sheriff Carl was a type of empath. She and her fox were able to calm people down. It was really neat to see."

Ripley snorted. "That would be neat to see. The only thing I can do is make people mad."

Paige started giggling.

Ripley stopped and turned around a frown on her face.

Paige held up a finger and pressed her other hand to her belly. "You almost said verbatim what I just said to myself."

A grin spread across Ripley's face. "Maybe you and I have more in common than we thought."

"I'm pretty sure Dexx knew." Paige took in a deep breath. She really missed him. She had no idea what they would be facing in Alaska, but she wanted him there with her. She was pretty sure he would love it there. "He's been telling me for months that I needed to get to know you."

Ripley smirked. "He's been telling me the same thing about you."

"Well, then I guess there will be one good thing that comes out of this trip."

"What's that?"

Paige moved to walk beside Ripley, slipping her arm in the crook of Ripley's elbow. "It looks like you and I are finally going to get the opportunity to meet."

Ripley met her stride. "It's about damn time."

It surely was. About damn time for a lot of things.

The main house looked pretty big from the back, with an obvious new addition going off to the side. It still had bare wood showing, but the roof looked good, and there didn't appear to be any holes anywhere. A swing hung in the backyard next to two rocking chairs. Smaller gardens peppered the surrounding land, all with freshly worked dirt. Paige didn't know a lot about gardening, but she'd been around her grandmother long enough to know that someone was getting ready to plant a whole bunch of stuff.

Ripley took them to the back door along the side, and walked right in. They stepped into what Paige had thought was the addition, but it was really the older part of the house. It still had old-style flooring, and antique looking appliances in the long kitchen that lined the back wall. The main room was devoid of furniture, and there was an opening to a hall right off the kitchen. She could *smell* the age in the house. It was oddly comforting.

Ripley led them up the three steps into the hall. There were two doors on either side that were closed, and one open doorway that Ripley disappeared into. It led into a small room with another door on the other side. Paige stepped through, wondering if she was traveling through Wonderland, only to find herself in yet another hallway. This one pointed to another door that obviously led outside. There was an entire rack for shoes and coats. Ripley took off her jacket and hung it up before kicking off her boots.

Paige followed suit and followed Ripley through yet another doorway.

The place was a frelling labyrinth.

However, as soon as she stepped through that door the smell of coffee greeted her. She took in the large kitchen with newer appliances, and the rest of what was obviously the living portion of the house.

Leslie sat at the square dining table nursing a cup of coffee.

Billie looked up from the stove and smiled. "Are you feeling better?"

"Yes. Much better. Thank you."

Billie gestured to the cabinet. "Make yourself at home. Mugs are in the cupboard. Coffee's in the carafe."

Ripley grabbed her cup, which was already sitting on the kitchen island, and moved to the dining table where she and Leslie broke immediately into hushed conversation.

Paige followed Billie's instructions and with cup in hand she paused for a long drink, savoring the nectar of the gods.

"Let me know when you're feeling human again." Ripley grinned then buried her nose back in her book.

Paige didn't say anything as she sipped her coffee. Black. No room for contaminates.

Billie puttered around the kitchen, cleaning up.

Paige felt like a schmuck standing there watching her. "Sure there isn't anything I can do?"

"Your sister asked the same thing." Billie wiped down the sink and turned. "I told her the same thing. No."

Paige was starting to feel a bit more normal. Her brain was waking up slightly. "You want to tell me what we're doing here?"

Billie narrowed her eyes. "You want to tell me why you agreed to come?"

"I just had a feeling."

"What kind?"

"That you could help us."

"Help you how?"

That's where Paige was stuck. "I don't know."

"Well then, let's start there."

Paige followed Billie to the dining room table. Paige didn't sit on a bench. She felt like standing. The moments where she was okay standing with all that extra weight were very rare.

"Do you know what kind of situation you're in?" Billie folded her hands around a glass of water.

Leslie looked over at Paige, her brown eyes clear, but tinged with worry.

Paige glanced at Leslie, then turned her attention to Billie. "I know that when Cawli picked me, he didn't do that out of the kindness of his heart."

Billie nodded. "What else?"

It was time to share some of the things Paige had learned in the spirit gave in Utah. "I know that what Leslie has is what's called an ancient."

Billie nodded again.

"I know that I am carrying two ancients. And I also know that there are more ancients out there."

Billie narrowed her eyes. "Do you know how many?"

"I only know of one other." A pegasus boy in Utah.

Billie bit her lip and rubbed her temple. She didn't look like she was upset, just that she was pondering the information she'd obtained.

Paige turned her cup in her hands. "What I don't know is why everyone thinks that the ancients are so— why everyone is so scared of them." Aside from how out of control Leslie seemed to be. "I realize that they're very powerful. But is everyone after the ancients because the ancients are a danger to humans? Or are they after the ancients because the humans are a danger to the ancients?"

Billie gave Paige a very direct look. "I don't know a lot about the ancients, but I do know that we've had one in our company for quite some time. He is an old dragon, and he has protected this realm for a very long time."

"Realm?" Because this sounded almost a little too much like Dungeons & dragons.

"Let's just say that he's been calling Alaska home long before it was ever known as Alaska."

"And is that the reason why you brought us here?"

Billie shook her head. "We brought you here because DoDO is hot on your trail, and you need to gain control of who and what you are before everyone else finds you."

"So, are we the danger? Or are they?" Paige hadn't forgotten about DoDO, but she had the ability to levitate cars now, so that might not be an issue.

Billie licked her lips. "That's something that only the dragon would know."

Paige was ready to get this show on the road. "Okay, then let's go meet the dragon."

Billie chuckled. "I almost forgot how gung-ho you were."

Leslie sighed. "I just need to know when I'm going to lose control again."

Billie gestured with her fingers. "While you're here, you really shouldn't. Wood witches are a bit different. I really can't explain it all to you right now, but let's just say that while you're within our protections, you should feel more in control of yourselves."

Ripley narrowed her eyes and leaned back on her bench. "Are you repressing the animal spirit?"

"No. We just have an odd way of making both the human and the animal spirit feel at home and at peace while on our lands."

Paige needed to figure out how to bottle that. She was going to need a whole lot of it at the Whiskey compound. "What are we waiting for?"

Billie chuckled and slammed her palms against the table lightly. "How do you feel about four-wheelers?"

After about twenty minutes of explanation, Leslie, Ripley, Billie, and Paige were outfitted with four wheelers and were on their way down the road. Paige had been a little bit concerned about being on a four-wheeler when she was so very pregnant. However, Billie assured her that women in Alaska were on four wheelers all the time. The trick was not to fall off.

They took several dirt roads along what Paige was able to see as a series of islands in the middle of a river. It was a bit chilly, and it seemed to be getting colder.

The stories of how cold it was in Alaska were starting to come back. She was just glad that she had put on two jackets and her boots.

However, when they came to a stop on the edge of town, Paige realized why it was so cold. They were at the base of a glacier.

A real glacier.

Billie got off her four-wheeler and gestured to the town. "Welcome to Cheechako."

Paige was a little taken aback. Out in the middle of nowhere, literally on an island in the middle of a river at the base of a glacier, was quite a quaint little town. It had a small town feel to it, not unlike Troutdale. The buildings might look a little more run down, but Paige had a feeling that it was because these buildings had more wear than they had tear. Or maybe more tear than wear. Paige really didn't know which way that one would go.

Billie started walking towards town. "Cheechako is a town for tourism. Motored vehicles stay here. We're only open during the summer. And it's a refuge for paranormals from all over the world. We do get the occasional mundane, but they tend to know about us. We haven't had a surprised mundane in a very long time."

Ripley skipped a step, shoving her hands in her back pockets with a grin on her face. "It's like a resort for paranormals."

"Though way out in the mountains." Leslie was starting to look a bit more like herself as well, though she was still far from what she was like before the griffin.

"Oh, I don't know," Paige said with a sigh, "I think I could be okay here for a while. Away from the stress."

"Good." Billie smiled at her. "Most of the paranormals here come because they need help. And us wood witches do what we can to put them back together."

"In what ways?" Because this was a very interesting idea.

Billie shrugged. "It really depends. We've got a couple that's here because they need help with their marriage. We've got one person here who needs help with the shift. We've got one who needs help starting a business."

Leslie shook her head. "This is amazing."

"Thank you." Billie led the way down the main street. "Over there, we have the apothecary. Over there is the drugstore. Although I don't know why they still call it a drugstore. There're no drugs there. If you want to go get that, you need you go to the apothecary."

This was need-to-know but Paige wanted to get on with fixing her own small, little world. She didn't want to stop and smell the dandelions.

"Maggie's got a pretty good sandwich shop. But at six, it turns into a diner."

The joys of the small town.

"Where's the bar?" Ripley asked.

"Got a hankering?" Billie gave Ripley a chiding expression.

"Not really. But I may get homesick and need to break up a fight or two."

Ripley was the owner of the one and only shapeshifter bar in Troutdale.

"You won't get much call for that here. We don't get too many fights."

"Where's the dragon?" Leslie asked. Her expression was sour.

"It's coming." Billie watched Leslie for a moment. "But I need to introduce you to someone else first."

Paige just hoped that this wasn't another trial situation. "Who?"

Billie took in a deep breath her smile tight and uncertain. "My coven?"

Oh yeah. This was definitely going to be another trial situation. Paige was ready for those to be over with.

Billie lead them down the street, pointing out different stores and telling them a little bit about who owned each one. She knew almost everyone in this town well, and they appreciated what she did for them. There were several times when people would pass by them, wave, and thank her for her special brand of help.

Leslie looked over at Billie with a questioning expression. "What exactly is your job here?"

Billie shrugged. "I own the local bookstore."

"Must be some kind of bookstore." Because as far as Paige knew, bookstores were going out of business.

"Well, it's not just a bookstore. It's also a bar, a winery, and I do crafts in the back on Tuesday."

Now that was diversity.

It didn't take them much longer before Billie finally led them to what looked like a small townhall.

It might have been a house at one point in time, but most of the common rooms had been opened into one large room. There were several tables and a couple of chairs, and along the back wall was a large desk. It wasn't really a desk. It was more of a glass case. And as they walked up toward it, Paige saw that there were several pieces of jewelry on display. Pretty random. It looked like they were tourist trap affairs. There was also a display case of keychains that all showed varying pictures that were very Alaska.

Behind the counter sat an older woman. She watched them approach with a smile on her face. But she did not rise. "You must be the Whiskeys."

Ripley waved. "I'm not a Whiskey. I'm just Ripley."

The woman's smile broadened. "It is very nice to meet you, just Ripley."

Ripley's eyebrows rose, and she gave Paige a pained look.

Ripley, apparently, wasn't used to being so openly and warmly received. Paige held out her hand. "I'm Paige, and this is my sister Leslie."

The woman took their hands each in turn. "My name is Opal."

"Nice to meet you Opal." But Paige wasn't really interested in getting to know more people. She wanted to get to the point of their stay. "Can you tell me why we're here?"

Opal leaned back in her chair and folded her fingers over her abdomen. "I'm sure that Billie told you a little bit."

"Oh, she did. However, I need a little bit more information, then we need to get moving. I don't know if you've noticed this, but I'm really pregnant. And I would like to get on a plane before I can't get on a plane. I'm having my kids at home."

Opal closed her blue eyes for a moment and nodded. "I understand. But that means that you'll have to learn quickly."

"I'm a pretty fast learner."

"And you?" Opal was looking right at Leslie.

Leslie lifted one shoulder and tossed her head to the side

almost flippantly. "I'm usually pretty quick. Though, I gotta admit, this one's kickin' my ass a little bit."

Opal nodded. "That's to be expected."

Billie gestured toward the back. "Is Glenda here?"

"I'm here," a high-pitched voice said from the back. "Ready to take over whenever you're ready to get the flock out of my store."

Paige chuckled. "I haven't heard that one used in a while."

Opal placed her hands on either side and backed up her wheelchair. "We like to keep things real over here." She wheeled out from behind the counter rolling down a short ramp.

Leslie stepped out of her way so that she could roll around the counter. "Where are we going?"

Opal gestured with her right hand then continued to wheel herself. "We've got some space around the back."

Billie smiled. "It's not much."

"Please tell me it's not another spirit cave." Because Paige wanted real answers. She didn't want to talk to more imaginary creatures. Even though she knew her spirit animal wasn't imaginary. He was just see-through.

He glared at her in the back of her mind.

Oh, good. He hadn't disappeared. She'd been wondering.

Opal threw a smile over her left shoulder. "Oh, no. You're going to be put through your paces."

"Put through her paces?" Leslie asked and gestured to Paige. "Maybe fewer paces."

"You think she's got an illness?" Opal asked with an incredulous look. "She's carrying a child."

"Two."

"Two children. That doesn't mean she's an invalid or that she gets special treatment."

Oh, great. This was going to be one of those.

"I'm not asking for her to get 'special treatment'," Leslie sneered, her full momma-bear out. "But if *I* feel you're pushing too hard, *I'll* end it."

Opal gave Leslie a genuine smile and a sharp tap on the shin before continuing to wheel herself. "That's the spirit."

Ripley frowned. "I'd offer to push, but…"

"Do I look like a cripple to you?"

Ripley raised her hands in defense and kept walking beside Leslie.

Paige was feeling nervous, though. Were they going to make them shift for the first time? Oh wait, this wasn't the first time for Leslie. It was just the first time for Paige.

"What am *I* supposed to do?" Ripley asked.

Opal glanced over at her. "You do whatever you want to. If you want to stay, stay. If you want to go, go."

"I'm feeling a little like a third wheel right now."

Paige glanced over at Ripley. "If you want to stay, I'd really like it."

Ripley frowned over her smile, but she nodded. "Okay."

Opal led the way down a long hall and out the back door to a landing that branched into a ramp and a stairwell. Opal took the ramp and Paige followed. Carrying this much extra weight, steps were not her friend.

Ripley, Billie, and Leslie took the stairs.

Paige's stomach was twisting into a knot that she couldn't ignore, and it had nothing to do with baby feet digging into her diaphragm. To divert her nerves and rising anxiety, she looked at Opal's wheelchair. "I'm going to ask the obvious question."

Opal looked up at her with the half grin. "I was wondering how long it would take you."

"It's like when a person sees you carrying children and asking you how far along you are. You just know it's going to happen."

Opal nodded. "Car accident. Not quite eleven years ago. I'm quite used to it."

"It looks like you're getting along quite well."

"Well, I've had eleven years to get used to it, so I should hope so."

Paige didn't feel any kind of remorse or empathy toward her. The woman was doing well, and it was just like anything else. If she was handling her lemons with sugar, Paige was going to just accept her for who she was. Because, after all, Paige was just hoping she would handle her lemons equally well. Eventually, anyway.

Opal led them to the back of a short parking lot that looked like it had weathered quite a few winters. It almost had more holes in it than it had flat asphalt.

"This has got to be difficult to traverse." Ripley gestured to the black top. "You almost need a four-wheel-drive wheelchair."

Opal laughed. "We've got someone who's going to come through and tear up the asphalt and just give us some good gravel."

"The asphalt? It seemed like a good idea at the time," Billie said.

"It just didn't weather well." Opal shook her head. "My husband tried to tell him. But Danny just wouldn't listen. He knew better because he was in construction."

"I've known more than a few of those kinds of men." As a matter of fact, Paige was thinking about marrying one of them.

"I think we all have," Leslie said. "I can't even tell you the conversations I've had with Tru over the years." Pain flashed across her face.

Paige really wished she had stayed around town more. Maybe she would've seen the signs. But the look on Leslie's face told Paige beyond a shadow of a doubt just how hard the transition had been for her. And through all of this, Leslie had probably needed her sister more than ever.

Guilt. Horrible, wracking guilt.

Yes. After this, Paige was going to put her foot down. She was going to tell the elders just how much she didn't appreciate them taking over her life.

They just had to survive this.

Billie stepped behind Opal's wheelchair and helped her along what had become a dirt path. Trees lined either side, and it was rutted, making wheeled travel difficult.

"That's it." Ripley's tone was full of snark "I'm going to rig you up a four-wheel-drive wheelchair."

"I'm sure you'd probably find one on the internet," Leslie said. "I'm pretty sure."

"They say you can buy anything on the internet nowadays." Except for mail-order order brides. No, wait. Now… really. That's where her mind went. Paige shook her head at herself.

Opal and Billie came to a stop in a wide patch of grass.

The grass came to Paige's waist, as did the dandelions. "I've never seen dandelions this tall in my entire life."

Opal laughed. "We grow everything bigger in Alaska."

"I thought that was Texas," Leslie said in a thick Texan drawl.

Paige wasn't about to let them get into a pissing contest. "Trust me. Both of you have got it pegged, okay? We're out in the middle of a dandelion field. What are we doing?"

Opal looked up at the sun peeking through the haze of clouds.

They could barely see the top of the rugged mountains over the tops of the trees. The rush of the river close by surrounded them. In that moment, they couldn't even hear the sound of other humans. No traffic. No conversation. Just nature.

Billie glanced over at Paige with a smile. "It's amazing here isn't it?"

It really was. Paige hadn't even realized just how much stress she carried around with her. Day in and day out. Always worried. Was she doing the right thing? Was her family safe? Did she know how to do her job? Was she going to be a good mother to her children? Was she currently a good mother to her current children?

"Feel nature and use it to keep you grounded. That's one of the ways of the wood witch."

That was, oddly, the way it was supposed to be for every witch, as far as Paige knew. But…the Eastwoods. Probably not.

"This doesn't help us."

Opal smiled up at her. "Reach down and touch your magick to the roots of the trees. Ground yourself in that."

Ground herself in the trees? "Opal, we're here because my sister is eating dogs and I'm levitating cars. We're here because DoDO wants to take us."

Opal's expression didn't change.

But Paige was all out of patience. "I don't need to fucking ground, Opal. I need fucking control!"

As she said that last word, a rush of energy surged through her in every direction. The trees bent back, leaves and pine needles falling to the ground.

A car alarm went off in the parking lot on the far end of town.

Paige breathed, her hands balled in a fist.

Opal nodded once then looked forward in her wheelchair. "So, like I was saying…"

Paige took in a deep breath to steady herself, her twins going still inside her womb. Opal might have a point.

"Okay, now, all three of you send your minds to the roots."

Ripley snorted. "I'm not a witch."

"I didn't call you one."

"But you—" Ripley shook her head and gestured to the ground. "Look, me sending my mind 'to the roots' or whatever isn't going to do anything."

Opal frowned up at her like she'd lost her mind and turned her wheelchair to face her. "Do you have *any* idea how the padfoot came to be?"

Ripley's expression told Opal she'd have a better time skipping. "No."

Opal flattened her lips. "Wow." She looked at Billie. "You weren't kidding."

Billie shrugged, her hands raised.

Ripley gave Paige a what-the-fuck look.

Paige was equally lost.

Leslie just seemed entertained with a soft smile on her face.

Ripley rolled her eyes and faced the trees, her posture telling everyone within sight that Opal was going to be massively disappointed.

Paige took in a deep breath and shook out her fingers. Her first magick had been her hands—the oozing black, door magick hands that gripped demons and sent them to hell. She didn't know how Opal and the other wood witches would react. Their magick was so...clean and pure, or at least, that's how Paige had always pictured it.

Paige's was...well, it was black.

You are not evil, Cawli said inside her head.

It's about time you show up. Where have you been?

Concentrate.

She hated when he did that. But she did as he commanded.

"Just touch the roots?" Paige asked, not quite sure of herself.

"Stop doubting," Billie said beside her. "And just look."

Paige opened her witch vision then shuddered it back to shifter vision almost in a force of habit.

The world around them changed.

The roots were a pulsing network of orange energy, all interconnected with the trees and the grasses and the wildflowers, which included the dandelions. It was like looking at life and how it all connected.

Billie's hands were almost like Paige's. They extended past her physical form and flowed away from her with orange, green, blue, and brown lines.

That's what it meant to be a wood witch. Her magick *was* wood, all of the elements coming together.

Billie smiled at Paige, her strange, webbed aura smiling. "There you go. Now, just touch."

She wasn't ready. Not yet.

Leslie's aura was different now. It had once been green, and now? Now it was golden, and the griffin towered over her, his large eagle head turned to meet her gaze with his blazing orange eyes. His gold wings were shot with blue lightening.

Paige realized too late that she shouldn't be looking at him with her shifter vision on. It tended to call the spirit animal out, or at least it had on everyone else.

He just looked at her.

Leslie stared at her magick as though she'd never seen it before.

What had to be going through her mind? Everything would be so different now. "You okay, Les?"

Leslie's glowing golden eyes met Paige's. She paused then blinked once. "It's just new."

"Yeah it is."

Ripley struggled. Her silver aura sluffed off her in tendrils of charred smoke. Her spirit animal looked around as if lost and terrified, her black eyes wide. Ripley was breathing hard and fast as she stared at her hands, then over at Leslie's. Her eyes glowed silver, almost a bright white.

Opal glowed with greener than any other color, but her aura was webbed as well. She reached for Ripley.

Ripley pulled away, silver fire rising around her.

She was losing control.

Paige didn't even think. She reached out with her black witch hand and caught Ripley's. *Calm yourself.*

What is going on? Ripley's voice was filled with terror.

We're fine, a new voice said, female and soft. *I think. I don't know.*

That's not helping, Decima.

None of this was helping. Paige didn't understand what was going on with Ripley. She was able to see the auras like a witch would and her aura hands were surging forward, away from her body, before being brought back.

Paige stepped around Opal and wrapped Ripley in her arms bringing her physical mouth to Ripley's ear. "You stay in control." *Both of you.* Her alpha will surged forward with Cawli's help.

Ripley fought, but after a moment, relaxed. *I don't understand.*

Neither did Paige. She pulled back because that really was a lot of pressure on her belly. *I have a feeling we have a lot to discover with you as well.*

Decima, Ripley's padfoot, lowered her head to meet Paige's gaze, her silver eyes glowing brightly, though not as wild. *It's been so long.*

Cryptic. Not loving that.

Since—I'm sorry. Decima looked away. *I haven't felt the All Mother's touch in so very, very long.*

Paige frowned, but stepped back. *Okay. Well, just extend*

your hands and touch the roots. Though, what would a death dog do by touching her death hands to those living roots?

But if the wood witches had invited it?

Paige stepped back into her position. "Okay, ladies. Are we all ready now?"

Leslie nodded.

Ripley and Decima both looked toward Opal.

Opal just sighed and gestured to the root system with her green, blue, brown, and orange witch hand.

Leslie was the first to touch her hand to the roots. Her power surged outward, running along the network of the forest, racing with white hot power. And then a calming orange power surged back through her hands and into her soul. Her wildly spiky golden aura settled and calmed, shoots of her old green aura poking through. Her shoulders sagged with relief.

Ripley closed her silver eyes and extended her hands. The silver energy shot out and the forest energy flared, wisps of dark shadow shooting off along the tips of the trees and the dandelion tops. The trees seemed to swell as the woods sent energy back to Ripley and Decima.

A silver tear fell from one of Decima's eyes.

Well, if they were both safe, then it was Paige's turn.

Her inky black hands reached forward and grabbed a hold of the orange roots.

Her energy—the extra stuff she struggled to carry and hadn't even realized was a struggle to contain—surged away from her. The trees, the grass, the dandelions, and other plants almost...chittered. She could feel them vibrate, hum.

And then the orange light surged back through her. The black of her magick glowed for a moment.

And then she was hit with so much information. She knew where everyone was and how everyone was doing. Well, those within the protection of the wood wards. She raced along the paths of magick, flinging her consciousness to the tops of the trees.

And then out.

The valley was beautiful from up there, all glittering in various shades of living magick.

This was the closest thing to flying she would ever experience. Well, maybe. She didn't know. Maybe—

She didn't want to think about maybes or the future. She was here, and this was the best she'd felt in a really long time.

A darkness hovered on the horizon, where Anchorage was, but it was distant.

She fell back along the lines of power and re-entered her own body, blinking her shifter vision off and pulling back her power, feeling more refreshed than she had in a very long time.

Opal raised an eyebrow. "There now. Don't you feel better?"

Okay. Paige could do with a little less of the attitude, but...

She wasn't wrong.

Opal returned to work after that.

Billie stepped out onto the sidewalk in front of the townhall and turned to them as they exited. "Well, I have things that I have to do. I leave you to your own."

Paige didn't like that. They weren't on a vacation. They were there to learn something. Otherwise, she needed to go home. Granted, the thing with the roots had been pretty cool. Relieving, even, but not worth the trip to Alaska. Though… that darkness on the horizon might not be something to blink at. "I'd prefer it if we could just get started."

Billie shook her head. "All in good time."

"We don't *have* time. When are we going to meet the dragon?"

"When he's ready."

Ripley held up a hand. The episode with the trees had changed her. Her eyes still glowed a soft silver, and her normally in-your-face attitude was feeling a bit muffled. "Now hold up. We could all probably use a little R&R."

Paige set her hands on her belly. "Do you see this? This

means that we need to hurry up." Also, there was the darkness. They had to be ready for whatever that was.

"I understand that, but at the same time, what are you gonna learn right now?" Ripley blinked her silver eyes with a sigh. "You haven't had the opportunity to sit down for longer than five minutes in weeks. I don't know if you've noticed this, but you're about to have babies. I think you're gonna want to have at least a little bit of rest time."

Okay. So maybe she wasn't as muted as Paige had thought, but her eyes were still silver.

Leslie studied Ripley in concern for a moment then turned to Paige. "She has a point."

They really didn't. Sluffing off some of her excess energy into the forest had been a great relief, but she had a bad feeling that DoDO was on their way. She'd been ignoring Billie's references to them, but she saw the darkness. She was worried. About her sister. About her babies. "I feel fine."

"I believe you forgot what it's like to give birth."

That very well might be true. But... "I still want to hurry this along if we can."

Billie shrugged. "You can try to force it if you want to, but it ain't gonna make it go any faster. Just be patient. And trust us. You're learning things right now. You just don't realize it."

"Like what?" Leslie asked frustrated.

It is about damn time. Paige was starting to wonder if her sister was even in her meat suit anymore.

Billie smiled. "You'll see. The trees are speaking to you if you give them time and listen." She spun on her heel and walked off. She raised a hand and waved. "Enjoy the town for a little while. When you're done, you know where we parked the four wheelers."

Leslie, Ripley, and Paige all stared at each other.

"I say we should go grab a beer…" Ripley looked significantly at Paige's belly. "Maybe a milkshake instead."

Leslie spun and slammed her palm into a mailbox. It didn't even rock.

Before all this ancient stuff had happened, that wouldn't have been even anything to take note of. But now? The wood witch magick was really working because the mailbox had stood up to Leslie's wrath…and lived.

Shoving her hands through her hair, Leslie turned back to Paige and Ripley. "I can't believe we're here."

"Upside," Ripley said holding up a finger, her eyes browner than silver finally, "you appear to be you again. You've been missed."

Leslie tugged on her hair, curling her fingers, and looking at her sister desperately. "What's been happening?"

Maybe Billie was onto something. They hadn't even had an opportunity to catch a breath lately. Just running from one thing to the next. It felt ridiculous to take a little bit of R&R. But maybe that was exactly what they needed.

"A lot." Paige turned around and actually took a look at the town. "Well, if we're here and being forced to sightsee…"

Ripley gave Paige half-cocked grin, back to herself. "Now, that's what I'm saying."

Leslie looked at them both like they were insane. "We need to get moving on a cure."

"Sweetie," Ripley said gently, "I don't think they have a cure for what you have."

Paige chuckled a little bit. "Rip's got a point. You are housing a very large spirit inside of you."

"But I didn't choose this."

That was actually something Paige had questioned. "What was that like?" She moved off in one direction not quite sure where she was going. But they really had no place to be at any particular time, so she had time to meander. Her body would tell her when to stop.

"What was what like?" Leslie asked irritably.

Paige stopped at a window, and looked in. They were definitely in a tourist trap. "Being chosen. Like, did anybody talk to you? Did your griffin come to you in a weird cloud? I mean, what was it like?"

"It was nothing. I didn't —" Leslie paused and glanced over at Paige. Her gaze was distant, as if she was trying to remember something. "I vaguely remember a dream."

Paige nodded, trying not to stare. Instead, she peered at the display case of jewelry. Common Western jewelry. Silver earrings, lots of feathers. However, there were things here that she hadn't seen anywhere else in the lower forty-eight. Like tribal pictures of whales, turtles, and some kind of bird that might have been a raven.

"I didn't really think much of it at the time."

She still was really providing a whole lot of detail. She was doing a lot more hesitating than telling.

"If you still remember it," Ripley said, "then it had to mean something."

Leslie chewed on the inside of her lip. "I don't remember a whole lot of it, though."

If Paige could push Leslie into giving them more information, she certainly would. "So, what do you remember?"

"Darkness. And a voice. His voice, the griffin."

"Do you remember anything he said?" Ripley pointed to a large, blue stone ring. "That's kinda pretty."

"It would make your hand disappear." And Paige was pretty sure it would. But the stone was gorgeous. It was blue and almost looked like there was fire shooting around it.

Leslie leaned over to take a look at it. She frowned then backed off again glancing at Paige. "I don't remember anything he said. I just remember feeling like I needed to protect him."

Paige nodded, turning to her sister. "Do you remember what you had to protect him from?"

"No. I just had to protect him from something."

Paige perched on the brick sill, lifting her belly with her hands. Her lower back was hinting it was almost time to sit. "And did you say yes at any point in time?"

Knowing Leslie, that's exactly what she'd done. If the griffin had asked her to protect him, Leslie would have agreed without thought, like she was rescuing kittens or something.

Leslie nodded. "I just didn't realize what I was saying yes to, apparently."

Ripley turned and kept moving on. "I don't think I can afford anything in that particular shop."

Paige had to agree. She wasn't making a whole grip of money. She was making enough to be comfortable. However, at this point, she was pretty sure Dexx was making more than she was. It didn't help she was having to pay for Well-Baby visits now. Her insurance wasn't the greatest. Who could afford to have babies anymore? "I could really go for coffee."

Ripley slowed a little and gestured toward her belly. "Isn't coffee bad for the baby?"

"The babies?"

"It would be kind of odd if caffeine was only bad for one of them."

There was a reason Dexx enjoyed Ripley. She had a very snarky personality. "It's like wine. You can have some. Just not all of it."

Leslie released a long breath and walked along beside them. "I'll buy you a drink if you get a tea."

"You do realize of course some of those teas have more

caffeine than coffee? Right?"

"Some do." Ripley scanned the street as the sun peeked out through the clouds. "Though, in Turkey, they have some pretty strong coffee."

Leslie stepped to the curb and pointed across the street. "You were in Turkey?" She pointed to a shop on the other side.

Sure enough. Coffee shop.

Ripley stepped into the street, looking for traffic that just wasn't there. "For a time. I enjoy going back there when I can."

Paige felt like a thousand-pound elephant as she stepped off the curb. She was ready to have these babies. As if under-standing her discomfort, they both stilled. She waddled across the street like a ridiculous duck.

"Wasn't it a little scary being over there?" Leslie asked.

"Sure." Ripley hopped onto the next sidewalk between two parked cars. "But there are still people there. People, just like you and me. Normal, just wanting to live. And hating the people who are destroying their homes and their way of life."

"In Turkey? Paige asked.

"Nope." Ripley gave Paige and Leslie a frank look. "But I knew what you were really asking about. You're wanting to know what it was like being in the Middle East."

Leslie raised her eyebrows. "I guess I'm showing some ignorance?"

"It's hard not to be ignorant over here." Ripley opened the door to the coffee shop and stepped aside. "When your news sources don't report the news."

That was a very true statement, but not something Paige really wanted to discuss. "I like rainbows."

Leslie paused midway through the door and glanced over at Paige behind her. She smirked then continued. "Changing the subject?"

"Aren't you? I'm curious about your griffin. And Ripley's buying the drinks. So, take your time." Paige sat gratefully down on the high stool. Why did babies have to be such a burden for so long?

Eventually, Ripley and Leslie came back with three paper cups.

"I had to listen to the barista tell me about how the beans were roasted," Leslie complained as she took her seat.

"Oh, good." That actually excited Paige.

Leslie gave her a look that asked her how she could be that excited about coffee beans.

"Okay. Look. The first time I got the pitch, it pissed me off. I get it. Coffee is coffee."

"Until it isn't." Ripley nodded once and saluted with her cup. "Cheers."

Leslie still didn't look impressed.

"Just try it." Paige shook her head and took a sip. It really was good. As good as the latte she'd had in Nederland? That was a bit of a stretch. That cup had ruined her, but it was good. "Okay. Rip, it's time you talk."

Ripley winced. "No."

Leslie sipped her coffee. "It tastes...like coffee."

"There's just no taming you." Paige gave her sister a mocking glare.

Leslie glared back but leaned in her chair and continued to sip.

"You're not done." Paige gave Ripley a level look.

Ripley groaned then draped herself non-dramatically over her cup. "Decima has been pretty quiet."

"Too bad." Paige blinked, calling up her shifter vision.

Someone in the shop let out a startled cry and a table tipped over as the animal spirits around her took over and initiated the shift in their human hosts.

Shit. So that still happened. She didn't understand why,

but when she slipped into shifter vision, sometimes, it would override the human's control over the animal spirit. It didn't happen with everyone, but it was annoying. Paige blinked her vision back to normal.

The man who'd stood turned around and glared at her, the front of his shirt and pants stained with coffee.

"Sorry." Paige held up her hand. "My bad." She looked at the barista. "Can you get him another coffee? I'll pay for it."

The barista gave her a flat look but went to work.

The man sat down, his wife consoling him.

Okay, so no shifter vision. Crap. "Decima, I need to talk to you."

I'm right here.

Ripley's eyes widened. "How can you do that?"

"I don't know." Because Paige didn't. "It's a new development. It might leave with the kids."

"You think you have a telepath in there?" Leslie asked, pointing to Paige's belly.

"I'm not reading everybody's thoughts."

"Oh, thank goodness."

Really? So, what had she been thinking that she didn't want Paige to hear?

Leslie just gave her a smile and sipped her coffee.

Paige shook her head. "Can *you* hear her?"

"Decima?" Leslie shook her head.

"Okay. Well, Decima," Paige started again, "I would have to say that you're part witch. Can you tell me if that's the case?"

I am not. No. But my original human was.

Ripley's eyes widened. "So, does that make me a witch?"

Leslie looked confused, so Paige filled her in. "Oh. Tell me it was a curse."

It was.

Ripley translated for Leslie.

A gypsy curse, a long time ago.

"Intriguing."

Only Leslie would think that was intriguing. "What happened?"

Well, you never want to wrong a gypsy. I don't remember a lot of it. It happened so long ago, but I remember that a family of witches had come into the area and upset the gypsy band. They may have even sacrificed a daughter. Yes. Yes, I think that was it.

Paige was getting flashes of visions in her head of a time long ago. A group of women surrounding another woman who lay on the ground, her blood seeping into the earth.

A gypsy woman arrived. Frankly, the vision was splintered and incomplete. She shouted something and the ten witches in the circle fell to their knees, death hounds appearing from the shadows, one for each of them. Their eyes glowed with silver as each dog stepped up to each woman.

And then the women seeped into the being of the dog.

The gypsy said something, but Paige couldn't understand. She could just tell words were said.

And then the vision ended. Paige shared with Leslie what she saw.

"So," Leslie said, blinking. "You're not really a death dog. You're...both a dog and a witch."

I believe so. Touching the All Mother...it awakened memories.

"Good ones?" Ripley asked.

Not all of them.

"Great. So," Paige looked at Leslie, "we have another witch in our...coven? Do we have a coven? Do they do meetings and stuff?"

"They—yes. For...crype's sake, Pea." Leslie tapped the table impatiently. "Yes. We have a coven, and if you were there more often, you could lead it."

"No." That was just a horrible idea. "Me, leading a coven. I don't know the first thing about any of this."

"And I do?"

Paige pulled her head back, her hands wide. "Yeah? And you're more than powerful enough."

Leslie gave her a very dry look.

"What is your griffin's name, anyway?" Ripley asked. "We've got a few suggestions."

"So did Dexx." Leslie pulled a face. "They were awful."

Paige chuckled. "Probably like the names he picked for the babies."

Leslie winced.

"Dexxie." Paige nodded, sucking her lips in.

"No." Ripley hung her head. "We're going to have to save those children."

"I know."

"Firebird and thunder lion?"

"No. Other way around. Thunderbird and fire lion."

"Oh, right. Okay. Um…Okay." Ripley widened her eyes and nodded. "Storm for the thunder birdie thing."

"Storm?" Paige wanted to rip that one, but she actually kind of liked it.

"Thor." Leslie raised a finger.

"Oh, goddess, no. It's like talking to Dexx."

Leslie smirked.

Ripley stared up at the ceiling. "Taren."

"Is that a boy or girl?"

"Uh…" Ripley shook her head. "I don't remember."

"Rai." Leslie raised her chin then lowered it. "I read that in a manga. It's a boy's name though."

"It's Chinese, though."

"Japanese, I think."

"So, we could use it for a girl and no one would know."

Leslie chuckled. "Yes."

"I like it." Ripley said. "A girl named Rai."

"Me, too." And she really did.

"Flint for a boy?" Ripley pulled the corners of her lips down. "Yeah. Rai and Flint."

It wasn't bad. "I'll write those down. And for the griffin?"

Leslie shook her head. "He won't give me a name."

Names are limiting, he said in Paige's head.

That was weird. Really weird.

Cawli drew forward, his voice soft. *You are their alpha and a very strong one at that.*

But Dexx is their alpha.

And you are his partner.

It still didn't make sense.

"Okay. Well, I'm making a decision and calling you—"

Leslie held up her hand. "He's mine—sorry. With me. So, I will name him."

Ripley rested her chin on her cup lid.

The barista came to their table. "I replaced the coffee and I'm not charging you."

Paige turned, startled. "It was really my fault."

The barista shrugged. "These things happen. Just don't… do whatever that was in here again?"

Paige nodded. "I can do that."

"I'm calling him Robin," Leslie said.

Paige snorted and turned back to her. "A little baby robin? That's his name?"

Leslie tipped her head. "No." She lowered her voice and made it husky. "I am Batman."

Ripley threw her head back and slapped the table. "That's good." She snapped her fingers and pointed at Paige. "That's good."

It was.

And…it was nice to just sit there and talk about silly things like naming the people in their lives.

Because only the goddess knew when they'd have that chance again.

They gathered in Billie's dining room. Billie disappeared, doing goodness only knew what, but this was her home, so there was no reason for her not to.

That gave the other three plenty of time to sit around and do absolutely nothing.

While Paige appreciated the time spent off her feet, she really didn't do boredom very well. She was used to having bad guys to chase, crimes to solve, or figuring out how to resolve differences.

She didn't know how to "resolve her sister." She didn't even know if her sister was something that needed to be resolved. The only thing she knew was that others were fairly afraid of her.

Of course, they should've been afraid of her before she'd invited the griffin—Robin—to share her body. If they'd been smart, anyway, they would be.

So, what was she supposed to do? Leslie wasn't sure how to handle Robin. Paige didn't think she was the right person to help her sister. After all, she didn't even know how to shift. How could she help Leslie with that?

Well, except that Leslie *knew* how to shift. *She* could probably help Paige out with that.

She really needed Chuck. She guessed she could have used Dexx's help as well. However, Dexx had his hands pretty full with other things.

No. She was a part of the shifter world now. She needed to start acting like it.

Which was all grand, but what did that even mean?

Paige pulled herself off the couch, which was an effort, and walked out the back door. The scenery was breathtaking. They were surrounded by tall, magnificent mountains. The trees blocked out all sounds of humanity. With her connection to the trees, she could hear them speaking to one another. Kind of. In tree speak, which she didn't understand.

For all she knew, the four of them could have been the only humans on the planet. She knew that wasn't the case, but it didn't matter. Here she could pretend as though they were. It kind of helped. She wasn't going to lie. Part of her was chafed. So many humans. So many people who needed things from her. She was tired. Tired of being pulled into so many different directions. She wanted some time to herself. She hoped beyond hope that she would get some time to spend with her twins once they were born.

But she knew how things were going to go. She knew things wouldn't slow down. She was going to have to come up with a plan. She needed rules. She needed to set boundaries. Too bad she wasn't better at doing all of that. She should really take a page out of Leslie's playbook.

And that brought her back to Leslie.

Paige was worried. She didn't know how to handle or help her sister. All she knew was that something in the wood magick was helping all of their animal spirits settle down.

Though, when were they going to meet the dragon? That also brought another question. The *dragon* was an ancient.

He'd been there, on earth this entire time. So…why was getting the ancients returned to earth such a hot priority?

What would happen when they returned to Troutdale? Would the wood witches be able to teach Leslie enough to live outside the protections of the wood witch wards?

This had to work.

"This is amazing." Ripley joined her with a smile. "I have never felt so relaxed."

Paige couldn't agree more, even though she still had a million worries battering down on her. "It feels as though my soul's being recharged a little."

"Too bad we can't bottle some of this and bring it back with us."

"I know. It would be amazing." Paige could almost imagine what it would be like if Leslie could somehow put some "Alaska" into a candle.

Paige didn't want to oversell it. Part of the draw of Alaska was the fact that there was so much open country. If too many humans got tuned in that Alaska was an amazing place, they would all come flocking in. And then where would they be? The things that made Alaska amazing would no longer be amazing. They would be trampled down, conquered, and have asphalt all over them. Just look at Colorado.

Paige took a seat on a rocky ledge and stared up at the nearest mountain. "I almost want to live here." And she did. Granted, her family was in Oregon. Not to mention the man she loved more than anything.

But it felt safe up here. She hadn't felt safe like that in a very long time.

Leslie stepped out of the house and joined them. "I need to figure out how to bottle this."

Paige chuckled. "I was just imagining what candle you would make."

Leslie thought about that for a moment, then smiled. "I may have to accept that challenge."

Ripley shoved her hands in her pockets. "I hate to be a killjoy…but what are we here for?"

Paige sighed

So did Leslie. "I appreciate the fact that by being here I'm in control again. But we need to figure out how I can gain control at home. I need to be with my kids."

Paige did too.

"Me too. But mine is more man-baby."

Paige looked at Ripley in surprise, an almost startled smile on her lips. "I never pictured Joe as a man-baby."

"Oh, he is. In every meaning of the word."

Leslie snorted. "It's hard to imagine. Him being a big ol' grizzly bear and everything."

Ripley leaned against the rock wall and clasped her hands in front of her. "Juliet should be around here someplace."

Paige held up her hand. "Juliet is in *Alaska*. She's nowhere near here. Alaska is a very huge place."

Leslie nodded. "Tyler just did a paper on Alaska. It's bigger than Texas."

"No way. Really?" Ripley smiled. "I feel like an idiot."

"Don't." Paige took in a large breath, enjoying the feel of the Alaskan air. "Pretty sure everyone has the same reaction.

"It doesn't help when it's so small on the map." Leslie shrugged. "It's like false advertising."

Paige chuckled. It kind of was. "I feel like I'm at a disadvantage with you, Rip."

Ripley looked over at her with a frown. "Why is that?"

"Every once in a while, I get an idea about where you've been, but I have no idea who you are." It probably was bad. Especially, since Ripley was part of her pack. "I mean, I'm supposed to be an alpha to you. Doesn't feel like it."

Leslie snorted. "I think you have to actually be there to be a pack alpha. Kind of like a coven leader."

"I hate you so much."

Leslie smiled.

"But you have a point there." However, it might just be something that was different and unique with their pack.

"I also keep wanting to call it the Whiskey pack." Ripley snorted. "I don't think Dexx would appreciate that much"

"No," Paige chuckled. "I don't think so."

"Which brings up an interesting point." Leslie smiled at her sister. "Who's changing their name?"

Oh, gosh. This. "I'm trying to get Dexx to change his."

"I don't think that's gonna happen." Ripley winced. "I don't know him that well, but I don't see that happening."

Neither did Paige. "I don't agree with the fact that the woman has to change her name every single time. It's like saying she's a piece of meat."

"That's not what it means." Leslie gave Paige a sour face.

"If we had signal, I would totally Google fight you over this." Because Paige was pretty certain that this was totally one of those things. "I just don't want to change my name."

"You could hyphenate." Leslie shrugged. "That's what I did, but I don't necessarily recommend it. It's an awful lot of writing."

Ripley looked over at her. "What made you decide to hyphenate anyway?"

"Tru absolutely refused to let me keep my name. I mean, if I had really put my foot down about it, he wouldn't have had any say. It really did upset him. So finally, in order to keep a little peace, I went ahead changed it. He wanted his kids to have his name."

"They couldn't have his name if you hadn't changed yours?" Ripley frowned.

Paige sighed. "You can put whatever name you want to on

the birth certificate. Within reason. I will say that Bobby is a Colt. He's not a Whiskey."

Leslie looked over at her in confusion. "Really?"

Paige nodded. "It was one of the things Dexx had insisted on. Originally the birth certificate had been written as Whiskey. But then he made Roxxie change it."

Ripley looked confused. "I didn't realize that was something you could do."

Paige really shouldn't tell anybody, but Ripley was part of the pack. And she seemed like the kind of person that Paige could trust. "Bobby really isn't ours."

Leslie didn't even look at Paige. She didn't second-guess her. She just nodded, her gaze distant. "Kind of a terrifying time."

Paige nodded. "Rachel had just gotten back into our lives. We were in Texas. Well, okay. Back-back-back. I had just gotten fired—"

"For exorcising the mayor or something."

"Yeah. In Denver. And Dexx had just been bitten. So, I've got this newly turned sabertooth cat shifter, I'd just been fired, and we headed down to Texas."

"Because Merry Eastwood was in Texas." Leslie raised her eyebrows and leaned back on her hands. "The sun never sets."

"Well, not now."

Ripley frowned at Paige. "Wow. That's...that's a lot."

"Yeah. If I was a character in a book, I'd be hating my author right now. Anyway, Rachel came back from New York with my daughter, Leah. I was fighting for custody of her. And then I found out that my best friend had been murdered."

Ripley frowned and tipped her head to the side. "Nothing happens in small degrees with you, does it?

Paige snorted. "No. Anyway, turns out that Bobby is a

prophet and his real mom had been murdered to get to him."

"As in Moses, or Daniel?"

"Yeah." Though, Paige didn't know Daniel.

Ripley blinked. "Being raised by witches."

Leslie sighed.

Paige nodded. "That's what I said. But a couple of angels placed him in our care then helped us set up all the paperwork that we needed with Rachel *right there*. They even went to people and altered their memories so that they remembered me being pregnant."

Ripley shook her head in wonder. "I always forget how powerful angels are supposed to be."

"Well, thankfully you weren't around when we were attacked by them."

Leslie frowned at Ripley. "Where were you during that time?"

"When was that?"

Leslie tipped her head and thought. "Shortly after we cured your brother-in-law."

"He's not my brother-in-law yet."

It seemed as though there were a lot of people who weren't quite married.

"We were working on the bar. My uncle left it in a bit of disarray. So, Joe and I were fixing it up."

Leslie shook her head. "Maybe it only felt as though it was a big deal because it was right in our back door."

"I heard about it a little bit from talk, but...." Ripley shook her head. "I heard about a big fire in the woods."

"That was djinn attacking the dryads," Leslie said, her eyes wide. "A big fire. Geez. Yeah. A portal was opened. The djinn were pouring through."

"Oh."

"Yeah. My son nearly died. Rainbow, Ethel. Grandma. I

mean, it was…" Leslie looked over at Paige. "It was bad. A lot bigger than a 'fire in the woods'."

It did sometimes amaze Paige how even the big stuff could be hidden right in plain sight.

"Where were *you* during all of that?" Ripley asked Paige.

She had to actually think about that. "I know I was in Portland for part of it. And in Utah. Oh, goddess. Utah. So. Funny story."

Ripley licked her lips, ready.

"So, when I was in Utah, I had to get this regional pack of alphas to like me, right?" It hadn't quite been that simple. "Anyway, I was in this trial and things were going well. Then Dexx decided to ram an angel into the wards."

Leslie narrowed her eyes. "Yeah. About that. You felt it?"

"Felt it? The wards were, like, screaming. I released this big old batch of power, knocked the alphas on their butts, and sent as much magick to the wards as I could."

Ripley closed one eye. "That didn't go over well."

"It *really* didn't."

Leslie looked up at Paige and frowned, thinking. "What were you doing in Portland?"

"Demons."

"Is the demon problem getting any better, or is it getting worse?"

When Paige had first gotten her abilities back, the demon situation had been getting out of hand. Unfortunately, she really hadn't done a whole lot to put a lid on it. She was the demon summoner. That didn't necessarily mean that she had to watch over all of them. Especially not when she had a family to look after, kids to grow, a man to watch. At some point, the demons needed to be dealt with on their own. "Worse and I don't know why."

Ripley narrowed her eyes. "I am never going to get used to any of this."

"At some point, you will. You'll have to." They all did.

Leslie opened her mouth to say something but stopped herself as she stared off into the horizon.

Paige turned her attention in the same direction.

A swarm of bugs was headed their way.

"Is this normal in Alaska?" Ripley asked.

Paige got to her feet. "I doubt it." She had a feeling she knew where this is coming from. And as the bugs got closer, her suspicion was cemented. Locusts. She turned to Leslie. "Get inside the house."

"What's going on?" Ripley asked.

Paige tugged on her magick, calling her witch hands. "This is McCree."

"I thought he was dead."

"It's Cooper's father. He's here for Leslie."

Leslie took one look at her sister and drew in a breath. "I'm not hiding."

Well, neither was Paige.

Paige searched along the web of magick she now had access to for any signs of McCree but found nothing except the swarm of locusts. She wasn't sure what was coming at them. She didn't know what to prepare for.

What could get through the wood witch wards? They likely weren't set up the same way the Whiskey wards were. After all, this was a tourist town. All the paranormals were welcome.

Why was it that trouble always seemed to follow them?

Ripley frowned up at the swarm of locusts as they came around. "Aren't these usually a harbinger of death?"

"Only in the fact that they eat entire crops." Paige had brushed up on her Bible studies since she'd taken Bobby in.

Ripley nodded. "I've got an idea."

Leslie moved to the side.

Ripley's body shimmered into dog form.

Paige looked towards the cloud of locusts. "Are you able to do anything?"

The dog growled. *Yes,* Decima's voice said.

What used to be a black dog transformed to grey fog. Embers, burning as if from hell, fell from her in small waves.

When an ember touched one of the locusts, it poofed into a flame.

Well that certainly was helpful. "You see if you can do more of that. I'm going to try something.

Paige's scry globe had been an amazing thing before Sven and Mike Jones had opened the door to hell inside her soul. Ever since then, her scry globe hadn't worked very well. However, a few months ago, she had tried to use it and it had worked. As least, for a moment. That was really all she needed. She reached inside herself and touched the core of her soul, where all her magick lay. In her mind's eye, it looked like a lotus flower. She reached in with her fingertip and touched the center, and light flew along the outside of each petal, going from the inside and flowing outward.

By the time that light touched her arms, the magic changed. It turned into inky black cords that almost looked like spider silk. The black was tinged with silvery blue and bright orange. In the back of her head, Paige knew those two magic colors, the blue and the orange, were the twins she carried.

She needed to give them names. The real kind.

But now wasn't the time.

Cupping her hands, she brought the magic together in a ball of shadow that quickly evaporated into clear liquid. It rose up in a bubble, forming a type of dome inside the palms of her hands.

In her mind's eye, she could see the map of the area. The wide river on her left, the smaller channel on her right. They converged directly in front of her. The island they stood on lay between the two.

She could see shadows of the different houses on the island, more than she originally thought there were.

She also saw the glows of certain people's souls. In town, there were many souls close. Blues, greens, pinks, reds, purples. There were so many colors. She'd never had that before. When she'd first had her scry globe, she'd had three colors. There had been a color for witches, a color for demons, and a color for angels. Because at that time, that was all she had in her world. Cawli had introduced her to so much since then.

However, it was now a lot more difficult to find what she was looking for—a witch. Before, she would've been looking for purple dots. Now, she had no idea what she was looking for.

Keeping the globe cupped in her palms, she focused on one dot at a time, using her own soul as the epicenter. She could always tell which one was hers. It was like there was a sticker on it that said, *you are here*.

As she pulled up the dots, faces floated in her eyes. Her mind's eye.

The green dot next to her was Leslie.

The silver dot next to her was Ripley.

A blue dot moved towards them, and when she pulled it up, she saw that it was Billie.

Along the riverbank, she saw a brown dot. When she it pulled up, she saw a face she'd only seen one other time.

McCree.

But how many of his pack did he bring?

Sifting through all of the dots, she saw people who lived on the island, doing their chores.

It appeared as though McCree had come on his own.

Paige wasn't really in the mood to wait. She banished the scry globe and looked over at Ripley. She and her padfoot were doing a remarkable job taking care of the locust cloud. There was still a considerable sum of bugs swarming around them, but the cloud wasn't so thick that they couldn't see through anymore.

Paige reached out with her mind and touched McCree. Something inside her... shifted. And suddenly McCree stood in front of them.

She'd done something similar with the car. This had to be a gift that one of her children had. Because teleportation wasn't something that Paige had ever been able to do. And she seriously doubted that she would ever become powerful enough to be able to acquire that gift on her own.

Still, it was something she would have to look into. If this was a developing trend of hers, she needed to control it better. She hadn't necessarily wanted to bring McCree to her. She had no idea what to do with him once he was there.

Probably do what she would do to anybody. Talk to them.

"Did you want to call off your bugs?"

McCree stood in front of them, slightly stooped. His shoulders slumped slightly each time Ripley killed more of his bugs.

If Paige was a gambling woman, she would bet those locusts were somehow tied to his power. And every single time Ripley killed the locusts, she was destroying his power.

"Because if you don't, I can just let the reaper take them out." Although, why he wasn't responding was annoying. It was almost like taking the father of your children to buy baby clothes.

McCree studied Paige and Leslie for a long moment. Then, he slid his muddy blue gaze to Ripley. "What is that?"

Paige was a sucker for accents. She loved them all. But the Australian accent was just lovely to listen to, even on her enemy. "She's a death dog. And she's a friend. Right now, she's really enjoying destroying your locusts. So, how about you take them back. And then we can have a conversation without bugs."

After a moment's thought, McCree gestured with his hands. The cloud of locusts dispersed from Ripley, then swarmed around him. By the dozens, they disappeared into his skin, as if they'd been sucked back into the well of his soul.

It was a little gross.

"Isn't that better?"

It was definitely better for Paige.

Leslie took a step forward. "You kidnapped me."

McCree folded his hands in front of him, very austere. "I was the one who released you. They were the ones who trapped you. I was trying to help."

"I seriously doubt you were trying to help."

Paige had to agree with her sister. "What's your deal? Why are you here?"

"I am trying to figure out why it is that one of my daughters is dead, the other is missing, and my son is in jail."

"Oh." Leslie turned to Paige. "I know the answer to all of that."

Which was good because Paige was a little fuzzy on the details. She'd been there for part of it but then she'd been taken away by angels. Even the parts that she'd been there for were a little bit fuzzy. Somehow, she was going to have to get her memories back. Her time in heaven, she was pretty sure, had not been a vacation.

"First," Leslie said ticking off her fingers, "your son decided he was going to take over the region."

McCree frowned, his bushy eyebrows furrowing together.

"Second, both of your daughters attacked Dexx. And then, one of them was killed by *your* crocodile."

"And where is my crocodile?"

"He's dead too. Bit off more than he could chew." Leslie looked pretty excited and happy about that. It was like having the old Leslie back.

Paige hadn't realized until that moment just how much she missed her sister.

"And then, we caught your son red-handed. He was arrested and thrown into the elder jail. His hearing is scheduled in another couple of months. They're still going over the evidence against him. He really doesn't have much of a defense, being caught a little too red-handed in murder, theft, burglary, kidnapping, and being an overall asshole."

Paige wasn't going to tell her that theft and burglary were pretty much the same thing. She knew what Leslie was going for. "Unfortunately, he decided to steal from a bank. A bank that was federally insured. So, we're trying to figure out jurisdiction. The elders are working on it. He might have to be tried in a real court. We're trying to keep that to a minimum. Especially since he was able to break in to the bank using his serpentine sisters."

And that was about the end of what Paige knew about what happened. Dexx was rather irate. She knew that about part two. Mostly because Jackie had been killed in the exchange.

Jackie was his 1970 Dodge Challenger. And now, thanks to Cooper, she had to be completely rebuilt. She was almost a pancake.

"How powerful is your pack?"

That wasn't something Paige wanted to get into with him. "Powerful enough to take out Cooper, your daughters, and his entire pack. He came with a lot of shifters, you know. And Dexx was able to take them all down. So, how about you tell me why you're here."

"Because," he said, staring at Leslie, "I have a feeling I know your source."

That didn't sound good. Paige put her hands on her belly. "Source?"

McCree narrowed his eyes and turned his gaze toward her. "Ancients."

This was one man she really did not want to have this conversation with. Because his son had figured out a way to go to the ancients playing plain and trapped one. That had been why Cooper had been so powerful. Did he know how to do that because of McCree? Or was Cooper the bad apple?

"We've seen what you've done with the ancients. Something tells me you're one of the people we have been asked to protect them against."

Ripley shimmered into human form as she stood next to Paige. Even though she was no longer a dog, the tips of her hair smoldered as though she still stood at the edge of the Hell mouth.

McCree glanced over at her, then turned his attention back to Paige. "What do you mean?"

"You're trying to tell me you don't know?"

"Know what?"

Well, maybe McCree wasn't as evil as she thought he was. Maybe he was a little like her. Just because he commanded locusts didn't mean he was evil. Same as just because she could summon demons didn't make her evil.

Leslie took a step forward. "Your son trapped an ancient. And then, he bound the alphas, so he could siphon their power. They died. He didn't count on Dexx."

McCree actually looked concerned. "Dexx did this?"

He was really ignorant of this? "You really didn't know?"

McCree shook his head. And then a light hit his eyes. "What about Jedda?"

Paige shook her head and glanced at Leslie.

Leslie raised her chin. "He's dead."

"Who's Jedda?" Because it felt like Paige was in the middle of a conversation that had been going on for a while.

"The aboriginal witch." Leslie glanced at Paige then

returned her focus on the older man. "He was killed at the warehouse."

McCree took two steps back and his entire stance shifted. He seemed to shrink in on himself. "I warned that boy."

"Warned him about what?"

McCree sighed then gestured toward Paige's belly. "Is the father a shifter?"

Paige nodded.

"My mate was a shifter. She gave me three children. One son and twin girls."

"Yeah," Leslie said with a snort, "we met them."

"Cooper was a witch. The girls were chosen by the spirit animals."

So, none of them had been shifter-witches.

"That had never been enough for Cooper. He always wanted more power. He wanted to shift like his sisters did."

That was neat. And valuable information for Paige and her unborn children. "Did you notice when he had the ability to change? When he could shift?"

"Because," Leslie said, "he was able to shift into every alpha he took. Did you know he could do that?"

McCree shook his head. "I did not. He went into the outback and came back different. All three of them did. I only knew that he was uncontrollable. So, I sent him on a walkabout."

Weren't walkabouts supposed to be vision quests?

"I had no idea he would come to the States and do this."

Leslie turned away from him in disgust. "He was trying to take over as regional alpha. Probably because of you."

"I am sorry for my part in that. None of that was my intention." He looked over at Paige with sincere regret. "I will leave you and your coven alone." He turned to walk away.

"Wait." This was the only other person Paige knew of

who had been in a similar relationship to the one that Paige was in.

He turned.

"Were you and your wife…okay?"

He frowned like it was a silly question. Then he nodded. "Yes. She and I have a very happy marriage."

"And your children? Were they okay?"

The sadness came over McCree's expression. "I thought they were. But apparently, I did not know my children as well as I thought."

That didn't help her nerves any at all.

"Watch them closely, Ms. Whiskey. Children of this mating have the potential to be very dangerous." And with that, he faded back into the woods.

No. That didn't help Paige's nerves at all.

2 2

Billie walked around the front of the house, looking around. "Is everything all right?"

Ripley waved. "Everything's fine, now."

Paige was still little bit frazzled. "Did something seem to be off?" Because she couldn't figure out what would have brought Billie out there. They were in a tourist town. Wards were moot.

"The wood magick let us know that there was something happening. Did we have a visitor?"

"We did. But he's gone now." At least Paige thought so.

"Who was it?" Billie asked joining their huddle.

Leslie practically growled. "Cooper McCree's father."

Billie shook her head with a frown. "I don't know the name."

"There's no reason you should." Paige wished there was a place on this earth they could go and escape everything that seemed to follow them. "He's a witch from Australia."

"Yeah." Leslie's tone was heated. "His son's pack came into town and tried to take over everything a couple of months ago. We're still rebuilding from it."

Ripley gave Billie a pained look. "It was really bad."

Billie's expression creased in concern. "Then, is everything okay?"

Paige sighed and flopped her hands against her thigh. "Apparently, he just wanted to talk."

"Really?"

"Really." Which was a surprise. A pleasant one. But still a surprise. So, that darkness on the horizon...wasn't him. Seemed like it could be. His son had done a lot of damage when he'd been in town. "Everything's fine." She was pretty sure. But hadn't that been too easy?

Billie shook her head. "Well, you girls are coming back into town to have dinner with us."

Really? "I just got back. All I want to do is sit down for the rest of the evening." Because Paige was carrying extra weight. She knew that the twins weren't that much. But by the end of the day, it felt as though she was carrying an extra fifty pounds at least. Each. Not to be a drama queen, but she was beat. "I'm not getting on a four-wheeler. And I'm not walking."

Billie gave her a very frank look. "We found this new invention. It's called a truck."

"Miraculous," Ripley said with a gasp.

Paige chuckled. She *liked* Ripley.

Billie walked toward the drive. "It's changed everyone's lives."

The trip back into town took a little bit longer. The four wheelers had been able to cut across the island, but in the truck, they'd had to go over the bridge up the mountain, onto the highway, back down the mountain, back over another bridge, and back onto the island. It was rather convoluted. Paige could understand why the four-wheelers were a good idea.

The town didn't look busy. There were very few vehicles in the lot and nobody on the street.

The sun hid behind a mountain, but still lit up the sky. They were well into the spring solstice where the sun would stay up for freaking forever.

She was sure she was exaggerating, but she was from the lower Forty-Eight, so she expected night to be *night*. Not dusk. She took off her sunglasses around 11p.m. Yippie. So, to her, it was still freaking *bright* when it should be *night*.

Billie led them into a rather adorable house. It almost felt as though they were intruding. To the left, just inside the door was the living room. A *real* lived in living room. To the right, was a rather large dining room with several small tables. It was very cutely furnished, but obvious that someone had taken the house they lived in and turned it into a part-time diner.

Paige took the first available chair. She didn't care. She just needed to get off her aching feet. She needed a pair of boots that slipped on easily and supported her back, knees, and hips. A girl could dream, right?

Ripley joined her and Billie dragged another table over where she and Leslie pulled up chairs.

"Sherry should be here any moment." Billie moved the saltshaker out from the edge of the table and put it in the middle.

"This is a really tiny town." Ripley looked out the big window beside them. "You must know everybody."

"Just about." Billie leaned forward and pointed across the street. "I was born in that house right over there."

Paige didn't even want to think about what it would be like to grow up in a town that small. Sometimes, it was bad enough living in Troutdale. And Troutdale was a rather large town. It was almost a city.

Okay. An evil angel had brought an entire pack of djinn to

take an ash grove and the only thing that was heard was that there was a forest fire. So, maybe it wasn't that big.

What was the dividing line between a town and a city anyway? She didn't know.

Billie thumped the table and looked over at Paige. "What are their names?"

Paige leaned back in her chair and rubbed her belly. The twins had awakened and were currently doing gymnastics in her womb. "I haven't quite thought about it yet. We've thrown around a few ideas." She gestured to Leslie and Ripley.

Billie frowned. "Why not?"

"Dexx absolutely refuses to think about it."

Leslie waved that off. "Tru did the same thing. Most people feel as though it's a father thing. He's not carrying the kid, so it's not super real yet."

Ripley chuckled. "I'm fairly certain that if we got pregnant, Joe would do the exact same thing."

Paige didn't get it. She only knew that it frustrated the fuck out of her. "I know I'm having a girl and a boy."

Billie grinned "Rose for a girl."

That actually wasn't bad. "I was kind of thinking of that one. Grandma's mother was named Rose."

Leslie pulled a face. "You mean the grandmother who went insane?"

Billie winced. "Maybe not that one."

Ripley tipped her head to the side. "I've always liked the name Doris."

Billie looked at her as though she lost her mind. "I believe you only name your baby that if you hate her."

Ripley shook her head. "I've only known one Doris, and she was amazing. Imagine. Having a name that no one had. You could create yourself."

"You do have a point." But at the same time, Paige didn't

want to come up with that name that was so original that it was annoying. Though, at some point, she was going to get tired of having this same conversation. Seriously. It was going to happen, but she *really* needed names. These kids could pop out any minute now and what was she going to do? Name them Golden Doornob and Broken Blinds? No. It wouldn't be *that* bad, but… "I like the old names like Mabel and Ira."

Leslie shook her head. "You're hopeless."

Ripley tipped her head to the side. "You should name her something that gives her courage."

Leslie's sneer said she lost her mind. "Like naming a girl Tom?"

Billie grinned. "Like naming a boy Sue?"

Leslie shrugged. "Yeah?"

Paige shook her head. "I like Ripley's idea for the girl. Rai. If we go that route, I'm going with Rai."

Billie took in a breath and looked upward. "Vicki."

"No."

"Kirsten." Ripley nodded very sure of herself. "And then she could be wooed by someone who was incredibly old and ancient and creepy."

"But then she would only have one expression on her face." Did saying that out loud make her a bad person? There were a few people who still liked *Twilight*, Paige was sure of it.

Leslie tapped her chin. "Vanessa."

"Did you get stuck on V?"

Billie chuckled. "What about boy names? I mean besides what we threw out earlier because that was just the tip of the iceberg."

"Jack." Ripley bit her bottom lip and nodded.

"That one is a problem because we already have too many Jacks." Paige held up a finger and counted them off. "Jackie, the car. And Jack Scott, the FBI agent. And I feel like there's another one and I just can't remember."

Ripley slumped in her chair, thinking.

Leslie stuck her tongue in her cheek in thought. "Harry."

"Potter." Paige made sure to give it a good English accent. "No."

"Kent." Billie nodded.

Ripley held up a finger. "That's my last name. So, I veto."

"You're part of my pack now." Paige smiled and looked at her. "That means you get to take my name now."

Ripley glared. "Just as soon as Dexx does."

And since that wasn't likely to happen... Paige looked around. "I thought you said Sherry was going to be here soon."

Billie twisted in her chair, a concerned look on her face. "She is. She's the whole reason why we're in town. She wanted to meet you."

Paige finally paid attention to their surroundings, her Spidey senses tingling. "I think something's wrong."

Ripley's gaze unfocused, and then her brown eyes turned silver, smoky tendrils rolling from beneath smoldering eyelashes. She blinked twice and her normal, human eyes returned. "No death."

"Has to be a first for everything." Paige turned around in her chair. She looked at the front door as if it was going to tell her something. Sighing, she stood. She'd really only needed to sit for a minute. "We should go check it out."

Billie rose and waved her back to the chair. "I'll go check it out. You just sit there."

Not likely. Paige waddled to the door. "I'm already up."

Billie tittered in frustration but followed close behind. Chairs scraped as Leslie and Ripley joined.

Outside, Paige listened

To silence. No wind. No cars. No people. No birds singing

or animals scurrying. Ugh. Things had *finally* settled, and now another shit storm.

She could call up her scry globe. It'd been nice to see the thing working again. Actually, it seemed to be working better than ever before. She didn't know if she should be concerned or excited. There was a part of her that really did not appreciate gaining all these new powers. She really didn't need the stress of wondering *why*.

Would she keep those powers after whatever she had to face showed up?

She hoped not.

The part of her soul that had touched the wood magick, the roots, the land, pointed her to the right. She had no idea what direction that was. East? Maybe. She only knew that it was right. Damn sun always up in the sky had really thrown her off. She still had no idea what time it was, or where she was. She gestured.

Billie nodded with a smile. "I agree."

Paige walked as fast as she could, which wasn't very quick at all. She was relatively in shape, but she was still pregnant.

Paige couldn't believe what she was seeing.

In the small park a family of lions fought against a horse, several birds, and a squirrel.

She wasn't kidding about the squirrel.

Though how that had been quiet was beyond Paige. She could see them, but there was still no sound.

A tiger leapt on a horse. The horse twisted with a kick, the dark mane flying.

A hawk launched into the air as a sparrow attacked it.

A litter of lion cubs crouched under the picnic table.

The squirrel attacked the lion, grabbing handfuls of mane.

And it was all silent.

Paige took one more step forward and the sound hit her.

All the roars, and cries, and screeches. Like someone had opened a soundproof door.

Cawli stirred as a lion roared. *This is bad.*

No Shit. What's going on?

The shifters are out of control.

"Is this something that happens often?" she asked.

Billie shook her head a confused frown on her face. "No. The wood witch magick calms the animal shifter down. It's one of the reasons why we get so many visitors. Those who are struggling with their animal come here to gain control."

Paige needed to know. *Is it because of us?*

Cawli paced in the back of Paige's mind and did not answer.

Paige looked at Billie. "If this is our fault, we need to fix this and leave. It's one thing to need help. It's another to do...this."

Billie shook her head fiercely. "No. You will stay. We'll figure this out."

Leslie looked at Paige, worried.

Billie headed towards the grass where the family of lions were fighting their shift.

Opal wheeled into the pavement beside the dumpster, another woman with the same dark hair by her side.

Another witch stepped over the curb.

It was time to figure out how to calm this down.

Paige had no idea what she was going to do, but she certainly wasn't leaving.

The look on Leslie's face said much the same. If this was their fault, and they were helping.

Okay, Cawli. What do we do?

Cawli seem to assess Paige for a moment. *Are you finally taking this seriously?*

I was always taking this seriously.

Not the shifter part.

He had her there. The "shifter thing" as he called it terrified her. *I understand witches.*

You are no longer merely a witch.

Oddly, that was one thing she'd been able to figure out on her own. *What do we do?*

Cawli raised his head and sniffed the air. Which was an odd thing to do since he was inside of her head. She never understood it. In order for him to smell anything, wouldn't he need to use her nose? Unless he was smelling something spiritual? He *did* disappear for long periods of time. It wasn't as if he lived inside her head every single second of the day. Actually, Paige was certain he spent more time wandering out wherever else than he did inside her head with her.

There are no other alphas. he said. *You are the only one.*

That didn't make Paige feel at ease at all. Not in the slightest.

They need your will.

That was the thing that irked her the most. She liked helping people find their independence. She didn't want to inflict her will upon anyone. Well, unless they were her children. And then she wanted to not only inflict her will, but sometimes the bottom side of her boot.

But, her soul knew what he was talking about. It wasn't as though she was learning how to walk for the first time. No. She knew exactly how to inflict her will upon something. She did it all the time with demons.

Demons were different, though. They were aliens on the wrong planet.

These were people just trying to be people.

It didn't help that the last time she'd put her witch abilities on a shifter, she'd nearly destroyed the shifter soul. Granted, that had been a year ago. But it wasn't something she would forget anytime soon. The fact that the shifter in question was also a part of her pack didn't help any, either.

Then, perhaps, you should shift, Cawli said.

Now that was different. Since Cawli had offered to bind himself to her, he told her repeatedly that she couldn't shift. After Leslie had been bitten and then chosen, and since Paige had become pregnant and her twins had been chosen by ancients, Cawli sung a different tune.

But, she still hadn't shifted.

Would it hurt the babies?

Shifter mothers do it all the time.

Keyword shifter.

You are a shifter.

She needed a different point of attack. *Why will it help if I shift?*

Because, he said simply, *when you're shifted you cannot access your witch abilities.*

She didn't believe that for anything. *Remember all those months where you told me I couldn't shift? You were lying to me then. What makes you think I believe you now?*

He sighed. *We need to build trust.*

I agree.

You need to understand that I had to lie to you. I did not agree with it. I did not want to. However, it was part of the agreement. In order for me to bond with you, I had to.

Another one of those times where I just have to trust you? It's a bit lopsided, don't you think?

Cawli pointedly looked at the lion family. Leslie and Billie where in the park with them. Billie was keeping her distance. Leslie was right in the middle of it. It was as if she didn't care. Well, maybe she didn't. She was a griffin after all.

Let me explain the physics of it.

Oh good. Because Paige always did so well with physics.

When you are in control, Cawli said slowly, *I have very little control. I can add to your senses a little bit, but not a lot.*

That made sense.

So, when I take control, when I shift your body into my shape, you become the passenger in my body.

That made an odd sort of sense. *So, my body doesn't change shape?*

It appears as though it does. And for others, that is exactly what happens. But for you and I, because you are able to cross planes rather easily, we simply trade places.

Paige looked over at Ripley as the light dawned. *I'll be able to keep my clothes.*

Cawli smiled. *Yes. I believe you will.*

So, Ripley? What Paige really wanted to know was if Ripley was a witch.

Cawli shrugged like only a cat can. *She is cursed. It is different for her. But she switches places with Decima in the same way you and I would change places.*

So, no pain.

No pain.

Paige sighed. *Okay. How do we do this?*

Well, first you should figure out which form we're going to take.

Well that just confused the hell out of her. *I thought you said we were taking your form.*

I am a spirit. I have no form.

But you always look like a cat to me. And he did.

That is how you see me.

So, what are you typically?

He paused as if thinking about that. *The last bonding, I was a tiger.*

Paige shook her head. *Fine. Let's be a tiger.* It might help her speak cat. After all she was trying to subdue lions. It only made sense.

All her fears and doubts about shifting dissipated as they merged, as they shifted, changed. She was no longer herself but was herself. Human, but cat, conscious, but not. She could see everything going on around her, but everything was more enhanced, crisper. It was as if she was looking through a magnifying glass and blind at the same time with the way her senses increased. She relaxed as she let Cawli take control and enjoyed the rest of the ride.

Cawli was right. Paige was still very much present, but she wasn't Paige. It was as if she had been put on mute. Her connection to the All Mother was very distant.

The network of information she hadn't even realized she

was getting from the trees, earth, water and air quieted. She couldn't hear the wind. She couldn't hear the earth.

She hadn't even realized they spoke. Any of them. The messages from the river, the whispers from the trees. The tingling from the sun's rays. It was like she was trying to listen to it through sound canceling headphones. It was still there. Just very, very quiet.

She and Cawli padded forward. She felt the power in his haunches. Gravel crunched into the pads of her feet. The wind tugged at her whiskers. The sun was brighter, but the shadows were darker. And the smells were almost over-whelming. Is this what Dexx felt?

And then she smelled fear.

Billie stood with a group of other women who looked remarkably like her. They were probably all related. They had similar cheekbones and build. Same hair. Two of them shared the same nose. And they all smelled relatively the same, despite the aroma of fear.

Leslie, however, did not. She was in the middle of a male lion, a female lion, and three cubs. One of those cubs was an adolescent.

Leslie. In human form. Without any of the protections the griffin could give her. Yet she stood among them, pushing them back, and somehow avoiding all of the claws.

She pushed her will out, doubting this would even work. She threw it out much like when she used her witch powers, and willed everybody to back off and shift back to human forms.

The lions stopped their attacks. One of the small ones sat down and licked a paw.

The horse pranced where she stood.

The sparrow landed on the dumpster.

The falcon folded his wings and transformed as soon as his feet touched the ground.

The male lion turned to her, his ears laid back.

With the lion family shifted back into human form, Paige shifted back. Wonder and excitement flowed through her as she stood on two feet again, pregnant and miserable. Maybe there was something to the whole shifting thing.

Her connection to the All Mother rushed back in. The elements spoke again with their messages.

Paige still had her clothes. Oh, Dexx was going to be *pissed!*

She turned to Billie more than a little surprised. "Cawli says that it's because of the ancients. We're in your network, and it's throwing things off balance. We should probably fix that."

A woman who could have been an exact replica of Billie if not for the heavy silver streaks in her dark hair, nodded. Her gaze was somber. "We will do what we can."

"The easiest thing to do would be to ask us to leave."

Leslie stepped up beside Paige. "I agree. If we're causing this much trouble, it would be best if we go. We need to figure this out without endangering others."

"If we forced everyone to leave who challenged us," the woman said, "then no one would be safe. No. You will stay." She turned. "Sherry, can you serve dinner?"

The only woman among them with different colored hair stepped forward. Sherry was a short strawberry blonde woman, in direct contrast with the Black clan. She smiled at them and walked back to the house. "If you will just follow me."

Ripley grinned as if nothing had happened. She just followed Sherry, linking her arm into the crook of Leslie's elbow.

Leslie seemed to be doing quite well herself. And that was good.

At least now she knew how to show Leslie how to shift. Shifting as a witch was different. Who knew?

But what Paige needed right then was to hear the sound of Dexx's voice. She took a seat on a bench and pulled out her phone. She had just enough bars to make the call.

2 4

Energy and excitement buzzed through Paige when she opened her eyes the next morning. She woke up without feeling the soreness in her back and legs. She doubted seriously that it had anything to do with the mattress.

No. She had a feeling it had something to do with shifting. She got an idea and hurried to put on her pants and boots.

The sun, to her untrained eye, looked like it was in the same location it was when she had gone to bed. That was the strange thing about Alaska. The sun wasn't straight overhead. It was off to her left. It looked like the sun was setting all day long.

Leslie was already up and about by the time Paige made it to her cabin. "Didn't expect to see you up so early."

Frankly, Paige could probably sleep a week and still not be caught up. "I was wondering if you wanted to do something with me."

"Get coffee?"

Funny. "No. Do you want to shift with me?" It sounded

really weird to ask her sister that. In all the years they had been together growing up they'd done many things together. They'd practiced magic together, and attempted spells together. They'd even gotten pregnant together.

This kind of felt like a pack thing though.

Leslie narrowed her eyes, but a slow smile slid onto her lips. "I would really love to do that right now."

A wild thrill ran through Paige. "Great. Let's go get Ripley and go play." She turned and headed out the door.

"You don't think will get in trouble for this, do you?" Leslie's footsteps paused at the door she slipped on her boots.

Which was fine because that gave Paige a little bit more time to make it down the stairs. She was doing just fine. She knew several other pregnant women who would never think to do half of the things she did while pregnant, but she wasn't going to let it slow her down. "No. We're in shifter territory."

"Even though I know we've got that in Troutdale, it still feels weird."

Paige stepped onto the gravel. "That's because you were raised by witches and around witches."

"Probably."

Ripley was sitting on her porch steps, a cup of coffee in one hand, and a book in the other.

"Are you still reading that one story?" Paige almost kicked herself for asking that. Obviously, she was.

Ripley just nodded though, taking a sip of her coffee and not even looking up. "It's getting really good."

"Has he gotten any smarter?"

"Not even a little bit." But that didn't seem to bother Ripley much.

Well, should she even bother? She should at least ask the question. "We were going to go shift. You want to go?"

Ripley looked up with a startled expression on her face. "Really?"

Paige nodded. She couldn't see Leslie's expression or what she was doing because she was standing behind her. Gauging from Ripley's reaction though, it was positive.

Ripley set down her book and coffee just inside the open door to the cabin and then closed it. "Let's go then."

Paige wasn't for sure where exactly they were going to go. Technically, they could shift right there. There were very few other houses around and it wasn't like they needed to take all their clothes off before shifting. So, they didn't need to hide.

She stopped in a sort of clearing behind the cabins. There were several downed trees laying on the ground, covered in a blanket of fallen leaves and needles. The undergrowth in Alaska was unlike anything Paige had ever seen before. It wasn't thick and lush like it was in Oregon. The earth almost felt thin. By that she meant that when she put her foot down, it sank a little. It was as if she was walking on a carpet.

She had a feeling that it was more do to with the blanket of deadfall, and less to do with how thick the dirt was.

Leslie looked at Paige, her shoulders tight. "Okay. What do we do?"

Paige licked her lips. "You've done this more than I have."

"Yeah, but I wasn't in control."

Ripley just shrugged deeply and shoved her hands in her pants pockets. "I just kind of sink into Decima? I don't know if that helps or not."

She is not wrong, Cawli said, his voice low and gentle.

Paige had done this just the night before. She wasn't necessarily nervous. Though, she kind of was. She didn't know why. Being in that animal form had been such a freeing experience. She didn't know why she was hesitating now..

"How do you decide?" Leslie's gaze was unfocused as she studied the ground.

Ripley raised one eyebrow. "Decide what?"

That's what Paige was asking too. "What shape to take." She looked up and met Ripley's gaze. "Last night, I chose a tiger because Cawli said that the last person he bonded to had chosen to be a tiger. So, do I just stay with that? Or do I try something else?"

Ripley looked at her as if she'd lost her mind. "I turn into a dog. That's the only thing I can turn into."

Well, she was going to be of absolutely no help at all.

Leslie looked at Paige's belly and pointed. "What about those?"

Paige waved off her concern. "They're just fine. They get moved over into the spirit plane or whatever you call it, and the animal just takes my place."

"What?"

Paige grinned and looked at both of them. "Yeah. That's how witches are able to keep their clothes and others aren't. Normal shapeshifters don't have the extra energy we do. It has to be sloughed off or relocated. It's very strange how the two dimensions work together, but they do."

Leslie leaned forward her eyes narrowed. "So, you're trying to tell me that when I shift, my human body goes to some other dimension while the griffin takes my place?"

"Kind of." Paige wasn't a scientist. She didn't know the physics of it. She just knew what Cawli had told her.

Ripley shook her head, blinking. "Well, if I had a choice, I would pick a bird."

Leslie nodded, thinking. "I do enjoy flying."

That actually gave Paige something to think about. If they took too long in Alaska and Paige was no longer able to get on board an airplane, there was the possibility that she could just shift shape and fly back home. Maybe. Would that work? Even going by plane, it was still an awful long way to go. She might get tired. And how long could her babies be in the other plane before getting affected?

By what?

Who knew?

It was time to figure out if she even enjoyed flying.

She just wished that Dexx was there to be with her.

"Okay. I think I'm going to be..." She shook her head.

Ripley held up a finger. "An astronaut."

Paige also held up a finger and frowned at her, saying in the same tone of voice, "no."

Leslie frowned at them both, held up a finger, and said in mom tone, "Why are we talking like this?"

"Because I'm nervous and I don't know why." She clawed her fingers.

Ripley imitated her gesture. "Then let's stop being nervous and just pick a shape."

That was probably a good plan. Paige settled with her feet shoulders width apart. She closed her eyes and inhaled deeply.

Just relax and do exactly what you did the last time.

Which was great advice, except she wasn't quite for sure how she had done it last time.

Ripley had said she just sort of fell into Decima.

Well, Paige guessed she could try that too.

It was very strange for her to not reach for her magick. In this, her magick was absolutely useless.

She felt Cawli's presence larger-than-life. But at the last minute, she chose a hawk.

White light surrounded her, warming every part of her. Her arms shortened and rolled back. Her chest muscles grew. Her nose and mouth elongated. Her legs slimmed and became shorter.

She felt all of this, even though she knew that her human

body, for all intents and purposes, was in a different dimension.

When she opened her eyes, the world looked completely different. Her perspective had changed, obviously.

However, she saw the world of ultraviolet. Who knew that's how hawks saw the world? It was rather brilliant, actually. She knew that the ground should be brown and green, but instead, everything was purple and blue.

Except for the dog standing next to her. She was bright white, as if she was on fire.

Leslie stood in eagle form the other side of her was a warm orange.

Well, wasn't that just interesting? Seeing the world through the eyes of others was going to be... eye opening.

Oh. That was so bad.

It was time to see if she could fly.

All it took was a thought and her body did the rest. She leaned forward, bending down a little. If she wasn't a bird, she would say she was crouching on her haunches. But she was a bird, so she was pretty sure she didn't have those.

Her wings went out and beat the air once, twice, and then she was in the air.

It didn't take her long to gain altitude. The eagle was a very powerful bird. With a long, strong beats of her wings, she was able to gain the air and soar over the tops of the trees. Elated, she let out a cry.

An eagles scream punctured the air.

As she circled around, catching the current, she caught sight of her sister winging behind her.

Flying was amazing. The freedom. Feeling the air beneath her wings. Up there, the only thing she could see were the purple and blues of the trees and a few red and orange dots from the people who lived below.

Not far from the cabins was a house that sat next to the river. They had a dog.

A little further away was a large cluster of small buildings. There were no dogs, there were people.

In a clearing on the other side of the island was a moose and her baby.

And all of these things, Paige was able to see using her ultraviolet sight.

She tried to switch into witch vision. From up there, she wanted to see if the darkness she'd noticed the day before was getting closer. Or if it had disappeared altogether. If they were really really lucky, that darkness could have been a representation of McCree, though she doubted it.

As soon as she attempted to switch to witch vision, she lost control of the air and started falling.

When you are in animal form, Cawli said his tone urgent, *you do not have access to your magick. If you attempt to use it, you will lose your form.*

Paige seized her attempt and regained altitude. As much as she might enjoy flying, she had to admit that she relied a little too healthily on her magical abilities. She felt naked and vulnerable without her magick.

Leslie circled with her in the air and let out an eagle cry.

Paige had to agree. Being up there was probably the most exhilarating thing she had ever experienced in her life.

But if she was going to survive, she should probably keep her feet on the ground.

Back on the ground, she wasn't quite ready to be finished. It was so freeing to be an animal form. So, instead, she decided to try a different form. Cawli said she could be anything she wanted, so this time she opted to be a bear.

Decima walked up to her then shifted into Ripley. "You sure that's a safe thing to shift into?"

Paige decided to feel out what it was like to be a bear. She rose up off her front feet then pounded back down again. The trees shook a little, needles falling around her. It was nice to be able to see in color again. Though, it was simple seeing the world in ultraviolet. And she appreciated how powerful her body felt. Every step she took her claws dug into the ground. There was a valid reason for people to be afraid of the bear.

Which meant Ripley probably had a valid reason for telling Paige that choosing a bear to go wander around human neighborhoods was a bad idea.

Okay. If she couldn't be a bear, she was going to be a horse.

Her limbs elongated, and her point of view shifted just a bit. However, the thing that freaked her out the most was the fact Ripley completely disappeared.

Paige shifted her head to the right and Ripley came back into view. She moved her head back to the left putting Ripley right in front of her, and Ripley disappeared again.

Okay. The horse was going to freak her out just a little bit. If she was going to walk around the neighborhood, she needed to be able to see. Why was it that people always rode horses? And they always said, "Trust the horse. He knows where he's putting his hooves."

Obviously, they were wrong.

So, instead, she chose to be a moose. This wasn't much better.

It's due to where your eyes are located on your head, Cawli said quietly.

Ripley chuckled.

This was frustrating, learning how to see with different types of eyes.

Ripley shook her head. "I say go with the horse or be a dog."

And with that, Ripley shifted again.

Paige hadn't realized there were dog shifters, then she remembered she could shift into a wolf. Wolves were quite common in the area and she wasn't sure if she would be immediately shot. Not like a bear.

But she didn't want to tempt fate. So, she pictured a golden retriever in her mind's eye and shifted.

Dogs saw in different colors. No. That wasn't quite right. They didn't see all the colors. She knew the trees were green. Or, at least they were supposed to be. The leaves were, that is. However, they were almost grayish-blue. Looking through the dog's eyes, was a little like seeing a different world. Like a child's world almost.

Paige had always imagined a child's world would have a lot more color to it, and the color would be brilliant and amazing. So, that particular comparison was probably wrong. But blue leaves on the tree? That was bizarre.

With her new form in place, and with the ability to see what was directly in front of her, she moved to follow Ripley through the woods and down the roads toward Billie's house.

Once they arrived, Paige shifted back into her human form, feeling more refreshed than ever. She didn't understand why she didn't do this earlier. Well, she knew. There had been a part of her that had been scared.

Well, she certainly wasn't scared anymore. If she could figure out how to bring her computer with her, this might be the way she traveled all the time. Then, she wouldn't have to worry about vehicles. Except when she had to go pick up the kids. Because she still had two of them that couldn't shift.

Billie greeted her at the back door with a warm smile. "I see you've been having some fun."

"I have." And her babies didn't seem to weigh as much. That was probably psychosomatic, but she would take it as a win. "I think it's time to see the dragon now."

Billie narrowed her eyes. "I'll see what I can do."

Leslie winged in and transformed before her feet hit the ground. "I think I'm getting the handle of this."

Which was good. They had been putting this off for how long now? She'd been a shifter for almost a year. And this was the first time she had attempted to do this? Okay. Yes. Cawli had been rather insistent she wasn't able to shift, but the reality was Paige wasn't the type of person who believed someone when they told her she couldn't do a thing. She really should have challenged this a lot sooner.

Ripley padded up and transformed into human, running her fingers through her hair. "I'm starting to figure out how to run on this plane without running through things like trees."

Wait. What? "You can run through trees?"

"Well, yes." Ripley shook her head. "When I'm Decima, it's like I'm more spirit than physical."

That did make a little bit of sense. "You *are* a death dog."

Leslie raised a finger and tipped her head to the side. "And you are really smoky. It kind of reminds me what Hell must be like."

"Even though," Paige said with a shrug, "I don't believe that Hell even exists."

"Oh, it exists." Ripley's expression was grim. "I'm pretty sure it's just here on earth."

This was another thing they had in common. Paige turned to Billie. "We really do need to get a move on. And it's time for me to get some information on DoDO."

Billie looked at them with a raised eyebrow. "Do you want breakfast?"

Breakfast sounded great. Paige put her hands on her belly and smiled. "Yeah. I think breakfast would be amazing."

They all tromped into the house and the four girls went to work making food. Billie had tried to get them to back off, but Paige, Leslie, and Ripley had been rather insistent. They were only going to be guests for so long. After that, they needed to pull their own weight.

With plates full of eggs, bacon, and pancakes—because making the decision to do one or the other had been too hard —they all sat down at the square table.

"Okay." Billie took a sip of her orange juice then set the glass back down. "DoDO. What do you know about them?"

Paige talked around the food she shoveled in her mouth. She didn't know how it was humanly possible to be any hungrier than she was when she was pregnant. But now she was a pregnant shapeshifter, and she felt like she could eat an entire cow. "I know they are witches. And they really do not like the fact that we are so closely tied with the shifters."

"Well, you're not wrong there."

Leslie picked up one of her dry pancakes and tore off a piece, shoving it in her mouth. "Where have you run into them?"

It was time to give them all the information she had, especially since she didn't have a lot. "I have had a feeling that I've been following them for a while. It's more about what we're not seeing, than what it is that we *are*, if that makes any sense at all."

Ripley shook her head, putting an entire slice of bacon in her mouth. "Not really."

Paige had thought they were silly to cook an entire half pound of bacon, but now she realized that even that may not have been enough. "I would get called out to locations for disappearances. But I wouldn't find anything. No clues. No trails. But one time, I did get a witness claiming to have seen a man in a black suit. And that is how I came to call them the men in black."

Leslie hummed a line to the *Men in Black* theme song, dancing in her chair and clapped twice. "I love that movie."

Paige vaguely remembered that movie. She didn't know if she'd actually watched the entire thing though. She may have slept through part of it. They were aliens. Aliens were boring. "Anyway, I couldn't get any more information about them. Until, that is, they came to visit us."

Leslie sat up in her seat on full alert. "What? When did this happen?"

The timeline was a little fuzzy for Paige. For whatever reason, and it really may be the pregnancy, she was having a tough time keeping track of days. Had it been two days ago? Three days ago? A week ago?

Probably not a week ago.

That was the best she could do. She was really looking forward to having her babies and getting her brain back. "A few days ago."

Billie set her fork down and leaned forward, her expression concerned. "What happened?"

"Well, it was really simple. I was on the phone with Mandy who was freaking out about her mom being there and not being her mom. We were discussing what the griffin was and why it would have chosen my sister."

Leslie slumped forward and rubbed her face with her hand. "It's going to take me forever to clean up this mess."

"But you will." Paige had every confidence in her sister. "Anyway, I heard gunfire over the phone. Somehow…" She looked around the table, her hands spread wide, not quite sure how to say what happened because saying it out loud made it sound ludicrous. "I teleported the car with Dexx and myself in it to the house."

Billie blinked.

Leslie dropped her hand and stared at Paige dumbfounded.

Ripley was the only one who seemed unaffected. She shoved a bite full of pancakes dripping with syrup into her mouth. She looked around, her cheeks full, and her eyes wide. "What? That isn't a normal?"

It was a little difficult trying to interpret the words around the pancakes.

Billie shook her head. "No. That's not normal."

That was about the reaction Paige was expecting. "So, anyway, we showed up. And then I kind of got very pissed off, and the trees came alive and started killing people."

Billie's lips went flat.

Leslie's eyes pinched at the corners. "Did you get any of the men who threatened my kids?"

"They claimed they were shooting into the air and into the woods."

"And my kids play in those woods." Leslie's voice was deadly cold.

To say that she had gotten a few of them must put it lightly. "Yes. I did."

"This is very serious." Billie glanced over at Leslie. "Just how powerful are you now?"

Some of the fear Paige was fighting so hard to ignore came to the forefront. "Very."

The realization of that very simple statement rolled over Billie. "We might be in more trouble than I thought."

Ripley shook her head, her face folded in a pained expression. "So, she's powerful. That's good. Right?"

Leslie pushed her still full plate away and sat back. "No. It means that something big is coming. We witches only get the kinds of power the world will need of us, at the moment it needs us."

"It's been bothering me for a while." Paige had wanted to talk about it of course. "But our kids are so strong. All of them. And early. I'm afraid to know why."

Billie shook her head as if to clear it. "We will be discussing that with the dragon shortly."

It didn't surprise Paige that her little statement had rushed the conversation timeline with the dragon.

"What happened with DoDO?"

Paige released a long breath and picked up her fork. "Mario introduced himself and told me he wasn't a danger. He wanted to see if we could join forces until he realized we were so close with the shifters."

Billie nodded.

"I didn't tell him about how out-of-control her situation really has become."

"That was probably a good idea. But I have a feeling they've probably figured out a lot of it by now."

It was time to get some answers. "Who are these guys?"

Billie pulled her plate closer to her then pushed it away. "There is secret organization that's been around for a long time. You may know them as the Brotherhood of Light."

Ripley frowned, something finally getting her attention. "They're like the Shadow Sisterhood except on the opposite side. They want the paranormals to come out into the light. They want the paranormals to stop living in the shadows and in fear."

"Well," Paige said, "that doesn't quite make sense. Because if that was the case, then why would they be so upset with the Whiskeys being close to the shifters?"

"They're connected to the Brotherhood of Light." Billie's tone was uncharacteristically solemn. "I didn't say that they were the Brotherhood of Light."

Well, this was certainly a tangle.

"The information we have says they are connected to the President of the United States."

Ripley slammed her hand against the table. "You've got to be fucking kidding me."

Billie raised an eyebrow and shook her head. "Did you ever wonder why it was the President of the United States knew about paranormals? Especially when she's not one?"

That had been a question Paige had been asking a lot lately, but she'd been trying to stay out of politics. "I haven't really been following too much."

Leslie just looked confused. "Me too. I guess I've just been so busy with everything."

Ripley snorted. "You have been helping Dexx blow up the town a little bit."

"It was just a warehouse. And it was just the one."

"You're starting to sound like Dexx." Paige chuckled but

then went sober again. "What does this mean? What do they want?"

Billie set her arms on either side of her plate, leaning forward. "The one thing that DoDO and the Brotherhood of Light both want is for the paranormals to come out into the open. The only difference is, DoDO wants the paranormals to be put in isolation camps as prisoners. I don't think the brotherhood even understands that yet."

"Or maybe they do." Ripley leaned back and crossed her arms over her chest. "It wouldn't surprise me in the least if the brotherhood was just trying to get to DoDO's resources. They probably think they could play this and make it right for the paranormal somehow."

"Whatever is going on," Billie said quietly, "you guys are playing right into their hands. You're shooting too loud and too fast. You're making too much noise. And that, I think, is exactly what the president and DoDO want."

Well, that was certainly a mood killer.

"Well, I guess if you want to," Billie said after breakfast, "you can shift and go with me. I'll be on the four-wheeler. That's the easiest way to get there."

Paige was eager to get back into animal form again.

"I do recommend that you be careful in which animal you choose." She looked at Paige and Leslie. "We're in Alaska. Not everyone in this area is shapeshifter friendly. If they see a bear, they're going to shoot it."

So being a bear in Alaska *was* a bad idea.

"I also wouldn't choose anything people can hunt. No moose, no deer."

"But we're not even in those hunting seasons." Leslie bent down to put on her boots.

Oh, Paige was looking forward to the day she could bend over to put on her boots without a fight.

Billie nodded. "But we live in an area where it's unlikely you will get caught. Unless, of course, you do something very stupid and leave evidence behind. Like a carcass. But here, we usually use everything we can."

More words of wisdom. Awesome.

Ripley open the door and walked down the steps outside. "I'm just going to stick with the dog."

"Oh, yeah." Paige realized she was being a horrible guest by keeping her boots on, but she hoped that Billie understood the dilemma. She stepped outside and took in the stormy setting. The sky was dark, and it looked like it could rain all day. "A smoky gray dog? That's not terrifying at all."

Ripley threw a glare over her shoulder and kept walking to the shed where the four wheelers were kept.

"I'm going to keep the bird form." Leslie stepped out into the driveway and stopped behind Billie's beat up truck. "I love flying."

Paige did too. "I enjoy being closer to the ground if, and when, I ever need my magick."

Leslie shrugged. "I'm used to not using it." She didn't say anything else and just leapt into the air, shifting into a hawk, and beating the air with her wings, gaining altitude quickly.

Billie headed to the shed and started up her four-wheeler.

Ripley was already in padfoot form and heading down the driveway.

Paige could be, literally, any animal she wanted. It was time to try out a fox.

Cawli chuckled in her head. *It pleases me that you are finding so much enjoyment in this.*

Well, it really is a lot of fun. Who knew how each of the animals would see differently or hear differently? Of course, it made sense now. But before? She'd never even thought to ask those things.

The shift into the fox was not difficult. Her vision was pretty good, and she could see through shadows better than she ever could as a human.

It is because the fox is related to the cat in many things. Cawli's voice was gentle and almost conversational. *I would say that for the future, it would be better to take this form at night.*

Thank you. I will keep that in mind.

She saw something moving in the thin grass up ahead. She lowered herself to the ground and crept forward, searching with her nose, listening with her big ears. She saw it again and pounced.

A mouse. Her every instinct was to eat it. However, her very human response was *no*.

Bringing a little bit of her human side forward, she put the mouse down and gave it a gentle lick before it scurried away.

Billie blazed past on the gravel road, kicking up rocks as she went.

Paige opened her mouth to bark and let out a scream. That startled her. She didn't realize foxes didn't bark.

Cawli just chuckled in the back of her head.

Paige gathered power in her small haunches and leapt forward, enjoying how easy it was to run. If running was this much fun as a human, she might do it more often.

They ended up taking the dirt road over the bridge and to the highway. For a moment, Paige thought they were heading into town and wondered why they just didn't cut along the island like they had the day before.

But Billie crossed the highway and went up the mountain, following a rough four-wheeler trail that Paige was very excited she wasn't driving on. Learning to shift now had been well-timed. This Alaska living was rough.

Paige wasn't sure how far they went, but eventually Billie turned off on a game trail, Paige and Ripley running beside her in the forest.

They broke through the trees and into a small clearing to find a large cabin. It was simple, and probably had about three or four rooms. But it was bigger than the ones Paige, Leslie, and Ripley were staying in.

Paige shifted to her human form, already regretting

leaving the fox behind. About halfway up the side of the mountain, she wished she had picked an animal with longer legs. But the fox was fun *and* fast.

Billie shut off the four-wheeler and got off. "Blake, are you around?"

Ripley came up beside them. "Did you see this view?"

Paige turned and walked around the four-wheeler to glimpse what Ripley saw. It was breathtaking. They were able to see over the tops of the trees below and into the valley. The river spilled from the glacier and surrounded the long island they'd just come from.

It was amazing. How did the island remain in the spring runoff? Or maybe it was the fact that it just never got that warm up there. It was in the middle of June and Paige was wearing jackets. The temperature hadn't gone over sixty since they'd arrived. She doubted this area ever had shorts weather. It didn't help they were *right next* to a glacier. "That *is* nice."

Leslie touched down beside them and shifted. "If you think this view is good, you should be up in the open air. Because that shit? It's amazeballs."

"Billie Black," a male voice said behind them.

Paige turned to take in the man who had walked into the clearing.

He was tall with dark hair. He was well-built and wore a red flannel over shirt. He looked from one to the next, his expression devoid of emotion. "You know how I feel about visitors."

"And I know Opal told you we were on our way." Billie wasn't taking any slack. "Now, normally I would wait until you got your scales out of your butt, but we don't have time. We've got a situation and we need your assistance."

Blake sighed. "I'm not letting any of you into my home."

Paige had been a part of many a conversation that started

off very similar to this. In those previous situations, she had a bit more patience. For whatever reason, she was all out of fucks for the day. Maybe even the next week. "Look, I don't even know if you'll be able to help us."

His gaze settled on hers and his eyes shifted. They turned to silver, and the pupils became slits. "Oh, I believe I can. The question is, do I want to."

Paige doubted she would be able to make a dragon, of all the mythical creatures, do what she wanted him to do. So, she pushed down her initial reaction to challenge him. It just wasn't smart. "What if we say please?"

"And put a cherry on top," Leslie said behind her. Her tone was probably a bit more flippant than it should be.

He studied the two of them. "So, the time has come."

Paige was really getting tired of listening to that. Like it was some prophesied event or something. "You've been an ancient in this world for a very long time."

"You have no idea how long I've been in this world."

Were they going to measure their dicks next? "That's great. That means you've got wisdom."

Blake narrowed his eyes and his expression changed. Instead of being judgmental, he was now intrigued. "Are you seeking more power?"

"No." Leslie's voice was firm.

Paige agreed with that sentiment one-hundred percent. "If anything, we're a little terrified by what it means to have this much power."

Blake relaxed. "Well chosen, Cawli."

Cawli purred.

"He says, 'thank you'." Because it was just weird to have someone talking to the being sharing your skin with you. "We have a few questions and we're hoping you can help."

He drummed his fingers against his jean-clad leg. "A griffin, a padfoot, a thunderbird, and a rajasi. What an interesting display."

It didn't escape Paige's attention he didn't mention what Cawli was. "We're also witches, the kind who understand that when the power rises, something will rise in opposition."

"The ancients need witches to bond with."

"Then, you're a witch?"

"I was." He took in Paige's belly. "I have a stump you can sit on."

Paige wasn't going to offend him by not accepting his offer. She walked over to the tree stump he pointed to and perched on it, resting her belly on her thighs. "Was. I didn't think that was something you could lose."

He chewed on the inside of his lip before answering. "I prefer being a shifter. As a witch, I can choose any form I wish. It is simply unwise for me to choose the dragon form."

"Not even where you think you're safe?" Leslie asked. "Like, in the forest where there are no other humans."

What *would* it be like to see Leslie as an actual griffin?

"It is always where you think no one exists that someone does. I've been hunted too long to make that mistake again. The humans think they killed off dragons. It is safer for us if they believe that."

And that was all very touching, but… "We need to go back home." Paige missed Dexx and she missed her kids. As much as she was enjoying this vacation, and it really was starting to feel kind of like a vacation, she wanted to be where *she* belonged, taking up *her* responsibilities instead of fostering them on others. "Leslie needs to learn how to control the griffin quickly. Now."

He nodded once. "The griffin was always volatile."

Leslie winced. "He's calling you names."

Blake chuckled. "I'm sure he is."

Paige wasn't done. "And I need to figure out how to teach my children how to control *their* abilities."

Blake met her gaze and held it for a long moment. "They are born ancients, so they will be much stronger."

"We thought we would have enough issues with shifter-witches. We ran into one of those before."

"You didn't." Leslie opened her hands and pulled her head back. "You decided to go spend some time with angels, while we were in the middle of being destroyed."

Ripley frowned at her. "Look who's being a drama queen."

"Drama queen?"

"She was *abducted*. She didn't go there by choice."

And that was something Paige still needed to handle. She would much rather be under the protections of *her* wards that helped keep angels out. She had no idea if she was safe from them here or not. She held up both of her hands to stop them both. "Ladies. We're running out of time. I would take it as a personal kindness if we stayed on task."

Leslie's hands curled into fists as she turned her attention to her sister, her eyes blazing orange. "She called me a drama queen."

Paige shot to her feet, her alpha will at the ready. "Do you need me to remind you why I need our family?"

Leslie blinked, and the orange light disappeared from her eyes.

Blake tipped his head at Paige. "I need to know what control you have over her."

Paige sank back to the stump, releasing her will. "It's nothing sick or evil. I just happen to be an alpha. I guess. It's a thing that I'm still learning about."

"You—" He blinked. "It's much more than a thing."

She realized that. Sort of. "Well, technically, Dexx is the alpha and I'm kind of his mate? We love each other and we both proposed to one another and I'm finally wearing his ring. So, yeah. I don't understand how any of that works together."

Blake nodded. "I am glad to hear it is only that."

Paige decided she wasn't going to ask for more details. She'd met other covens. She knew what some of them called control. "Can you teach us or not?"

He looked to each of them in turn. "Yes. But it will take time."

Paige put her hands on her belly. "That's one thing we don't have a lot of. I'm having my babies at home. And I have a feeling when we get there shit is going to hit the fan. DoDO has already shown up on our doorstep."

He went still. "They are aware of you?"

"Yeah."

He straightened. "I hope you're capable of learning quickly."

They trained for the next several days. Each morning they shifted and made the trek to Blake's cabin. They worked on the basics, mostly. Everything from shifting to controlling the elements in their human form. Everything they had taken for granted was now new.

Paige's extra abilities were starting to make sense now. Apparently, Cawli wasn't the typical animal spirit. He wasn't an ancient. So, she didn't have to worry about having that power, on top of helping her sister harness *her* power, on top of helping her babies harness *their* power. That was a lot of power to harness. The thought of all of it was kind of over-whelming.

No. Cawli was what Blake called *the herald*. He had no single shape. Unlike the griffin or the stag or the dragon, in his world, he could be any shape he wanted. That made him the perfect herald.

He would go out into the world every few generations to see if it was safe for the ancients to come out. The last time he had said it was safe, he'd been wrong.

The ancients needed to get out, though the why still hid.

They lived in an alternate dimension called the Vaada Bhoomi, which was Hindi for Promised Land. That sounded really neat and everything—except, apparently, the Vaada Bhoomi was under attack. The ancients didn't know how this was happening, but they knew it was.

Ancients, like the stag who had been bound by Cooper McCree, were disappearing more and nore often. The ancients were now looking at the human dimension as a sort of exodus. If they didn't get out of Vaada Bhoomi now, they might never leave.

There were stories of guardian cats dying. This was a relatively new development. Bastet was the goddess of these cats and had hundreds of them. In the last few months, however, they had been disappearing never to be seen again.

That was only one situation.

Cawli, with Blake's assistance, was able bring Paige with him. Under any other normal circumstance, they would merely switch places.

Vaada Bhoomi didn't smell like earth. The colors weren't the same either. It was almost as if she was looking at the world through a dog's eyes. Cawli had brought them to a desert. To the right was a giant pyramid. Behind them stretched a line of jagged mountains.

Cawli walked beside her in the form of a Siberian tiger. *It changes. Vaada Bhoomi is not like your world. It is what we needed to be.*

"And you need pyramids?"

That is Bastet. Cawli growled. *I stay away from there as much as I can.*

"Why is that?" Part of Paige was tickled by the idea that someone else had upset Cawli. Of course, that was a horrible thing to say, and a worse one to think. But she couldn't help herself. She was a person.

Because I enjoy the form of the cat so much, she thinks I should serve her.

Paige vaguely recalled she was some Egyptian goddess of cats or something. "And she's the one who's losing her cats."

Yes. Cawli's voice sounded grim.

"Do you think that's something that we should investigate?"

No. On this side, you have no authority. You have no witch abilities. You must be careful while you're here.

"Okay." She stepped into the desert, her feet sinking into the sand. The extra weight of her pregnancy didn't feel as heavy there. "What are we doing here? Sightseeing?"

Cawli glared at her then bumped his head against her leg.

The landscape shifted. They were now in a tropical forest, standing beside a gigantic mountain.

A roar filled the air so loud and so massive it vibrated ground around her.

Paige crouched down, her eyes wide. "Was that a T-rex?"

No. Cawli walked forward a little bit. *That's the Argentinosaurus. He's not even a meat eater.*

"Are you trying to tell me that dinosaurs could be coming through? That is going to change everything. And I can tell you, there is no way to hide whatever that was from DoDO."

We are aware. Also, there are not enough witches willing to bind themselves to us so we can all escape.

That was something Paige hadn't even taken into consideration. "How do we help them?"

Most of the animals who live here want to stay.

He touched her leg again and the landscape shifted. The rain forest's trees disappeared and became a forest she was more used to. Normal-sized pine trees and a few others that had leaves she couldn't put a name to, but she knew she had seen.

Playing among the tree trunks was a herd of unicorns.

It is the more exotic ones, like the griffin, pegasus, dragon, and unicorn. They are the ones being hunted.

"That and Bastet's cats."

Her cats are confusing. There is nothing unique about them. I do not know why they are being targeted.

"But the rest? It makes sense they would be?"

She had to admit, that watching unicorns play was unlike anything she thought she would see in her entire life. They looked like horses. Only two of them were white. One was black. Most of the rest were painted. But each of them had a single horn spiraling from their head.

The horns weren't all straight though. Some were curved. Some were dark in color. Few were white.

Each one of them was unique. Some had long manes and tails. Some had short. Some were tall and slender. Some were shorter and bulkier.

The gray one with the splotch covered rump was the largest. The only horse she could compare it to, and this was coming from someone who didn't know horses, was the Clydesdale. His horn was also the longest and the base nearly touched both ears. It spiraled up like branches and she was almost disappointed she didn't see leaves. It curved its way upward to a point.

"How many have been taken?"

This is the last unicorn herd. Cawli sat. *We don't know who is taking them or where they are going.*

"And that big one there didn't want a free ride with my babies?"

Do you think that just because you had children that you should get the biggest and, as you would say, coolest of the ancients?

Okay. That one hurt a little. "No." Yes. Maybe. "It just seems as though he would want to find a safe place."

For his herd, yes. He is their leader. He protects them.

"And there are more like these."

Of course.

The scene shifted, and they stood on top of the mountain, in the middle of a rocky crevice. All around them were other griffins.

Some had black feathers, some had gold. One even had white feathers, while another had blue.

"All of these creatures are in danger?"

Yes. And that is the real reason we are sending ancients out to you. We know we cannot save everyone by sending them to your world. There just are not enough people like you to make that happen.

"But you want me to figure out who is taking them."

Not just you. But anyone we send out. Those we release into your world are carefully chosen. We did not release the griffin to you lightly.

"And the pegasus in Utah?"

He also was chosen. There are many others all over the world. You are not unique in this. We need to find who is picking us off one by one and bring an end to it.

That actually made her feel better. It made sense. Sending them out to be protected? That didn't. "Why all the secrets?"

I wasn't at the liberty to share. You are the only one getting our true story.

"Well, that makes me feel special."

That was not my intent. I need you to understand that the knowledge of the Vaada Bhoomi is highly guarded.

She could understand why. If others knew of this other dimension and that there was a way to get there, how long would it take for intrepid explorers to want to discover everything they could? "I will keep it a secret."

You do not need to keep it from your mate. He is bonded to an ancient who hunts demons. She has brought him over here quite a few times.

Well, there were quite a few things that suddenly made sense.

There is something else you should probably know.

Oh great. Because she hadn't learned enough. "What is it?"

He turned his large cat head toward her. *The ancients just rocked the world around them. There is no amount of grounding or balancing that will help this.*

"That was actually something you could have warned us about sooner."

Honestly, it was something I had forgotten.

"Forgotten? That sounds convenient."

He lowered his head. *It's important that we figure out who was behind the attacks on the Vaada Bhoomi. If someone has discovered her location, it could be detrimental.*

"Yeah. I understand that. But what does that mean to the people around us? The people in our town? The people here?" She was thinking about what happened the night when all the shapeshifters had gone crazy.

It is my hope that the wood witches can give you something that will help.

"Something you didn't have before?"

Exactly.

"What did happen the last time? I mean, the sand women tried to tell me. But they were more about keeping the mystery mysterious than they were about giving real answers. I found it to be a little frustrating."

Well, the world became wild. A kind of wild that scared a lot of people

"And we all know how people react to things that scare them."

Yes. We do unfortunately, this hasn't changed much over time.

"So, what? It killed a whole bunch of ancients?"

No. They started killing each other. We are the reason the paranormals must live in the shadows now. The humans nearly destroyed the paranormals. It was the dark ages for all of us.

Alarm crashed through Paige and an energy tugged at her.

Cawli looked up at her. *The wood magic is calling. Something is wrong.*

Together, they slipped back to where Blake had left them, on the side of a mountain that looked remarkably like the one he had on earth.

But here, he was allowed to be himself, a large, blue dragon. He laid in the grass, his wings open to soak up the light from the sky. She couldn't call it a sun because she had never actually seen it.

Paige walked up to him as quickly as she could. "We need to get home. Now."

Blake didn't ask questions. He rose to all four feet, his wings spread.

As soon her hand touched his scales, she was back in her world.

The wood wards were screaming.

Ripley had already shifted and was running towards town.

Leslie appeared to be waiting for her. "We don't know what's going on. We only know that whatever it is, it's in town."

That was all Paige needed. She reached into herself and fell into the form of a great horned owl.

P aige could hear the screams and cries of the shifters before she'd flown into town. It was almost as bad as the scene from Nederland when Sven had control of the shifters.

She touched down in the street and shifted immediately. She knew she couldn't save the shifters the same way she had the last time. And by last time, she meant when she had saved them in Nederland. Then, she had gone after Sven and destroyed the box that was controlling the shifters. They were then able to regain control of themselves and their spirit animals and stop attacking each other.

Before, she had let her alpha out. That had worked for a small group. This was not a small group.

Paige hadn't even realized this many shifters were in town. Who would've thought so many people would be in Cheechako? She certainly didn't.

The first thing she did was to set up a type of dome like shield around her. She needed to assess the situation without dying. She didn't want to react. With as strong as she was, she had a feeling she could kill someone without meaning to do so.

Leslie joined her. "What is this?"

"I think this might be what Cawli was trying to warn us about."

"Trying to warn *you* about." Leslie shook her head. "We have to do something."

Paige agreed, but what?

Ripley ran to them and straightened. "Do you see that big lion there?"

Paige had seen him the other night, too. "Yeah? What of him?"

"The death I see is centered around him."

That was rather handy. "So, what are you saying? Is he infected?"

"Not that I can see. But he is where the death starts."

It could just be the fact that he had the biggest sets of teeth and claws out in the field at the moment.

Leslie looked at Paige. "There is no way you are going out into that fight."

"Why not? I'll be just fine."

Leslie gestured to her belly, her expression wide with surprise. "Because you're pregnant?"

"If I go out there in shifter form, the babies will be just fine."

"And what are you going to go out there as?"

That was a good question. But then again, why did she have to pick just one thing? She opted to start off as a tiger.

"I'm going to keep the shield open. You," she said to Ripley, "get as many of the kids in here as you can."

Ripley's eyes widened until she realized that somehow, the shifters really were staying outside of it.

Paige would love to take credit for that, but she really had no idea what she was doing. She'd really only thought of protecting herself in the best way possible when she thought the shield up. And this was what appeared.

Leslie looked at her. "What do you need me to do?"

"You're very strong and powerful. You also are very capable witch, and that's what we need right now. Get together with Billie and see what we can do you about fixing the wood witch wards."

Leslie didn't even nod. She just spun on her heel and took flight.

Ripley went in the other direction, staying in human form.

Taking a deep breath to calm her doubting thoughts, Paige closed her eyes and fell back into Cawli.

What is the plan?

Get the bigger guy to stop trying to kill people and buy Leslie enough time to fix the wards.

That's a decent plan.

Do you really think that this is us? Are we doing this to them?

On this scale? Cawli's voice did not sound convinced. *No. Something else is at play here.*

That was something else that she would have to figure out later. For right now, she needed to take down a lion.

She ran out of the shield circle in the form of a large, Siberian tiger.

The lion was fighting off a lioness.

Paige hoped that it wasn't his wife, but she had a feeling that it was. How many lions were there out there anyway?

She let out her alpha roar and watched as it washed over the shifters on the street. A few of them turned to her. The horse, the bear.

A few seemed completely unfazed.

That was, until the lion put all four paws on the ground and turned to her.

The lion was large. His mane made his head look even

bigger than she knew it had to be. How was she going to take him down without killing him? That was the question. Because it wasn't as if he was doing this on purpose. He wasn't enraged to kill because he wanted to. At least, she didn't believe that.

So, she needed to knock him out. How did anyone knock out a lion? It was time to figure it out. Power gathered in her rear haunches as she ran to him, wishing she had access to her magick. As a witch, she could defeat a lion without any worries, but Leslie was right. Fighting as a *pregnant* witch was a really bad idea. It was irresponsible at best.

The lion charged her.

She shifted into a rhinoceros, ramming her head into him, trying to be careful not to hit him with her horn. The rhino was strong, but the horn was an issue. She needed an animal that was large but wouldn't kill the lion.

The lion went tumbling along the pavement like a ragdoll.

The lioness roared a challenge.

Yeah, yeah. I know. Paige hoped the lioness could hear her. She didn't know how talking to other shifters worked. Could she only do that with her own pack?

I have most of the kids, Ripley said. *Or, at least, all of them I can find.*

See if you can help Leslie.

I'll help another way.

Paige didn't' have time to talk more. The lion shook himself, rising to his feet and turned to her. She couldn't risk using the horn, but what else could fight against a lion?

She'd watched Discovery Channel once. She slipped into a hippo.

Hippos were fast and strong and had a jaw that could snap just about anything in two.

The lion launched himself at her. His claws sank into the

flesh on her back. She spun, snapping at him with her hippo teeth. She didn't break his skin.

But she did break his leg.

He roared and fell to the ground.

Paige pulled her head back and let out a roar. The hippo roar was long and loud, there was no mistaking that.

Two wolves to her left whimpered and scurried away.

The lioness circled her.

The hippo had been a promising idea, but she didn't quite enjoy it. She opted for another large animal, though she wasn't sure it was going to do her much good. She slipped into the skin of an elephant.

Her vision was amazing, and she could hear everything as if in ultra-high definition. She towered over everyone.

The lioness came at her, rumbling low in her throat.

Paige was nearly done playing. She reared back and landed on her front feet, stomping heavily. She lashed out with her trunk and hit the lion in the side. The trunk was pretty strong, like she'd hoped it would be. She'd seen videos of elephants lifting trees with it, so she'd thought it would buy her something.

She wasn't wrong.

Letting out an elephant trumpet that was louder than she'd bargained for, she chased the lioness.

The female feline scurried out of the way.

The other animals seemed to be tiring. Whatever had triggered them was starting to wear off.

It was time to end this.

She shifted into a tiger and released a roar, calling on her alpha will and throwing it on the crowd like a dousing agent.

The lion shuddered as he lay on the street in front of her.

The lioness cowered to the ground, her ears laid back.

The two wolves lowered themselves to the ground and bared their necks.

The other animals reacted similarly, showing obedience per their own animal's instinct.

That was going to keep them down.

She walked toward the lion, shifting into human as she went. It was dangerous, yes, but she had to find what was controlling him. An implant? Like Nederland? If that was the case, there was little to no way she'd be able to find it. She would need a scanner.

What if it was magickal?

She switched to witch vision, which was difficult. In witch vision, she didn't see solid objects. She saw energy. The asphalt of the road had none, so all she saw was darkness.

But the lioness burned with a blue fire.

The wolf on the left was pink water.

The wolf on the right green electricity.

The horse was swirls of red as if the winds swept his aura away.

The male lion was a mass of red and brown splotches. Something was definitely wrong with him.

She reached toward him.

He reacted with teeth and claws.

Fuck. She should have known.

She stumbled back, not even bringing her witch hands to bear. They'd be great if she wanted to kill him, which she didn't. Instead, she circled toward his back.

He flipped onto it, rolling over.

But she's seen what she was looking for. *Ripley, do you have a spare hand or paw?*

Yes. What do you need?

A distraction.

There underneath his mane was a collar, and on that collar, something dark spread from it. All she needed to do was sever it. Somehow.

Ripley ran out to her as a padfoot, her large eyes glowing silver and shooting off shadowy wisps of death flame.

I need to get behind him.

As a human?

Yeah.

Great.

That wasn't what Paige had said.

Ripley crouched, her hind quarters raised, and growled, getting the lion's attention.

The lion was still too focused on Paige.

With good reason. Paige had been the hippo who had broken his leg.

The lioness inched forward, her attention on Paige.

Paige crouched, her belly extended in front of her, and looked the lioness in the eye. She growled low in her throat, pulling her alpha will to the front. *I'm trying to help.*

The lioness made a kind of gurgling sound almost and crawled backward, still not rising from her belly.

Ripley lunged forward, snapping with her teeth.

If you bite him, will you kill him?

Huh? Ripley asked, jumping back.

You're a death dog. I'm just wondering how much death you…you know, have.

I'm still a dog. They're just teeth. Ripley leapt forward again, snapping at the lion.

He snapped back, pulling himself toward her before collapsing to the ground again.

You might want to hurry, Ripley said. *Unless you want me dead.*

I don't.

Then, do what you need to.

Paige waited for her opening. She pulled her pocket knife out and opened it. She hoped that whatever was infecting him was an actual collar she could cut because that would be a simple remedy.

The lion lunged at Ripley again.

Paige got her opening and she went for it. There, just under his massive mane, was the collar. She grabbed for it, losing her footing and slipping. She landed hard against the lion's back.

The lioness leapt for her.

Paige just needed to cut the damned thing off. Her feet slipped as she fought the roll of the lion with only the weight of a pretty small woman. It was a losing battle. She got her fingers under the collar.

The lioness hit her hard in the side.

Paige growled, reached for her magick, and slammed the hand that held the knife out, pushing the lioness back. She also reached for the earth, careful not to reach too far and grab fire. She used it to keep herself firm, bracing against the lion.

The lioness's eyes caught Paige's movement. They flared, and she looked at her mate.

Paige projected her alpha will again. "Yeah. I'm trying to *help*. So, *help* me."

Ripley went in again, trying to draw the lion's attention back to her.

The lioness nodded and snapped at her mate.

With the lion no longer fighting Paige, she got the pocketknife worked underneath the collar, hoping to hell she didn't cut him with him flopping around all over. Not that he was flopping but trying to hold him was like trying wrestle a—well, a lion. She was wrestling a *lion*.

The collar was made of thick plastic. With the lion's resistance and the sharpness of her blade—which probably wasn't as sharp as it could have been...she didn't remember the last time she'd actually done something with it—the collar came off.

The roars and cries, whinnies and screams stopped. Paige hadn't even realized just how noisy it had gotten.

The lion shifted into a man, his naked back to her.

She didn't see any blood where she'd cut the collar off him. She released the earth magick, closed her pocketknife, and pushed herself to her feet. "You okay?"

The lion twisted around his expression pained as he looked at her, his eyes pausing on her belly. "I'm so sorry."

He looked fucking terrified. She offered her hand to help him up.

He frowned but took it, rising to his feet.

By this time, she'd been around enough naked people to just see a body no matter what part of the anatomy was flashing her. She held out the collar. "Do you recognize this?"

He nodded, reaching for it.

She held it away from him and shook her head. "Where did you get it?"

The lioness had shifted and stood beside her mate, her blonde hair cascading down her back. "He got it from someone who said they were trying to help."

"Okay. Did that someone have a name?"

He shook his head. "I don't remember."

The lioness took a step forward. "He said he was with DoDO."

Shit. "Okay. I'm going to keep this. Do you have any more of them?"

"Yes." The lioness sighed, glancing at her mate. "We've been having troubles with our shifts lately. I don't know why. Our oldest is about to turn thirteen. We've never had problems before."

Paige narrowed her eyes. "Has anything in your routine changed at all?"

They exchanged looks.

Ripley came to stand next to them.

Two kids, one a teen and the other maybe two or three years younger, plowed past them to get to their parents.

The lion wrapped an arm around his son. "I got a new job. It's a start-up company that I'd never heard of."

"And did you start losing control of your shift after that?"

The lioness hugged her daughter close but looked up at her mate. "Yeah, actually."

"Okay." Great. That news sucked balls. Big, hairy ones. "DoDO is bad, so stay away from them if you can. And…get rid of these. All of them."

He nodded. "I'm very sorry."

"Well, I'm—" Paige gestured to the arm that hung from his side. "—sorry about that."

He shrugged. "It'll heal."

"I can help with that."

He shook his head. "We'll set it and let it heal naturally."

"Not because you're scared of me?" Because while she'd been having a lot of fun switching from one animal to the next, she didn't know how the other shifters were going to respond to that.

"No." He pressed a kiss onto the top of his lioness' head. "Because I need the reminder." He gathered his family to him and padded naked back to their cabin.

Well, at least she had managed to settle things peacefully.

But, what in the hell *were* DoDO's plans?

Most of the shifters left long enough to retrieve clothes then came back. Cheechako was a mess, and it was really going to take everyone to help clean it up.

Paige had other things to do though. Like trying to figure out what DoDO was really up to.

Leslie took the bench next to her and set another collar on the picnic table. "We have even more of these."

"It can't be the same story as the lions." By now, the lion family had a name. And that was good. She had a lot of names, and it was taking everything she had not to mix them all up.

Leslie shook her head. "Not quite. This couple is newlywed and they just moved to a new town."

"Anywhere near that one company?" Paige kept the rest of it pretty vague because she wasn't taking notes and she was having a hard time with all of the names.

"Teltech?" Leslie gave her a look that said she understood exactly what was going on. "No. Not even in the same state."

Somewhere there had to be a pattern. But dang if Paige was seeing it.

"Shortly after they arrived in the new town, he started losing control of the shift."

Now that was a pattern. The last three stories that people had brought to her it was the male who had lost control of the shift first. "Okay. And then after that, DoDO shows up and offers the collar?"

"Exactly."

"And somehow all of these people decided they were going to come here." That was something Paige wasn't sure if she should be concerned about or not. It could be a coincidence. Or, it could be a plan. But was that giving them too much credit? There was a part of her that really hoped the answer to that question was no

Ripley knelt on the bench across from Paige. "Okay. I've talked to four families. Each of them had a major change in their life. It was either a job, relocation, or a new baby. The new baby was adopted."

Paige pulled her hands in front of her. If she spread her legs and let her belly go between them, it wasn't an uncomfortable position. "Same story as everybody else?"

"Yup. They lost control of their shift shortly afterward."

"Starting with the male."

Ripley nodded. "DoDO showed up, offered the collar, and left."

"Did any of the DoDO personnel mention Cheechako?"

Ripley glanced over at Leslie and shook her head.

Leslie shook her head as well. "It was always someone else who said, 'this isn't working. Let's go see Billie.' Like the lion's wife. She's the one who packed up their family to come here."

"To see Billie." That *had* to be something.

"Yup," Ripley confirmed.

That was it. "They said they were going to go see Billie.

Not go to Cheechako. Not talk to Opal, Sherry, or anyone else."

A sense of alarm washed over Leslie's face. "Exactly. What does that mean?"

"It means," Paige said, rising to her feet. "That Billie is the target."

Ripley and Leslie were quick to rise.

"We need to do something, like protect Billie."

"I'll go to the townhall." Ripley turned and jogged down the street.

Leslie waved her off. "There's no way I'm running. I'm walking…fastly as a human. I'm beat."

"Me, too." Paige appreciated Leslie's grammar choice, but didn't say anything. She was… tired. She set off at a slow waddle, following Ripley's disappearing form much slower. "I mean, I'll shift and run that way, but other than that?" She wasn't exhausted, not like she had been after other fights she'd had, but her human body gently reminded her she was still pregnant.

Leslie slashed her hand, killing that thought. "You were just a rhino, a hippo, and an elephant."

Yeah. She had been. "It was pretty bad ass."

"Also, they were all animals bigger than a house. I think your subconsciousness is trying to tell you something."

That *was* possible. "Yes. That I needed to be something big and powerful so I could disable a frelling lion and not kill him."

Leslie tipped her head to the side but didn't change her expression. "You need to be a human carrying little human-shifter babies for a bit."

She might be onto something. "Fine."

"Besides, what happened with Cawli when you two went to the other place?"

"The shifter world?"

"Yeah. That place."

Right. Paige hadn't had a chance to fill her in. As long as Ripley didn't come back with a report of Billie's demise—which was highly unlikely—they had time for a little catch-up. She was getting entirely too much practice at all this fighting-for-her-life stuff. "They're sending ancients because they need to discover who's behind the attacks on their dimension."

"What?" Leslie's expression showed her complete surprise.

Which was about the way Paige had felt. "Apparently, they're disappearing. He showed me dinosaurs while he was talking about it, so there might even be dinosaurs running around? I don't know."

"I... hope not?"

"Me, too. That would be super hard to hide. Can you imagine the blowback from that?"

They made it to Sherry's Diner. Several people were in the streets, cleaning up and talking to one another. Someone was setting up tables near the parking lot and putting out food.

Oh, the joys of a small town.

Paige stepped into the diner and held the door for Leslie to grab.

Sherry was just headed to the back. She stopped, smiled at them, and said, "Rip and Bill are in the back. You can go on up if you want."

The back was the upstairs. Paige guessed they called it the back because the stairs started there? She didn't know. Anyway, she led the way up.

"So, how many are disappearing?"

It took Paige a minute to catch up. Right. Ancients. "That I don't know. Cawli wasn't too specific. But enough to be concerned. I even got to see unicorns. The real ones are super pretty."

"Too bad you're not giving birth to a unicorn."

"Right?" Though Paige cringed a little recalling what Cawli had said. His words had cut a little too close to home. A part of her was a little disappointed she was giving birth to a fiery lion and a bird of thunder, even though—why? For reals. Why? Because she wanted something more powerful? She thought she'd *earned* that? It was stupid.

Also, the thunderbird and the rajasi had been the two who had nearly closed the door to Heaven and Hell, so maybe she could get over herself and just enjoy the fact that *any* animal spirit had chosen her to bring it into the world.

Vanity, if *that's* what this was, was stupid. "However, each one that's being sent through to our side serves a purpose and, apparently the unicorns don't have one."

"Okay. So, they're sending through a thunderbird and a rajasi… as babies." Leslie's tone said she was confused.

Paige was too, now that she had time to think about it. "Why would they choose to send through two of their agents as babies if they need to solve a missing person's case?"

"Yeah."

Paige got to the top landing. It was like a half a hexagon, or—whatever six sides was. She didn't know. It wasn't square. There were three doors all cut in at odd angles. Paige picked the door with the light shining underneath and opened it further.

Billie was gathering books and handing them to Ripley who was shoving them in a bag.

"You got the message."

Billie nodded, picking up a thick tome.

Ripley looked up, her hands pausing. "She's a little shook up."

"They're targeting my friends," Billie said, her tone harsh. "You'd be upset, too."

"My question is why they're targeting you," Leslie said,

stepping up to the work table and setting her hands on it. "Can I help?"

"I'm getting out of Cheechako, so I don't pose a greater threat to the town. So, just grab anything that might be helpful."

Paige decided she'd leave that to the two witches who were actually...witches. She just threw elements around and had no idea what *helpful* might look like, what herbs or books or spells would be deemed worthy. "What about these people that are coming to you? How do you know them?"

"Karen and Todd?" Billie shrugged, handing Ripley a large green book.

Ripley took it and tried to shove it in the bag. It didn't fit. "Have you thought about packing lightly?"

Leslie looked around and grabbed a box. "Here."

With a smile, Ripley started shoving more books in there.

"Anyway," Paige prodded. "The...lions."

Billie nodded. "I've known them since forever. Todd and I went to school together. Karen and I met in college."

"Okay. Did either of them ever do anything that would have maybe put them on someone's radar?"

Billie shook her head. "No. I mean, we—" She stopped and turned to Paige. "Todd and Karen. Gary and Elsie. John. Daren and Darla?"

"You know how they're all tied together." Brilliant.

"We were at a rally. The...the Brotherhood came into town when we were all in college. Well, some of us were attending college. The rest of us were just in town visiting friends or family. But we all went to one of their rallies."

That was surprising. "You don't strike me as the 'go to rallies to support the Brotherhood' sort." The Brotherhood of Light wanted to bring all paranormals into the open and Billie seemed to be a big proponent of keeping one's nose in one's own business.

"Not now, but then?" Billie closed her eye, clasping her book to her chest. "I was…a rather loud supporter."

"But what put you on DoDO's radar this time?"

Billie let out a long breath. "I flew down to Seattle to visit some friends. Ran into a DoDO agent while I was there. He wanted me to join him. Said that things were getting too out of hand and they could use the help of another witch like myself."

"That sounds about right. But you didn't smell like shifter." Because Paige was carrying two. Her man and her sister were shifters.

"No. But he'd heard of Cheechako and he wanted to learn more about it."

"And?" Paige didn't like where this was going.

"I told him it was a sanctuary from people like him. We helped those who needed help. We provided calm in chaos."

"And? What did he say?"

"That it sounded great and that he wanted to see it for himself. That if he could see what we did here, that maybe they could do it in other places."

There was something in that statement that gave Paige a very bad feeling, but she couldn't put her finger what it was. "What else? What information was he trying to get?"

"Our location."

"And did you give it to him?"

"No." Billie jumped back into action, hurrying as if they were running out of time.

"How hard did he push?"

Billie froze. "He tagged me."

"What do you mean?"

"He put a magickal tracker on my bag. I caught it before I even left the airport, though."

A magickal tracker? Paige didn't know if *she* could have found that. "Wood magick?"

Billie shrugged, then went back to packing up her books.

They weren't *running out of time.* They were already out of it. "Billie."

She grabbed another book and handed it to Ripley.

Paige grabbed Billie's hand. "Bill."

She looked up and met Paige's gaze.

"If they put trackers on those people to get to you, they're trying to find your location." And Paige was willing to bet that the collars *had* that device on them. "They're already here."

Billie stopped.

Leslie froze.

Ripley paused, then looked up at Paige. "Okay, boss. What do we do?"

"Prepare for war." Because that's exactly what Mario had been after.

C heechako was more than just a tourist town. It was a community and it showed.

Paige, Leslie, and Ripley were invited to help strengthen the wards. At first, Ripley had told them absolutely not. No way. Nuh-uh.

"But we could use your death whatever in the wards," Paige said, pushing away her empty plate. Dinner had been an odd mix of whatever everyone had been cooking at the time, everyone sharing what they had.

Ripley shook her head, extending her neck out. "I'm not a witch."

"Decima might disagree with you. You're...kind of like a witch." Though, what that meant, Paige was clueless.

Shit. She was clueless about a lot, but to be fair, they were talking about some pretty extreme stuff. This wasn't a grocery list or hunting vamps or whatever. This was...stuff that...centuries ago...lost to memory and...

When was she giving birth, so she could have her damned brain back?

"Look," Paige said, trying again. "One of the reasons the

Whiskey wards are so strong is because each of us puts our gift into them."

"Okay. But I don't have a gift."

"You do," Opal said as she wheeled past. "And if you haven't figured that out yet, you should. Quickly."

Ripley glared. "I'm not making you the four-wheel drive chair."

"Do or don't. I've survived this long without it."

Ripley gave her a sour face.

"It doesn't matter if you know how to use it or not." Paige leaned back, stretching her back. Not too far because she was a little top heavy, but enough to unwork—well, no, to touch a kink in her back and remind her it was there. "Bobby and Kammy were able to do it and they're babies."

Ripley glared.

A very large raven winged in then shifted into Blake. He walked over to them. "I heard we have a situation. Is it because of you?"

"For once?" Paige was so incredibly grateful for this answer. "No." Because it usually was. "Though, we might have helped lead them here. I don't know."

"Mario didn't give you anything," Ripley grumbled.

"Accept the…" Paige patted her pockets. Had she brought that damned card with her? "A business card. You can't put a tracker spell on a card, can you?"

"I don't see why not," Blake said.

"It doesn't matter." Ripley stood and placed a booted foot on the bench, resting her elbow on her bend knee. "He had scientific trackers on everyone else. So…" She glared at Paige.

Oh, that woman had a hard time working through things. She'd fit in just fine with the Whiskeys. "My thought is that we boost the wards, keep them out."

"And how do we do that?" Blake crossed his beefy arms over his chest.

"We each add what we have to the wards."

"Witches and shifters?"

That was a thought Paige had been toying around with actually. "I know how to do it with witches, but I think we should be able to do it with the shifters too."

"We don't have powers," Ripley said louder.

"Except that you do," Paige said equally loud. "You don't see what I do. You see that woman over there?" She pointed.

Blake nodded. "Ginny."

"Yeah. Well, Ginny is a pink water wolf."

"I assure you, she's a timber wolf."

"But to my witch vision, her aura is pink. She's an empath. She makes people feel better. And her element is water."

Blake narrowed his eyes at her.

"I think that if I switch into what I call shifter vision—"

His face folded in confusion.

"It's this thing." Words were hard. "I can see auras and I can see the real world and I can see the shifter spirit. Anyway, sometimes, it brings the animal out and I have to be careful. If there's a shifter who's struggling with his shift, my shifter vision will force the shift."

Blake licked his lips and shook his head. "Okay. And with this, you can tell that Ginny is an empathic water summoner."

She wouldn't have used those words, but sure. "Yeah."

Blake walked away.

Paige didn't know what that meant. She turned to Ripley. "I'm not going to force you. Okay."

"You could."

There were a lot of shifters who said that she could force others to her will, but it didn't make sense that she would be able to make people do things against their—well, not their will, but their...natural tendencies? Like, could she force someone to kill who really loathed the thought of killing? Was that something she could do?

She hoped not, though she had a feeling she could. There were too many shifters with the same opinion. That meant someone somewhere had done exactly that.

And then she recalled Cooper. She hadn't known him for long, but he seemed pretty damned slimy. He might have done something like that.

Or what if they got into a situation with DoDO? What would she do to protect her kids? Her sister? Her packmates? What might she demand? What would she force a person to do?

Power, for all that most people sought it like it was candy, was terrifying.

Blake returned with Leslie, most of the wood witch coven, and several shifters. "Okay. We're here to try...whatever this is."

Paige's eyebrows rose into her hairline. Okay. Not quite but they were high. "Who's the coven leader?"

Opal rolled forward. "What are we doing?"

Paige talked her through it as quickly as she could.

"This goes against most witch wards," Opal said, but her expression said she was interested.

"Right. They're only as strong as the person who casts it." Like Alma's wards. She'd been a strong witch in her day and everyone—including herself—had remarked on how strong those wards were. "Chuck gave me the idea. As a coven, we're only as strong as the strongest member. We're all supporting that one person."

"But in a pack," Ripley said, dawning slowly spreading across her face, "we're strongest when we're all together supporting one another."

"The alpha isn't the strongest because he takes strength."

"He's the strongest because he gives it," Ripley finished for her.

More or less, which was the reason Paige really didn't under the whole alpha-dick character thing happening in a lot of the books she'd attempted to read lately. Just because they had power didn't mean they had to abuse it, nor that the abuse was a turn-on. "So, the basic premise is the same with the shields. We let each person put a little bit of themselves into the wards."

"And then it's strong because of *everyone* who is supporting it."

"Exactly."

"The logic doesn't quite track," Ripley said. "But I guess I'll try. I won't promise I'll be able to do anything."

"That's what the other shifters said," Blake added. "But they're willing to try."

"Okay," Paige called out. She wasn't standing up for this. She just wasn't. It was the end of the day and she didn't know if there was going to be a big battle or not. She was staying seated as long as she could to conserve energy. "I'm going to start by turning on what I call shifter vision. If there are any of you who struggle with your shift, you might feel your animal spirit move forward. Don't fight it."

Todd stepped forward, his face flush with concern. "You've already seen what happens when my lion is out of control. This is a bad idea."

"But you weren't out of control your whole life." Paige needed him to see that, for everyone to see that. "You were whole once. You and your animal spirit lived in harmony, no matter what spirit you have or how strong he or she is. You used to be one."

Todd nodded, his eyes bare slits.

"And then someone stepped in and made you off-balance."

"DoDO," Ginny said, looking at her mate.

Paige nodded. "I can't be certain, but right now, that's where the evidence is pointing."

"We need to be sure if we make an attack," Karen said. "We can't be the kind of people who just run off and kill people because of an opinion."

"Exactly right." Paige was so glad Billie tended to collect well-balanced people. "But, if we're defending ourselves, the only thing we can do is to go on the information we have and prepare for the best."

"Okay." Opal wheeled herself next to Paige. "What are we doing?"

Paige shrugged. "Follow my lead and open your ward. Everyone else, be prepared. I'm about to switch to shifter vision."

A murmur went through the gathered crowd.

Paige blinked to witch vision. All she saw was auras and life energy. She blinked again, and the real world came into focus behind it all. The picnic tables. A paper plate that had been left behind by someone. Opal's wheelchair.

She also saw everyone's animal spirits. They rose above their human hosts like ghostly images of fairy flame.

Be calm and don't surge forward. Paige didn't know if they could hear her or not. She hoped so.

Todd's lion nodded but rose just a little higher. He was no longer splotchy and that was good. Paige had to assume that something in the collar had been what had messed with his aura. He was not a brilliant red with shoots of electricity. Not lightening, exactly. Just…balls of electricity.

Opal glowed green with veins of blue, brown, and orange. A pillar of energy ran from her chest to the wards high above, which flowed in her same colors.

Taking in a deep breath, Paige called on the elements. Not

with all the power she had because she didn't want to blow the place up.

Water came to her with the power of change, forceful and impatient.

Air danced like a child around her, wanting to play like a fox.

Earth came to her with the ferocious roar of a mother protecting her young.

And the fire that came with it was hot as lava.

With all the elements collected, she extended her witch hands, the door magick, laced with her silver demon magick and reached out to touch Opal's pillar.

Someone in the crowd gasped.

As Paige's magic traveled upward, intertwining with Opal's, she looked around. The spirit animals watched the magick work its way upward, their human's glowing eyes traveling up afterward, as if the humans were able to see through the shifter's eyes.

How the hell did her shifter vision work? Would she ever figure that out?

She doubted it.

"That's all you have to do," Paige said quietly. "Who would like to go next?"

Todd pushed his way past Ginny, his red electricity already balled up in one hand. He reached out and touched it, his real hand extending. As soon as his electricity touched the pillar, the pillar connecting to Opal flared.

Opal jerked and her eyes glowed white as two of the threads of magick that had started at her chest broke away and danced their way to the ground.

"Are you okay?" Paige asked, watching the threads to see if the break was a bad thing.

The wards flared in answer, and the electricity cascaded down, chasing Paige's magick.

Opal nodded, gripping the arms of her chair. "The wards are getting stronger."

As Paige watched, her magick, followed by Todd's energies, touched the ground and raced back to them via the roots. The magick and the energy met in the middle of the circle. Nothing happened.

Opal released a breath. "I'm okay. This is good. The trees are happy."

And that's when Paige saw. Her magick, as well as Todd's energy, were racing back up the trunks of each of the trees, running out to the branches and through the leaves and needles.

Paige had never seen anything so incredible in her life. Everything glowed…brighter.

Ginny stepped up next, the wolf adding her pink water to the pillar. Followed by the red wind horse, the green lightning wolf, the blue fire lioness, and the purple earth raccoon. Everyone who had gathered took their turn, and with each of them the threads fell away from Opal's chest, taking root in the soil near the picnic table.

Finally, Blake stepped forward, his blue dragon flexing his fire wings. He touched his energy to the threads which were now thick around enough to be a trunk.

Shaking her head, Ripley did the same. Her death energy flew through the channels, giving everything, including the wards, a smoky flare.

Leslie stepped up, her red griffin smoldering. "Blessed Mother, hear our prayer. With our combined energies, keep out all those who intend to do us harm. Keep us grounded so that we do not fail, and guide us to the right decision."

"That's rather open-ended," Opal muttered.

"She likes to keep it that way," Paige murmured back. "So that the All Mother doesn't feel we're trapping her in a corner. As Leslie puts it, when the All Mother feels trapped, she gets creative."

"That's valid."

Leslie put both her hands to the threads. The griffin joined her with is claws. Their combined powers flowed through it like they were powerlines, reaching up to the wards. The red and orange energy flowed up, then cascaded down, only to roll back to the center.

It coalesced at the roots of everyone's energies and rose back up, creating a type of loop.

It still ran up the other trees, creating an explosion of red lights.

Before everyone's eyes, the magick they'd created solidified and became a large tree that grew and blossomed, bathing them all in the dusting lights of their combined might.

The wards flared once, sending out an almost bell-like toll.

Paige blinked and returned her vision to normal, staring at everyone almost as stupidly as they were staring at each other.

Opal looked up and cleared her throat. "Well, isn't that somethin'?"

They'd created a tree.

A massive tree not nearly the size of a redwood, but huge. Not that she'd met a redwood tree to compare it to. She needed to add that to her to do list. The branches were large and wide. They covered a generous portion of the small park. It was an odd mix of evergreen and deciduous that she couldn't quite figure out. The bark and the limbs looked like a pine, but the leaves were almost that of a maple, if smaller and more abundant.

Looking at it with her witch vision the next morning, Paige could see the lines of every person who'd added their essence to it. And, moreover, she could feel the soul currents of others who hadn't been there. Had others been able to add themselves after it was all said and done?

And was this something she could do to the Whiskey wards?

She was going to give a shot, that was for sure.

Paige couldn't tell where DoDO was. No one could. They didn't know if they were close, or if they were even a threat.

No. They knew DoDO was a threat. Why else track so many people to Billie's door?

And why target her? Were they intending to fight her? Talk it out? What?

They'd all slept in town. Billie's cabins were located outside of the shields, something that would probably need to be fixed, and the one thing they intended to rectify that morning. Paige had a belly full of bacon, eggs, and potatoes. People who lived here loved bacon, that was for sure.

Opal wheeled herself next to Paige, her eyes on the branches of the tree. "I'll say it again, that's impressive."

Paige had a challenging time looking away as well. "It was all you."

"But your idea."

Paige shrugged. "I think maybe we work together better than apart."

Opal gave Paige a frown.

"Okay. I see here everyone lives together, but you're not *really* together." And that was something that Paige was only just now realizing. "The wood witches all have their own homes and eat separately and live—" She gestured with her hands. "—out there. And that's fine. You guys need a life. I get that."

Opal narrowed her eyes and raised her chin. "But you live with shifters."

"And we *are* shifters." Which...they were.

"And you work closely with other paranormals."

"They're like family." And they were. Rainbow, Tarik, and Michelle were at the Whiskey house more often than not. Anytime they didn't want to cook but didn't want to go out either? Or anytime Rainbow wanted to watch a show? Or anytime Michelle just wanted to hang out in Alma's garden?

Paige looked up, trying to see just how far up she could

see through the thick limbs. "I wonder if DoDO isn't afraid of that closeness."

"That's a new light." Opal's expression was pensive.

"And only one that I've thought of lately. The elders didn't even think of bringing everyone together—the other packs, the covens. The... elves?" Because, one day, she might get over that one, For the moment, elves were still an oddity. "None of that until we showed up."

"And you do have a very odd family."

Paige nodded. "Everyone is welcome. I think we adopt more than we...well, do we keep anyone out that wants in? There was Cooper, but he wanted to take over, not come in."

Opal shook her head. "We built Cheechako to be a refuge area for those who had no other place to go. Then it became a safe place for people who were struggling, or a vacation place where you could be whoever you were."

That all sounded great. "What was it, do you think, that put Billie on DoDO's radar?"

Opal went still, her eyes on the ground as she thought about that, chewing on her top lip.

"It had to be something." And what *was* DoDO after anyway? Really. Because, according to what Paige had been able to gather, they'd only started ramping up whatever they were doing recently.

Right before the new president had been elected. During the –whatever it was called when the candidates bashed each other and refused to talk about the genuine issues. There was a word for that. She knew it. Somewhere.

It didn't matter.

Somehow, the president was behind it, and that was scary enough.

Paige needed to break out her detective hat again and figure out what was really at stake, what they were really up to, because she knew she wasn't seeing it.

With a sudden light in her eye, Opal turned to Paige. "Billie was called to Kansas a few months ago."

"Really. Where?"

"Topeka."

What weqre the odds? "Elves?"

Opal nodded. "They wanted wood wards, but they couldn't figure out who they were trying to keep out."

"Because of the disappearances."

"Yeah."

"And were the wards able to help at all?"

"Nope. Whoever was behind the disappearances kept getting through."

That was the thing about elves that frustrated Paige the most. They were able to travel to different dimensions. That's the only thing she could attribute Underhill to. Because she doubted seriously they lived under the ground. With all the fracking and mining and drilling? No. It just didn't make sense. But an alternate dimension?

And people were still disappearing.

As were the residents of Vaada Bhoomi.

Those two had to be connected. Didn't they?

Not necessarily, but maybe. It made sense.

Which meant that if they could get into Underhill and into Vaada Bhoomi they would be able to get through the Cheechako wards, even with all the modifications.

She looked at the ground, recalling how the ward had cascaded back around. Maybe not.

And how was that going to affect their ability to move the shields forward?

Before she had a chance to delve further into that, two black SUV's rolled through town, leaving the parking lot behind and pulling right up to the park

Paige had a sneaky suspicion she knew who they were. She got to her feet and started walking toward them.

Opal rolled forward. "Remember, this isn't your juris-diction."

Good reminder. "I'll follow your lead."

Mario stepped out of the vehicle and approached, four others fanning out around the SUV's in dark suits with empty hands. He didn't seem surprised to see Paige there, but he kept his attention on Opal. "Hello. I'm Mario Kester from the Department of Delicate Operations." He offered his hand.

Opal ignored it, keeping her hands on her wheels. "I know who you are."

His smile tightened. He clasped his hands in front of him and finally looked at Paige. "Ms. Whiskey."

"Mario." Paige wasn't in the mood to dance around, but she wasn't the one to ask the questions.

"What are you doing here, DoDO?" Opal asked.

Mario winced, flinched, then raised his eyebrows, closing his eyes momentarily. "Ah. Well, I'm here for a number of reasons. Can we talk somewhere privately?"

"We can talk here." Opal's tone was final.

Mario gave her a look of displeasure as his gaze flicked upward. "Okay."

Opal nodded once, her lips pursed.

It was like a Wild West shoot out.

"I'm sure you've noticed an increase of shifters unable to control their shift lately."

Opal narrowed her eyes.

A smiled flickered on his lips. "We at DoDO believe we know why, and we need help combatting the disease."

Oh, there he went. Now the ancients were a disease.

Opal nodded but said nothing.

Mario took a deep breath, ignoring Paige. "There is an upsurge of ancients in the paranormal community. We know you are harboring at least one of them."

"I wasn't aware ancients needed to be 'harbored,'" Opal said.

"They are a danger."

"Says who?"

"Anyone who's run across one." Mario's cheeks sank a little as he pursed his lips.

"And you've run across one before?" Opal tipped her head to the side. "Last I heard, ancients weren't around until just recently."

Something shifted in the back of his eyes. It wasn't that he noticed he'd been caught in a lie. It was more like he simply wasn't pleased with what he was hearing. "There have always been a few around. More than they would like us to believe."

"And witches willing to bond with them," Opal said flatly.

"Yes." He turned his lips up as if the thought disgusted him.

Opal pushed her lips out, glancing up at Paige for a moment. She shrugged. "Well, I don't see an issue with them being around. They have just as much right to be here as any of the other shifters."

He paused, eyes narrowed.

What *was* he going to say to that? How *would* he respond?

Finally, he said, "I worry they should be allowed in our society at all."

"You do realize where you are, right?" Opal didn't seem surprised by his statement.

Frankly, neither was Paige.

"This is a sanctuary for shifters."

"A safe place for you to contain them," he agreed.

Opal went still. "We help them find their control then we send them back."

"But some stay."

"Some do." She gestured with one hand. "But we're not a

big town, Mr. DoDO. We don't have a lot of space for new residents. Not a lot of jobs, and we still live in a society where money is required."

He pulled his head back and assessed her. "Where is Billie Black?"

"Not here at the moment."

He blinked his gaze to Paige. "Where is Billie Black?"

Why the fuck was he asking her? Because he thought she'd give him a different answer? She met his gaze, her alpha will rising.

He raised a pale eyebrow then turned his attention back to Opal. "Billie Black is wanted on suspicion for murder."

Paige let out a startled chuckle. "Billie?"

His gaze was cold as it settled on Paige. "Yes."

"Not here," Opal said.

He returned his gaze to her and stretched his neck. "We *will* find her."

"I doubt it."

He gave her a cold smile. "She's not that good."

"She doesn't have to be."

Paige didn't want to know what Opal meant by that, or if she meant anything.

Mario didn't react for a long moment, but then he straightened himself, pushing his shoulders forward. "Well, things would have gone a lot easier on Billie, and on all of you, if you had cooperated."

"And because we didn't?"

His bright blue eyes were downright frigid. "You'll never know how much easier this could have been for you."

"You probably shouldn't have come here."

"You're knowingly ignoring the danger these people represent."

"We're not ignoring the trackers." Opal's voice was like a bullet, her gaze like a dagger. "Or the fact that you somehow had something to do with their inability to control their shift."

He dipped his head, moving his gaze to Paige. He nodded to her once.

In acknowledgement? As if, "Good job for finding out we're assholes and douchebags?"

"They *are* a danger."

"When you make them one," Opal said. "Yes. They can be. So, too, can you. Should we hunt you down? Should we eradicate you?"

Mario narrowed his eyes. "I will see this through."

"I'm sure you will."

"One last chance. Where is Billie Black?"

Opal said nothing.

Paige shook her head. "You really went with murder. Billie. You've met the woman. You couldn't believe any of us would fall for that."

His gaze slid to hers. "None of us know what another might be capable of."

Valid. Except he was completely full of shit. "What are you really after?"

Something shifted across his face, and he stank of dark smoke, but he remained quiet.

Paige was almost certain, though she didn't know how, that Billie had found something—information or an object— and he wanted it. Whatever the case, Billie was in trouble. "Unless you have a warrant, I think it's time for you to leave."

He looked at her for a moment then turned and walked back to his SUV, gesturing to the others to get in. He stopped at the vehicle and turned back to them, gesturing around them. "Nice wards, by the way."

It was nice he'd noticed, but Paige didn't like the fact he'd still been able to get through anyway.

They watched as the SUV's tail lights disappeared around the last building at the parking lot.

Several people came out of the stores, including Billie.

Paige looked at Opal. "We need to get those shields extended. Now."

"I agree." She wheeled herself to the tree.

The sound of large wings beating the air drew Paige's attention to the other end of town.

A large, black, winged horse landed, running down the street, tucking his wings in. As he came to the park, he shifted into a young man.

Paige knew who he was. Max. He'd been the young man Doe's pack had been protecting in Utah. Or, at least, she assumed it was him. She didn't know of another pegasus.

"Paige."

Also, there was the fact that he knew her name. "Yeah. What's up, Max?"

Relief rolled over his expression, but he didn't slow until he reached her. "Doe's been attacked."

What? "By who?"

He looked over his shoulder where the SUV's disappeared. "Them." He turned back to her. "I talked to Chuck. He's already sending some people down to help her, but he wanted me to come and warn you. It's time to get back home. Things are…well, things are getting strange."

"Strange how?"

His expression pinched, his dark brows drawing together. "Several members of her pack were taken right before DoDO attacked. But…Doe says it wasn't them. Someone else took them. Someone that smells like a demon."

Great. Just great. Because Paige didn't just need *one* enemy. She needed two. "Tell Chuck we'll be there as soon as we can."

"Is everything…" Max shrugged and looked around.

Paige narrowed her eyes. "Have you been struggling with your power? Your pegasus?"

He shook his head. "We're a good match. I mean, I'm more powerful. I can call on all the elements now and I can choose any shape and that's neat, but no. We're fine."

Too bad a flying horse couldn't have chosen them then. "Okay. Well, we've got work to do and you might actually be safer elsewhere."

Max nodded and headed back to the street.

"And, Max," Paige called after him.

"Yeah." He paused and looked at her.

"Fly over as something real in this world. Let's not start a panic with flying horses."

He rolled his eyes like a teenager, then ran into the street, transforming into a pegasus as soon as he was past the town hall.

Teenagers.

But before he left the protection of the wards, his shape shifted, and he became a bird.

At least he'd listened.

$\mathbf{P}$aige pulled her phone out of her back pocket and searched for Dexx's contact.

He answered on the second ring. "Hey, babe. What's up?"

"I'm just checking to see how things are going over there."

She could almost see him shrug in his pause. "Things are going well. Tony is fitting in quite well. I'm still not used to having him as a boss, but none of us are."

"You're not making his job harder, are you?"

"Who me?"

Yeah. That's what she thought. "How are the kids?"

"They're good. They're hoping you get back in time. Leah will be very upset if you have those kids in Alaska."

Paige would be really upset if that happened. "Were working as fast as we can."

"What are you learning?"

A lot more than she could say over the phone. "Just some general stuff. But it's good."

"Great." His tone said that he didn't believe it was going that well.

She didn't believe it was going that well on his end either. "I heard word that Chuck has some trouble in Utah."

"If he does, he's keeping it to himself. I haven't heard anything."

Which meant that Jack was able to take care of it on his own. Or he thought he could. "Okay. Well I'll be over soon as I can."

"Be sure you do. How is Leslie?"

"Doing really good."

"Have you been able to talk to her all? I mean, has she been… herself?"

"Yeah. These wards are amazing. That is one thing that we are going to be doing when I get home."

"Oh yeah?"

He sounded about as interested as she did when he was talking about car parts. "Anyway, I've got to go. Mario was just here we might have trouble."

"Way to bury the lead, babe. DoDO is there?"

"Yeah. Apparently, they're trying to get a hold of Billie."

"Billie? Why?"

"My guess is that she has something they want. I have no idea how bad it's going to get."

"Are you in danger?"

She probably should've kept her mouth shut. "No. We've got this under control."

"I almost feel as though you're telling me that the zombie apocalypse just started, but that everything will be fine because it's just a *little* virus."

Paige laughed. She couldn't help herself. "I'm about to see just how bad DoDO can be, I think."

"That's it. I'm getting on a plane and heading over there right now."

"No. You're not. You're staying right there and keeping our team and family safe."

He was silent for a moment. "You're going to be okay?"

How could she make him feel better? "You're talking to the woman who teleported a car with two people inside of it."

"Right." A little more silence. "Okay, babe. Don't die. Love you."

"Same goes for you. But… Try not to die while not blowing the town apart."

He sighed. "Will that ever go away?"

"Probably not." She didn't know how it was possible, but just hearing his voice made her feel as though she really could succeed. She was confident in herself. She didn't need another man to fill her with value. But he still did that. And all she needed was the sound of his voice. "Are the kids around?"

"No. I'm at the station. Kids are in school."

"Okay. I just miss their faces."

"Well, see if you can video call again tonight. They loved it last night."

"So did I."

"You should stay home more often."

"I really should." But she didn't know if that was going to happen anytime soon. She was about to give birth and needed to be a mom doing mom things, but her reality was that she might not have time for that.

"Love you, babe."

"Love you, too. Jerk."

He chuckled. "Hanging up now." And then the line went dead.

She and Opal spent the next part of the afternoon extending the wards. With the shields extended, the branches on the trees also grew. Looking at that tree, it was easy to see how and where they were weakening their shields. The longer the branches, the more fragile they were at the ends. They pushed it as far as they thought was feasible. It didn't cover the entire island, the Cheechako sanctuary, but it was a pretty good start. Paige was fairly certain with more people adding their strength to the tree, the shields would be able to be pushed out further.

They just didn't have any more people to add.

That was something she was going to have to think about with her own wards. She had basically a small town living at her home. And, it was possible she could even do this for the shields around Troutdale and the surrounding area. If she was able to get everybody from the town, well, everyone who was paranormal, to add their energy to the tree, they could quite possibly have very large powerful wards.

But that was something to worry about on another day.

With the wards in place, it was safe for Billie, Leslie, Ripley, and Paige to return to the cabins for some much-needed sleep.

Rested, at least as much as they could be given the circumstances, it seemed as though maybe they were all over-reacting. Nothing new on the horizon. None of the sensors had gone off. And Blake couldn't see anything going on around them. Apparently, his dragon senses were one more defense.

Paige decided to shift into the fox. It seemed safest. And she enjoyed how easy and fun the fox was. Though, she still preferred the big cat. It just felt more natural. But they did not belong in Alaska. She didn't know the area, or how many of the residents were of paranormals versus mundanes, so she wasn't going to push her luck. DoDO was already at the door.

Billie sat at the dining table staring at her phone.

Paige walked into the kitchen and grabbed a cup of coffee. "Reading a book?"

"Yeah."

"Anything fun?"

"Yeah. I'm a little annoyed with this character, though, but the story is really good."

"Oh. Well, that happens." Paige needed to find more time to read. Like on the plane. She could read a book on the plane. Her problem was that she couldn't focus while reading. Her mind would wander in a million directions.

Billie turned the screen off and looked over at Paige. "Did you sleep well?"

"Yup. You?"

"No." Billie held her head in her hand and frowned. "How do you sleep through stuff like this?"

"Well, if you don't, you'll die. That usually helps."

Billie shook her head.

"No? Okay." Paige brought her cup of coffee to the table and sat. "You've got to push it from your mind before you sleep."

"How?"

"I didn't say it was easy, but I usually just tell myself that I can't do anything about it at that time, then allow myself some downtime. Without it, you run yourself thin, and you can't do anything."

"That sounds like meditation."

"There's actually—" Paige dug in her pocket. She probably shouldn't be going into this at the moment, but it was kind of neat and exciting and made meditation easy. "There's an app."

Billie chuckled. "Of course there is."

Paige joined her in the laughter. "But no. Really. It helps." She found the big orange circle icon and opened it. "Okay, so see? There's meditation cycles for anxiety and stress and changing habits and self-esteem and productivity. I mean, it's great."

"And you do this?" Billie took the phone and flipped through the screen.

"Well..." That was the thing. She knew it was a great idea, but she rarely *actually* took the time to *do* it. "I'm intending to."

Billie laughed and handed the phone back to her. "That sounds about like what I would do."

Paige grunted. She really *did* need to do something with it. She was paying a monthly subscription for it and it was good health. With as hard as she was playing, she needed to take care of herself. She wasn't a young chicken who could go galivanting all over the world while eating snickers and drinking sodas.

Not that she ever really did that, but there were times where she caught herself looking for that quick fix. She just needed a cup of coffee and a muffin—then that was all she had all day because she didn't have time for anything else.

Yeah. A healthier lifestyle. How the *hell* was she going to fit that in? "Do you have any veggies? I could scramble up some eggs."

Billie raised her eyebrows, her lips pulled down as she gestured to the fridge. "Use whatever you find."

Several minutes later, they had two plates of eggs scrambled with healthy looking veggies. See? Small steps.

"So," Paige said, tucking in, her twins doing what had to be cartwheels in her belly. She knew they weren't *full* cartwheels, but those damned little *feet* could find every organ in her body. "What did you find that DoDO wants so bad?"

Billie looked at her out of the corner of her eye.

"They said you're a suspect for murder." And if everyone wasn't already so overwhelmed, they would have been all over that a lot sooner. This felt like a delayed reaction, mostly because it was. No one believed Billie Black could be capable of murder, so it wasn't even a thought worth their energy at the moment.

But Billie didn't look surprised. She just groaned and concentrated on her eggs. "I *found* a body and some…pretty valuable information besides."

"And what is that information?"

"If I told you, they'd be after you, too."

"They'll be after me anyway. I'm giving birth to two powerful ancients and I house a—well, I don't know what. A herald of the ancients? Whatever. Not on their Christmas list."

Billie chuckled, then sobered. "You don't understand."

"Then make me."

Taking in a deep breath, Billie revealed her left shoulder. There was a green circle with foreign letters inscribed within it. It looked like an occult tattoo, but it…had energy.

Paige didn't want to touch it. "What is it?"

Billie put her shirt back. "Let's just say the information I found marked me, so I'm not going to share it."

"Marked you how? Just the tattoo?"

Billie shook her head. "Here, too." She pointed at her chest. "It's like a door to something opened."

Paige knew a thing or two about that. "Was there a ceremony?" Because when the door to Hell had been opened in her soul, there had been incantations and magic mushrooms and all sorts of stuff.

"No. Just…There was a thumb drive with information that was in the man's hand. I took the thumb drive from him. I don't know why I did it. I wasn't there for that. And then, when I read what was on the drive, I had a horrible nightmare. And then the next day, there was this and…it feels like I can hear people."

"Inside you? Like you're possessed?" Because that could be bad, but a kind of bad that Paige knew how to handle.

"No."

Well, poop.

"It's like there's a wall. A really thin wall and I can hear what's on the other side."

"And what is that?"

Billie shook her head. "Again, I don't want to tell you because…it could get you hurt."

Paige appreciated that thought, but she knew—

No. She didn't have to *save* every damned person in the freaking world. She had enough on her plate. There was someone attacking shifters in her region, a region she should be helping to protect. And there was a group of people attacking paranormals. Or making them disappear. She didn't know which. Maybe both, but she had a feeling she was about to find out.

Billie—whatever it was that she was into—might have to deal with that on her own. Paige was in over her head—per normal—with…angels and demons and shifters and men in black and…kids and a maybe-soon time husband and babies. That? That was a lot.

No. Paige nodded and took in a deep breath. "I'm going to respect that. If you need help, ask." After all, Billie *was* helping them. She couldn't ignore that.

But…she needed to take care of her own first.

33

A deep, round roar rocked Billie's house.

Billie's wide, dark eyes met Paige's. "The wards."

Yup. She was already scrambling off the bench, maneuvering her large belly to get out the door. Billie's house was right at the edge of the wards, so they should be able to see what was going on just outside them.

Paige rounded the house and cleared the backyard to see four men with guns standing in the gravel road that interconnected all the houses on the island. Their weapons were pointed at the house, their eyes on the air in front of them as if they could see the ward through their goggles.

Perhaps they could. Paige wasn't going to say it wasn't possible.

Paige switched to witch vision. The ward was hot, mini waves running out and crashing into one another from where the men were touching the wards with their hands and guns. No bullets, though.

Leslie flew in and shifted as her feet touched the ground. "They're over by the cabins, too. They can't seem to get in, though."

That was odd. The Whiskey wards had always allowed witches to come through. It was other things like angels and demons who weren't allowed.

"It's because of their intent," Billie said quietly. "That's the key to our wards."

"You're going to have to help us with that, because that is brilliant." Though, they were going to have to survive first. "Where's Mario?"

Billie walked around the garage, staring at the men just on the other side of the wards. "Have no idea. In town?"

Probably. Or maybe he was right outside these wards, trying to get his hands on Billie.

Shit. They were there for Billie. Having her right there in the open, probably wasn't a great idea.

As if on cue, one the men keyed the mic hanging from his utility belt and raised it to his mouth.

Yeah. If Mario wasn't standing outside those wards now, he would be very soon.

Paige needed her damned brain back. She should have seen that one sooner, but the damage was already done. No hope for it now. "How do those wards work on bullets?"

"Never had them tried against bullets before." Billie's voice was strong, her hands clenched at her sides, her tree magick coiling around them like whips.

Paige turned her witch vision off because it wasn't giving her anything. She couldn't *see* the auras of the men outside the wards. Somehow the wards were blocking those off? She didn't know why, but the men were showing up as...men in her witch vision.

That was odd.

"What are they waiting for?" Leslie stepped between Paige and Billie, balls of green magick in her hands.

Paige didn't know.

I'm heading into town, Ripley's voice said over the pack bond. *I'll let you know what I see.*

Do you see death? Paige knew what the answer was already.

Ripley didn't answer immediately. *Yes and no. I see that it should be there, but it's hiding from me.*

How did death hide from death?

It's strange. I don't like these people.

Paige didn't either. *Tell me what you see.*

Will do.

"Rip's heading into town," Paige told Billie and Leslie. "We'll know what's going on there soon enough."

"All this for me?" Billie shook her head.

Paige looked at her out of the corner of her eye. "For the information you hold. Sure you don't want to share it?"

"It's best if I don't."

Paige wasn't going to second guess the woman. She'd proven herself a valuable friend and asset too many times.

Paige's phone rang. She pulled it out of her back pocket. She didn't recognize the area code. She swiped the green icon and put the phone to her ear. "Whiskey."

"It's Mario Kester."

She turned to look at Billie. "We were just talking about you."

"Were you really?" His tone was dry.

"I see you've arrived in force."

"I did, and I've gotta say, your wards surprised me a little. Are these new?"

"Since the last time you were here?" She wasn't going to tell him they were. Because he'd been able to get through while they'd been up the last time. Probably because he hadn't intended anything bad to happen during that conversation.

He grunted. "Our demands are simple. Hand over Billie Black."

"Because she's a murderer."

A tall, heavily tattooed man strolled into the back yard. He wore no clothes, so Paige figured him for a shifter.

A few more joined him, breaking out of the woods and shifting as soon as their feet touched the mowed grass.

Well, at least they'd have a few friends to help. But how beneficial would they be in a bullet battle? Magick? Maybe. Bullets? Magick didn't fight those well. There was this trivial matter of physics to overcome.

"That is what I said." Mario's tone hadn't changed.

"Yes. It is."

"You don't believe me."

"Nope."

"She's a good liar. She has a pretty face to hide behind."

"Are you talking to me like I have a dick to be led by?"

He didn't respond.

It was a low blow, but Dexx had let her into his head and she knew what *he* thought about, so…the blow wasn't too far from home. "I know why you're really after her."

His silence continued, but only briefly. "No, you really don't."

"She hasn't shown me the information she tripped on, but I know that's what you're after, and it has nothing to do with the body she found."

"The stories of your detective abilities are not unfounded."

"Glad to know I could meet your…" She lost the word. "…rumors." Lame. So, fucking lame. Goddamn baby brain.

"Yes." He didn't seem pleased.

"Well, I have the thumb drive. So kill her if you think that's a good idea, but then you're just going to have to get through the Whiskey Coven. And if you think getting through the wood witches is hard, I think you've got a whole other thing comin' to you, buddy."

"You think the wood witches are going to be a problem for me."

"I think you have no idea the pile of shit you're about to step in." At least, she really hoped so. He had come to a witch battle with bullets, so it was possible he did know.

"Last chance, Paige. Hand over Billie Black and no one gets hurt."

"No."

"Think about your sister." His tone changed slightly. "Your unborn children."

"Oh. So low, Mario, but…still no."

"You give me no other options." The line went silent.

Paige stowed the phone. "Do we have any way to knock these guys out without killing them?" Because Paige was better at killing than knocking out.

Billie turned toward the gathered shifters. "They're each outfitted with a pouch that will go with them when they shift. They dip their claws or beaks into it and all they have to do is scratch the skin and the target drops. Paralyzed."

"Got any more of that?" Leslie asked.

Billie shook her head. "Not handy. It's all in town."

No matter. Paige had magick, and she was going to be using that as much as she possibly could.

A man without any guns walked up to the wards and placed his hands against him. The other men stepped back as inky blackness oozed out from him.

Shit. Door magick. "Get ready. He's opening the wards."

"He can't." Billie said.

"Hell yes he can, and he's about to." Paige released her witch hands, her own inky black magick writhing forward.

With the same door magick Paige had inherited from the Blackman side of the family, the man opened a door.

To the ward's credit, the man obviously struggled to get it

open,, and it was only as wide as his arms spread open. The other men had to wiggle by him one at a time.

"Death only if necessary," Paige ordered. "We're not murderers."

"We're at war," the tall blonde man said with a thick Texan accent. "We'd be shootin' ourselves in the foot if we let them live."

But he was already moving forward, his figure stooping into a small, fuzzy squirrel.

Paige had not seen that one coming. Big, tall, burly man? She figured he'd be a bear. Nope. Squirrel.

She didn't have time to think about it.

The men raised their semi-automatic rifles and took aim as soon as they were through.

Paige should have told the shifters to kill. It was obvious the men weren't intending on taking hostages. Well, except *maybe* Billie.

Wind whipped around them as Leslie called on the air, shooting pellets of dirt in their faces as they stepped through the wards.

Hard to take aim when they couldn't see. Good thinking.

Paige wasn't nearly so subtle. She called power to her hands and it coiled around her witch hands in golden, crackling energy.

That was new.

One of the men waved an arm and a blue shield rose in front of him, keeping the dirt from his face. He raised the rifle and pointed at Leslie.

Like hell. Paige lobbed an energy glob at him.

It pierced his shield and hit him, sending him writhing to the ground.

It didn't look like he was dead.

Billie was taking care of herself, her magick flowing from her like limbs on a tree.

One of the men let out a cry as he pointed his rifle at his own legs. He flailed and fell to the ground. The squirrel came running out of the downed man's pant leg and went to find another victim.

As long as they came at them one a time like this, they'd be okay. Paige wasn't tiring, and it didn't appear as though Leslie was either. And they had backup. A bear, a lion, a horse, and a llama.

Yeah. A llama.

Eight men in utility vests, guns aimed, entered the yard from the east. Maybe the east? Whatever. From the rear. Paige spun in time to throw up a shield as three of the men opened fire.

The shield didn't do shit. Bullets whizzed by her, one nicking her arm.

Shit. That was close.

I need something that's bullet proof.

Trust me. Cawli crawled forward and shifted into something small.

An armadillo? Paige couldn't believe it. They were in a damned gunfight and Cawli, one of the most powerful spirit animals she knew of, had shifted into a damned armadillo.

A bullet bounced right off him. She felt the impact, but nothing...

Blessed Mother. Armadillos are bullet proof?

Cawli was almost smug.

Too bad they're so damned slow.

Watch this.

Before Paige had a chance to do much more than blink in her own mind, they were across the yard and at the feet of the first armed man.

Cawli pushed Paige forward.

She gripped her power and clapped two energy crackling hands around the man's head.

He went down, making a choking sound, his body twitching.

She spun, her arms up, and deflected a blow she had no idea how she'd seen coming.

Animal reflexes. Less thinking. More fighting.

Right. She punched the man in the face with her left power-filled hand.

He went flying and crumpled to the ground.

An eagle's scream filled the air. A man cried out.

Leslie must be doing okay.

Paige spun on the third man.

He gave her a cocky grin and clawed his left hand. It was full of a red, sickly magick.

Don't let that touch you.

No shit.

She lobbed an energy ball at him.

He dodged.

He was too far away for her to touch him with her energy charged hands. Maybe the squirrel and armadillo were onto something.

She shifted into a squirrel and scurried toward him.

He frowned at her as if trying to figure out what the hell she was doing.

As soon as she was close enough, she shifted back to human, her energy already called up. Staying close to the ground so he wouldn't touch her with...whatever magick *that* was, she lit up his legs like they were fireworks.

He toppled backward away from her.

Thank goodness.

She tried picking herself off the ground. There was a fourth man and he was coming at her.

Human form wasn't cutting it.

He raised his rifle and pointed it at her.

She shifted into an armadillo.

Trust me on this one?

She shrugged.

As soon as they got close, Cawli pulled himself forward and shifted into something quadrupedal and furry. He climbed up the man like a primate and jammed his elbow into the man's neck.

The man went down.

As soon as Paige's feet touched the ground, she shifted into human, her magick in her hands. She turned, scanning the area.

Leslie was fine, attacking a man with her eagle claws.

But Billie?

She was nowhere to be seen.

But Paige saw a set of taillights heading away. Something crackled over the men's radios, and those who were still upright left through the same opening the door magick man had made.

With the last man through—there had only been two remaining—the door man looked at Paige from across the yard then dropped his hands, letting the door close.

Shit.

They fucking had Billie.

3 4

Leslie landed and shifted back to human.

Paige shifted into a tiger and ran over to Leslie. This being a shifter thing was *amazing*. She was kicking herself for not doing this sooner. For Pete's sake. Seriously. She morphed back to human—a very pregnant and still kick ass human—as soon as she got to her sister. "They took Billie."

Leslie glared at the place the SUV had disappeared. "Plan?"

"You and I fly after them. Attack them with our super witch skills. Get her back."

"And then what do we do with the humans?"

Opal rolled up to them. "You leave them to us. Just bring them back and we'll handle their memories."

"Memories." Paige needed more to go on than that.

Opal leaned reached toward one of the fallen men. Her magic flowed from her fingertips, visible to the even the normal eye. It looked like vines that reached into his ears, nose, and mouth.

Paige switched to witch vision and watched as beads of

golden energy rolled down each vine, stopped, then rolled back up.

Opal retracted her magick and sat up. "We can deal with the memories. I believe you said you could teleport people now?"

Paige had done it only the one time. It would have to do. She nodded and turned to Leslie. "You up for this?"

Leslie gave her a you-betcha, kick-ass shrug and leapt into the air, shifting into a golden eagle.

Eagle. Cawli scoffed. *Let's try something a little faster.*

Taking the lead, Cawli shifted into a peregrine falcon.

It looks like I need to start researching animals, Paige told him. *Find their benefits. What did you do while we were the monkey? How did you knock him out with your elbow?*

I was a loris, Cawli said as they gained altitude. *They shoot toxin out of their elbow. Normally, it's just irritating to humans, but we're…a little more.*

So, the toxin knocked him out.

Precisely.

His tone made her feel like a school kid who had provided the right answer.

She and Cawli took off after Leslie, quickly gaining in speed. They grabbed the same current racing down the mountain and climbed out of the ravine where the river threaded. About midway up the mountain, they came to the highway.

The SUV's were already speeding down it, going faster than the speed limit, which was obvious by the way they handled the curves. There were four, with another three working to catch up quickly. Mario was probably in one of those. Paige guessed they'd come from Cheechako.

Just how many of these guys were Leslie and Paige going to have to fight on their own?

Paige gained more speed and flew further up ahead on the

highway. The problem with having a magick fight on a public highway was—well, first, it would be a Federal offense. Second, it would likely bring the Shadow Sisterhood to her doorstep and might actually land her in jail, no matter who the hell she was to the Elder Council. Third, it really could put others in danger.

Where do you need me? Ripley asked.

Paige was seriously going to have to stop forgetting the fact she had a pack. *Keep people off the road. Things are about to get explody.*

Explody. Roger that.

Paige didn't know how Ripley was going make it happen and, frankly, she couldn't care less. She was about to have a fight with a very physical, fast moving vehicle. How in the hell was she going to manage that?

Her mind traveled down the pathways of her magick and an answer came to her like it was second nature, or breathing. All she had to do was trust it.

What the hell was going on with her? This amount of power? It was fucking terrifying.

But if it kept her alive, she'd stop sniveling like a child and use it.

Wise decision.

Oh, for crying out loud. *You've been silent for how long and now you're a chatty Catty?* She chuckled to herself at her own wit, but only because she was buying time. She couldn't believe she was attempting to do something so reckless.

She sank into her magick in a way she'd never done before. She fell into it like she did with Cawli, trusting it the way she trusted her spirit animal.

You and I are much closer now. His voice was almost like arms holding her close like a treasured family member.

She belonged. She was comforted. She was safe.

Her magick coalesced around her, touching her in ways it

had never had a chance to before. She didn't have to call the wind. She *was* the wind. Water flowed through her, creating a stronger, more fluid being. Earth's fire roared in her soul, giving her strength, courage, and stability. The ground itself crawled up through her feet, her legs, her abdomen, around her womb, her chest, her shoulders, arms, hands, fingers, neck, and finally swarmed over her head.

She was a rock with the fiery mantle of Earth's fire. She breathed the wind and moved like water.

She opened her eyes.

Everything looked different. Colors were muted and almost ultraviolet. She could enahance her vision, zooming in like an eagle, and pulling it back out again.

Sounds sharpened. She heard Ripley's feet wisping through the undergrowth, swooshing through trees. The footsteps of those who followed her pattered in the soggy deadfall.

Paige's skin was alive, telling her things she'd never known were possible to know. She could *feel* the air currents from Leslie's wing beats as she flew in and shifted beside her.

Tastes settled on her tongue. Freshly turned earth from the steps of the shifters running ahead to keep any mundanes out of the witch fight. The cutting tang of oil and burned gas hanging stagnant above the asphalt.

The first SUV came into view, barreling down at them.

Paige and Leslie were in a straight patch a half mile or so downhill from the blind curve.

Taking a deep breath, gathering, becoming, and changing, Paige brought her clawed hands forward, summoning a shield she'd never even imagined possible. It came from the depths of this new her. It was strong and flexible like rubber, and her magick assured her it would repel a physical weapon like a car.

She just had to make sure Billie remained undamaged.

Her magick whispered in her ear a hiss that was more of an emotion. It accepted the challenge.

The first SUV sped up.

Paige focused her eagle vision, spying the driver.

He grinned cockily.

She didn't care about him. She searched inside the SUV for Billie. But the vehicle was dark in the back and too full of shadow. Even with her slight UV vision, she couldn't determine if Billie was inside.

A tendril of her magick raced forward like a hound.

"Paige?" Leslie's voice was hesitant.

"Be ready." Paige barely recalled how to make her voice work. Voice boxes were so…ineffective and unnecessary. Limiting.

Her magick was almost intoxicating.

Paige steeled herself, preparing for the impact of the first vehicle.

It slammed into her shield, the engine compartment accordioning in on itself, rising up in slow motion.

The second, hot on its tail, slammed on the brakes, smoke rising from his tires.

Paige pushed the tail end of the vehicle in midair to the side, letting it fall on its own into the ditch on the mountain side.

The other side was a several hundred-foot drop and would certainly lead to death.

She didn't want to be a killer that day. Maybe one day soon, but not this one.

The other SUV's ground to a halt and men and women in military vests carrying semi-automatic rifles emerged like cockroaches.

A small voice in the back of Paige's mind cringed, knowing they were wildly outnumbered and quite possibly outmatched.

Her magick smothered that voice. They were fine.

Mario stepped out of one of the rear SUVs' and walked up to the front, balls of magick in either hand.

Take out the leader, Cawli said.

Paige was good with that. Golden energy balls already in hand, she lobbed them at Mario.

Leslie's green magick flowed toward the men directly in front of them.

They opened fire…

On a pregnant woman. How…rude.

Paige snarled, pulled her shield back and punched forward with it.

The people hit with it flew backward. One man hit the SUV directly behind him. He scrambled on top of it as the shield continued its punch and slammed into the nose of the SUV itself. The SUV moved, the wheels resisting a little.

Mario paused, watching. He blinked once then his eyes widened.

Leslie's magick hit another woman in the chest, knocking her gun out of her hands.

Paige kept walking forward the shield rising and curling up and around her and Leslie to keep the aggressors who were now behind them from shooting them in the back. Her feet crunched on the bullets her shield had captured and let fall to the ground.

Mario took a step back.

Too damned late. "Where is Billie?"

His magick blinked, faded, then lit back up. It was like watching a string of lights with a loose wire. He took in a deep breath and stepped forward. "I can't let you have her."

"I won't let you take her."

"She is dangerous."

Paige lowered her head. "So am I."

His expression widened a little with fear. "Yes," he said quietly. "You are."

"Billie," Paige called.

The back door opened in an SUV near the rear and Billie fell out. She crouched behind the opened door, her hands out as she shot something Paige couldn't see.

The SUV sparked.

Billie walked toward Paige, her expression firm and pissed.

The SUV caught fire behind her.

Paige wasn't going to let anything hurt her friend.

Her magick answered. The tendril that had gone in search of her rolled out of the SUV now on fire and engulfed Billy in an opalescent cocoon.

The SUV exploded.

The force blew Billie's black hair over her shoulders, but she kept walking.

Two men near the explosion were blown back further onto the mountain. Paige couldn't see who was affected on other side of the SUV's to her right.

Mario glanced around him.

His men were a lot fewer than they had been at the beginning.

Paige stopped in front of him. "I'm going to give you an opportunity to save as many of your men as you can."

He met her gaze levelly. "You wouldn't kill them."

"You fired bullets at me and my sister, knowing we had nothing more than magick to protect us." Which normally didn't stand a rat's chance in hell of defending against them. "I believe you intended to kill us."

Mario's expression strengthened. "I did. You're a danger to the world and someone needs to stop you."

"I am not."

"I believe that's what Merry Eastwood said and you put *her* away."

Paige wanted to roll her eyes but refrained. "She killed people in blood magick rituals. What I do isn't even close."

"No." Mario ground his jaw. "It's worse. You taint the life magick that flows in the Whiskey blood. The Blackman magick. The..." He shifted his shoulders, his lip curling. "The spirit inside you."

Paige leaned forward and whispered. "And let's not forget the door to Hell in my bones or the demon magick I wield."

His eyes grew large.

Yeah. If he wanted to call her a danger, he had damned well better understand just how big of one she was. On her own. Without Cawli's assistance. She pulled back and smiled grimly.

"I will do whatever I need to," he said, his voice quivering, "to keep the world safe from the likes of you."

"I'm pretty sure I was born to answer the threat you bring."

He scoffed and turned his gaze away. "You're disgusting."

"Not nearly as disgusting as you."

Billie's wood magick whipped out and inserted itself into his ear, up his nose, and into his mouth.

He let out a startled noise before he fell to the ground.

Billie took a step forward and looked down at him while her magick worked. "Normally, I wait for them to be asleep first."

Paige certainly hoped so.

More wood witches stepped out of the trees, their vines snaking out and snatching the memories of the men and women who were sprawled on the ground.

Billie extracted her magick and looked to Paige. "Would you do the honors of disposing of them?"

The trick was not to raise suspicion. "Do you know how many more trackers they have?"

Billie nodded. "I'll take care of that."

"Good." Paige closed her eyes and let her magick take over. Each body was lifted and put into one of the SUV's, even the beat-up ones. The one that was still smoldering, however, was left alone.

Then she closed the doors, grabbed all the SUV's, even the one that was in pieces, and sent them on with a thought.

Anchorage airport.

Her magick sighed.

And then left her along with the SUV's.

Instantly, Paige had zero energy. She remained on her feet for a moment, but then her eyes drifted closed and the only thing she felt was the pavement.

Paige opened her eyes to sunlight and a warm bed that wasn't hers. She moved and wished she hadn't. Every muscle in her body ached. Maybe not every single one of them. There might have been one in her face—like the one that controlled the corner of her eye or something—that didn't hurt, but she really couldn't tell. She moaned and fell back into the bed.

Leslie burst through, a worried expression on her face. "You okay?" Her voice was thick with her Texan accent.

Yeah. She was worried. "Pretty okay." Paige pushed herself to a sitting position, leaning against the headboard. That wasn't too comfortable, though because of the pillow, but she just hurt too damned much to rearrange the damned pillow.

Leslie came forward in two strides and helped with that.

"Thank you," Paige said with relief.

"You're welcome." She pulled back then perched on the side of the bed.

That actually hurt, because Paige had to balance or fall off the damned bed. She scooted herself away, so she wasn't falling.

Leslie scooted backward but remained on the bed. "That was a lot of magick."

Paige closed her eyes and replayed what had happened. "That…was fucking insane."

"Yeah."

Paige groaned and opened her eyes. "I can't even begin to describe it."

"You looked like a Hollywood action hero."

Oh. "I felt a little like one, too."

Leslie shook her head, her expression worried. "What does this mean?"

Paige knew what she was really asking. "I doubt it's Mario or DoDO that we have this power for."

"Then who?"

Paige shook her head. She really didn't know. But there were so many things she hadn't quite buttoned down in the past. Like the Scribe of Hell or Sven.

But she'd faced off with both of them and been okay. So, she didn't see how or why she needed this much power to face off with them now. What could be worse than either of them?

She really didn't want to know. She was afraid she was going to anyway.

Dammit.

Leslie took in a deep breath and released it. "How are the twins?"

Still. Paige put her hands on her belly. "They're either laying low because they realized we nearly died or it's almost time."

Leslie looked worried. "If you're going to have them at home, you need to get to a plane quickly."

"About that," Billie said, stepping in and leaning against

the doorframe. "I could probably fly you. We'll have to make another landing to refuel, but we wouldn't have to worry about flight regulations or airport security."

That would be rather nice.

Oh, Blessed Mother. Having access to a plane. How nice was that? "I may need your services more often."

Billie gave her a sad smile. "I may have to relocate anyway."

What? "Why?"

Billie drew her shoulders up to her ears. "The coven has asked me to leave."

"No," Leslie said with a breath.

"Yeah. I bring too much danger to Cheechako."

"But..." Paige shook her head, not quite understanding. "You're a part of their coven. I see how they are with you. You're a tight unit of supreme witches."

"Yes. And Cheechako is a town of sanctuary. I got one person seriously injured and another twelve besides. Also, all the shifters who are here for 'sanctuary' are here because of me. Not because they need real help."

"That's shit." Leslie rolled her head on her neck. "Well, you're welcome at our place." She looked at Paige. "She can have—"

"Nick's old room," Paige finished for her. She looked up at Billie. "It's a guest room that everyone seems to live in for a time."

Billie smiled tightly. "Thanks."

"Besides," Paige said, trying to make light of the fact that Billie's family was basically throwing her out—with reason or not, it was still throwing her out—though there was no good way to make light of it, "we need to set up wood wards at Troutdale and on the Whiskey lands."

The corners of Billie's lips went down as she nodded. "Okay. I think we can do that."

Ripley slid through the doorway and fast-walked to the other side of the bed where she plopped down.

Holy fucking crap. That fucking hurt.

"Rip," Leslie chided.

Ripley gave her a toothy smile, putting her head on Paige's lap, folding her hands on her own abdomen, and looking up at Paige past her bulging belly. "Where are the dudes anyway?"

Paige stroked Ripley's hair. It was too damned hard to be mad at that woman. "I don't know. The airport? That's where I sent them, but...who knows?"

Ripley shook her head, pushing it into Paige's fingers at the same time. "And we're safe?"

"The information they gathered while they were here is missing." Billie's tone was final. "There might be some digital footprint, but they have no memories and all the trackers here are destroyed."

"Good." Paige rested her head back.

One of the twins dug a toe into her diaphragm.

Rubbing her belly with her right hand, her left still stroking Ripley's hair, her sister on her bed, and Billie unharmed, Paige felt pretty damned good. She'd kicked some major ass for a pregnant chick.

Billie straightened. "Hungry?"

Paige gave her a look that asked if that was a real question.

She chuckled. "I'll go fix you a plate."

Ripley got out of the bed to follow.

"Rip," Paige called.

"Yeah." Ripley stopped at the door.

Paige didn't know what she wanted to say, but she knew Ripley was someone who hadn't *belonged* in a very long time and she knew what that felt like. "Thank you for being here."

Ripley beamed. "Well, thanks for...inviting me along."

That look was all Paige needed.

Ripley turned to leave again.

"Oh, and I'm hungry enough I could eat an entire cow," Paige called.

"On it," Ripley yelled back.

Leslie took Paige's fingers and squeezed them. "For real. No blustering. Are you okay?"

It was such a relief to be able to just be herself around her sister. "I'm tired as hell. My power is terrifying, and oddly reassuring at the same time. The babies are okay. We won. So, yeah, I think I'm fine."

Leslie studied her for a long moment, then finally nodded. "Also, shifting is *amazing.*"

Leslie joined Paige in a chuckle. "Yeah. It *really* is."

"I mean, why was I so scared of it before?"

"I don't know. Like, oh my god, how many different animals have you shifted into so far?"

"A lot." Paige was quite proud of that. "And the loris was rather surprising. I venomed a guy with my elbow."

"That's not a thing."

"Oh, it is, and I did it."

Leslie chuckled.

"And I was squirrel for a bit. They're fast as shit. And an armadillo. Who knew they could *move*?"

"Not me. I only ever see them as roadkill on the side of the highway."

"Right?" Paige curled her nose. "Bulletproof."

"Yes."

"Shit."

They chuckled again.

Paige bit her lip and sank into her sad-needed-more-stuffing-to-be-comfortable pillow. "We are so incredibly fucked."

Leslie sagged, her gaze unfocused. "Yeah." She closed her

eyes then opened them again, staring at Paige. "What the hell is coming?"

Who the fuck knew, but Paige had a sinking feeling in her gut that they were about to find out.

And soon.

The day held promise for Dexx. According to the online tracker, his parts for Jackie, his 1970 Dodge Challenger, were out for delivery. She'd been smashed in his last investigation while fighting a shifter-witch. Who knew shifter witches were so darned powerful? Or big? One body slam had been enough to total Dexx's prized car.

He missed that car. So bad. But he was going to build her back up better than she was before.

Paige, his big-as-a-house, pregnant fiancée, was still waking. He'd learned the hard way to let her get up on her own, but to be ready for her needs as soon as her bare feet hit the wooden kitchen floor.

Not that she was high-maintenance. She was just beyond ready to give birth.

That was something he could understand. He felt bad just sleeping next to her. She was carrying twins. Shifter twins. Well, shifter-*witch* twins. And he had put them there, so his pregnancy duties were keeping her happy. It was the least he could do. Right?

Remember that shifter-witch he'd fought earlier that had totaled his car? Yeah.

Dexx's shifter sperm had impregnated Paige's witch eggs, and now two more ultra-powerful shifter witches were on the way. Just . . .hopefully, these two wouldn't be evil. Like the one who'd smashed his car.

He tromped the last few steps to the kitchen, following the smell of bacon, eggs, and skillet-fried taters. Alma was making magic at the stove already. Most likely adding real magick to them.

"Mornin'. Is there coffee yet? Paige is making noises up there."

"I'm not your short order cook." Alma's tone was curt, but normal. She was Paige's grandmother and had been around long enough to serve in the Second World War as a nurse. She was also a practicing witch and had been the Whiskey coven leader for most of her life. "You can make coffee your own damned self."

He filled water to the line and grabbed a single-serve cup

for the machine. The coffee maker had far more buttons and complications than the one Paige had killed in Denver. It sported a touchscreen and flashing lights.

The last drops plipped in the cup as Paige's footsteps announced her arrival.

Dexx pulled the cup out and presented it handle first to her. "Morning, love."

Paige mumbled something that didn't sound anything like, "I love you," and grabbed the cup from him. She'd only managed to open one eye on the trip down the stairs. She waddled to the table, sipping the hot coffee. It was a reduced-caffeine blend due to her pregnancy, but Dexx suspected that just the taste would be enough to brighten her up. She sat slowly, bracing herself as she did. "Oh, Blessed Mother, I want these things out of me."

"Well that's what happens." Alma spoke without sympathy, which was her standard. She was a simple and brusque woman.

Paige drew her brows down and sipped more of the life-saving liquid.

Dexx sat across from her at the old and very large table. He knew how to get under her skin in a good way, bringing out the best in the woman he was going to marry. "Mornin', babe?"

"Better. Why are you so happy? Not wearing my favorite underwear, are you?"

"Psh, no." Dexx lifted the waistband of his jeans to check. Paige was more than a little miffed that her good undies were dwindling because he *occasionally* wore them. Only the *once*.

He owed her some new underwear and, boy, did he have some ideas on what to get her. "Nope. Good ol' boy stuff."

Alma snorted from the kitchen. "In my day, boys didn't do that."

"Pretty sure boys have been doing it since they invented

girl clothes, Alma." Women's underwear was made out of finer materials than men's.

Alma grumbled.

Paige just shook her head with a smirk. He'd worn her underwear *one time*, but the joke would never, ever die. She enjoyed needling him with it every time.

Something exploded outside, small or distant. "Is Tyler already out there?"

"Been out there since before daybreak." Alma paused and looked out the kitchen window above the sink. "He's setting up those stick dummies to blow up. His little friend must have shown up."

Griff and Tyler's favorite game all summer had been attacking stick figures with their abilities, pretending the dummies were bad guys of different sorts.

Tyler was a bard—common sounding enough, except *he* was the one making things explode . . . with his *voice*. He was becoming quite an artist with it. He'd progressed beyond blowing up entire dummies and had started picking smaller targets, like hands and feet.

Paige turned her one eye to Dexx. "Why are you so happy?"

She had got a lot crankier with the pregnancy, and her trip to Alaska hadn't helped. His hope had been that some time in the wilderness would be good for her soul.

But she'd ended up having a big blow-out fight with the Department of Delicate Operations—DoDO, a government-run agency determined to take down the paranormals. And she'd learned to shift for the first time, all the while eight months pregnant. With twins. With shifter-witch twins. Had he mentioned yet that she was as big-as-a-house? "Got parts coming in." Dexx grinned widely at her scowl.

Paige raised her eyebrows. She'd listen to him talk about

cars, but he knew she didn't appreciate it. "You're really going to rebuild her?"

"How is that even a question?" Paige hadn't given him the full Alaska story and it was time to get it. "What else happened up there that you haven't mentioned?"

In her defense, she'd only been back a few hours. Her plane had touched down and she'd come home and passed out immediately.

She sighed and shook her head. "We've got problems."

Great. Because they needed more of *those*.

"DoDO is setting up shifters to lose control of their spirit animals, and then using that as an excuse to make them disappear. They were tracking down Billie because she learned something she shouldn't have. She's coming down here with Leslie when she's got better control of her shift."

Leslie was yet another shifter-witch they all hoped wasn't going to be evil. Before Leslie had been bitten, she was the heart and soul of the Whiskey clan. After she was chosen by the griffin, things had changed and not for the better. He *hoped* she got control of her shift because if she didn't, they'd have some tough decisions to make that *no one* wanted to even *think* about.

Dexx tapped the table with his thumb. "So, we're hiding Billie, the mad wood witch, here." *Here.* "In a place we normally blow up."

Paige nodded like that was an obvious statement. "Yes. It's the safest place for her."

"Sometimes, Pea, I think your brain is broken."

She shrugged and sipped her coffee. "DoDO's turning out to be a bigger problem than we expected."

"And what about Sven?" Alma asked.

Paige gave Dexx a where-the-fuck-did-that-come-from look and set her cup down. "When he shows up, we'll deal with him."

"And do you know how? Because he will show eventually, and by my reckoning, he's long overdue."

Alma wasn't wrong.

The look on Paige's face said she didn't have a plan yet.

Alma raised her chin, her wrinkled lips pursed. "Reece and I have been doing some research into the old Whiskey grimoires and—"

The back door slid open. Tyler and Griff spilled in with all the excitement of young boys having fun blowing things up. In Griff's case, attacking sticks as a bear.

Griff's robe fit too loosely on his body. It had been Dexx's robe, so it was way too big for his slight frame.

"Hey, Grandma," Tyler said through an exuberant grin, "Can Griff stay for breakfast?"

Alma passed her gaze from Paige to Dexx. "You bought yourselves some time. Tonight, we talk about this."

Paige flared her eyes wide. She was obviously thrilled. Though, part of that probably had to do with Reece. She'd just discovered he was her grandfather who had abandoned Alma to raise their child, Rachel, on her own. That probably would have been okay because Reece *had* been married to God at the time, so . . . it was a little understandable, though, imagine *that* conversation when Reece got to the Pearly Gates.

God: "You cheated on me with a woman."

Reece: "Seriously, why did you wire our brains the way you did if you didn't expect it to happen?"

Probably wasn't going to work in Reece's favor.

What made it tough for Paige was that Reece and Alma's daughter, Rachel, had abandoned her two daughters, Paige and Leslie, taking only her youngest son, Nick. Alma had then been responsible for raising a second generation of Whiskey children on her own. Dexx was pretty sure Paige blamed Reece for that.

So, Paige had some serious abandonment issues to work out with her newly discovered grandfather. The thought of working with him on anything? Probably not great.

Tyler gave each of the adults a look. "What is it? Can I help?"

"No." Alma pointed to the kitchen with her wooden spoon. "Get a plate and dish yourself. You, too, Griff."

They hurried to the kitchen for plates.

Dexx left the table. He walked through the kitchen to the garage. He should be leaving for the station, but it could wait.

Today, he'd be turning the reins of the Red Star Division over to someone else, someone with more experience in police procedures. Sure, Dexx had many skills hunting all kinds of paranormal beasties, but police procedures were like thorns in all the wrong places. But the turnover didn't have to be at a certain time.

Leah stood at the workbench wiping down tools.

"You know you can't do anything until the parts come in, right?"

Leah was becoming quite the little mechanic, which was a big surprise to Dexx. He'd first met her in New York where she was being raised by Rachel freshly taken from Paige. Yeah. Rachel. The woman who'd abandoned her two daughters had still managed to win custody of her granddaughter.

And Dexx had been there, thinking Rachel was God's answer to bacon sandwiches. He could be a really stupid asshat. Anyway, when he'd first met Leah, she'd been into My Little Ponies and Monster High dolls. Now, she preferred spark plugs and wrenches. That was *his* kind of girl. "Those parts, by the way, should be here today."

Leah put the rag down and jumped up, letting Dexx catch her in a hug.

He squeezed, his hand tangled in her long, blonde braid.

He shook her lightly, then set her down. "Good morning, Little Leah."

"Not as little anymore."

"You'll *always* be little to me." She was right, though. She'd begun to bud into womanhood. How long would she stay interested in mechanics after her first boyfriend?

"Morning, Dad."

Dexx's heart swelled. Since she'd begun calling him Dad, it always hit him. He liked it. "You can only polish those things so much before the chrome wears off. You know that, right?"

"Ha, ha. Jackie needs to be on the road soon. Then we can work on Cab."

"Cab?"

"Yeah. It's short for *caballo*, Spanish for horse. Figured we could call him Cab for short."

"Cab. Works for me, but shouldn't it be a girl's name?"

"*I'm* a girl. So, no, Cab is a boy."

Dexx raised his hands in surrender. "Understood. Loud and clear, daughter dear. Cab it is."

She narrowed her big, blue eyes at him. "You should be paying me for using him."

With his car out of commission, he'd been forced to use Leah's project car that he'd saved from a junkyard, to rebuild together. "Really? I thought keeping the rust knocked off was payment enough. And I'm the one that keeps you fed, remember?"

"Wear and tear is a real thing. I looked it up."

"Nope." Dexx leaned against the bench, crossing his arms. "Until you figure out how to start her—him—you don't get to claim him. After that, we'll talk." Some carbureted cars had extra "personality" and were harder to start.

Leah cocked her hip with a fist on it. "You think I haven't

paid attention? I know how to flutter the gas before turning the key."

Damn, she had *all* the Whiskey glare. She ruined it after a second with a smile she couldn't contain.

"You're not even sixteen yet," Paige said from the doorway.

Leah's smile slipped only a fraction. "Hey, Mom."

Paige looked miserable waddling through the cars.

Leah hugged Paige awkwardly around the baby bump. *Babies* bump.

Since Dexx hadn't made it to the car yet, he and Paige could ride together. "I'll drive."

Paige froze him with a look. "No. I'll drive. You have too much tendency to wreck the city."

Dexx turned innocent eyes to Leah. "See what I gotta put up with?"

Leah laughed.

Paige grinned. "Get in. We're taking my car. Leah can have hers for the day. Besides, I don't get to drive you very often. It'll be a treat."

"Not if I'm screaming 'look out' all the time." Dexx mimed imminent-crash posture.

"Funny. Get in." Paige hugged Leah one more time and slipped—wiggled, rather—into the driver seat of her little Mazda.

They backed out of the garage, Leah waving until the car turned around.

Dexx smiled and waved back, blowing kisses every few seconds.

"I'm so glad you two are close. I don't think she's quite there with me, yet." Paige glanced at Dexx while maintaining eye contact with the gravel driveway.

They needed to do some fill work since the rains had washed out two big holes the week before. "She's still coming around. Rachel worked her magic on that girl. She doesn't trust Rachel or you like she should. Just give her more time. She's ready, I think."

"Thanks, Dexx. I love you."

"I love you, too."

Dexx loved the peace and quiet they seemed to have at the moment. Paige could really use the time to invest into bonding with Leah. He really hoped the quiet would last long enough for Paige to give birth to their kids.

He had a feeling it wouldn't. That was just how their luck went.

Don't forget to leave reviews! Let us know what you think!

Shifting Heart Romances

by Hattie Hunt & F.J. Blooding

Bear Moon

Grizzly Attraction

Here's the reading order to make it even easier to catch up!

https://www.fjblooding.com/reading-order

Other Books by F.J. Blooding

Devices of War Trilogy

Fall of Sky City

Sky Games

Whispers of the Skyborne

Discover more, sign up for updates and gifts, and join the forum discussions at www.fjblooding.com.

WHISKEY MAGICK & MENTAL HEALTH

Sign up to learn more about our books and receive this free e-zine about Whiskey Magick and Mental Health.
https://www.fjblooding.com/books-lp

F.J. Blooding lives in hard-as-nails Alaska growing grey hair in the midnight sun with Shane, her writing partner and husband, his two part-time kids, his BrotherTwin, SistaWitch, TeenMan, and SnarkGirl, along with a small menagerie of animals which includes several cats, an army of chickens, a rabbit or two, but only one dog.

She enjoys writing and creating with her wonderful husband and dreaming about sleeping. She's dated vampires, werewolves, sorcerers, weapons smugglers, U.S. Government assassins, and slingshot terrorists. No. She is *not* kidding. She even married one of them.

Sign up for her newsletter, get free books, and join the discussions on the forums when you visit her website at FJBlooding.com